THE
COSSACKS

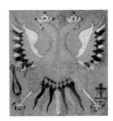

THE
COSSACKS

AN ILLUSTRATED HISTORY

JOHN URE

THE OVERLOOK PRESS
WOODSTOCK & NEW YORK

First published in the United States in 2002 by
The Overlook Press, Peter Mayer Publishers, Inc.
Woodstock & New York

WOODSTOCK:
One Overlook Drive
Woodstock, NY 12498
www.overlookpress.com
[for individual orders, bulk and special sales, contact our Woodstock office]

NEW YORK:
141 Wooster Street
New York, NY 10012

Library of Congress Cataloging-in-Publication Data

Ure, John
The Cossacks : an illustrated history : John Ure.
p. cm.
1. Cossacks—History. I. Title
DK35 . U74 2001   958'.00491714—dc21   2001036819

Book design and type formatting by Bernard Schleifer
Manufactured in Spain
FIRST EDITION
10 9 8 7 6 5 4 3 2 1
ISBN 1-58567-138-X

PICTURE CREDITS
pp. 2, 31, 147, 160, 161 (left), 161 (right), 189, 199, 201, 212, 215, 219, 231, 233, 234-235, 236, 239, 252 Mary
Evans Picture Library; p. 16-17 Musée Carnavalet/ Bridgeman Art Library; p. 19 Author's Collection; p. 23
Novosti Press Agency; p. 29 © Estate of Aleksandr Mihajlovic Gerasimov/Licensed by VAGA, New York, NY;
p. 39 Hermitage, St. Petersburg, Russia/ Bridgeman Art Library; p. 45 Odessa Fine Arts Museum, Ukraine/
Bridgeman Art Library; p. 57, 140 State Russian Museum, St. Petersburg, Russia/ Bridgeman Art Library;
p. 60 Blackburn Museum and Art Gallery, Lancashire, UK/ Bridgeman Art Library; p. 78 Pushkin Museum,
Moscow, Russia/ Bridgeman Art Library; p. 82-83 Private Collection/The Stapleton Collection/ Bridgeman Art
Library; pp. 90-91, 273 Corbis; p. 121 Royal Palace, Drottingholm, Sweden/ Bridgeman Art Library; pp. 125
Hermitage Museum, St. Petersburg, Russia; p. 129 Drottingholm Palace Collection, Sweden/ Bridgeman Art
Library; p. 134-135 Nationalmuseum, Stockholm, Sweden/ Bridgeman Art Library; p. 145 Musée des Beaux-
Arts, Chartres, France/ Bridgeman Art Library; p. 149, 169, 174 Stapleton Collection, UK/ Bridgeman Art
Library; p. 159 E.T. Archive; p. 165, 166, 243 Christie's Images/ Bridgeman Art Library; p. 177 Institute of
Russian Literature, Pushkin House, St. Petersburg; p.196-197 Private Collection/ Bridgeman Art Library; p.
204 Collection Kharbine-Tapabor, Paris, France/ Bridgeman Art Library; pp. 206-207 Bridgeman Art
Library; p. 211 National Army Museum; p. 224 National Portrait Gallery, London, UK; p. 241 Russian State
Archive Film and Documents, Krasnogorsk; pp. 265, 267, 271, 277 © Gerd Ludwig

This book is dedicated
to the memory of
SIR FITZROY MACLEAN
traveller, adventurer,
Russian scholar
and good friend

CONTENTS

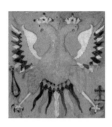

ACKNOWLEDGMENTS

I AM INDEBTED TO ALL THOSE WHO HAVE ENGENDERED MY INTEREST IN THE Cossacks and in the Caucasus, Central Asia and the other regions of southern Russia associated with them. Foremost among these must be the Dadiani family (descendants of the unhappy Prince Dadiani who features briefly in my chapter on the Conquest of the Caucasus) who endeavoured to teach me the Russian language throughout a hot summer in Paris in 1957. Sir Patrick Reilly, then H.M. Ambassador in Moscow, took me with him on a tour of the Ukraine, the Don and Caucasus later in the same year, and allowed me – as a junior member of his staff – to make an independent trip to Central Asia the following year. Sir Fitzroy Maclean also encouraged my burgeoning interest in the region on his visits to Russia at that time. More recent visits to Central Asian Russia have been sponsored by various tour companies for whom I have travelled as a guest lecturer – notably by *Steppes East* in 1996.

In writing this book I have also been much encouraged by many friends with a special knowledge of the subject, including Prince Rostislav Romanov, one of the closest descendants of the Russian Imperial family; H.E. Mr Yuri Fokine, the Russian Ambassador in London; Peter Hopkirk, who helped me track down Cossacks involved in the Great Game; and Neal Ascherson, whose pages about contemporary Cossacks in his *Black Sea* and whose generous advice have been especially percipient and helpful.

My researches have also been greatly assisted by the friendly help of the staff at the London Library and – in relation to the contemporary scene – the library staff at the Royal Institute of International Affairs (Chatham House).

To all these and many others my thanks are due.

PROLOGUE: STRANGERS IN THE PARK

THE summer of 1814 was a lively time to be in Regency London. The capital was seething with people, many of them foreigners. Creativity was in the air. John Nash was designing the terraces around the new Regent's Park, and fifty miles to the south of the city the exotic pleasure domes of the Brighton Pavilion were rising by the seaside. A country parson's daughter – Miss Jane Austen – had just published her novel *Pride and Prejudice*, and an Edinburgh lawyer and poet – Walter Scott, not yet a baronet – was publishing anonymously an historical novel called *Waverley*.

On the 20th of June a greater crowd than ever seen before had gathered in Hyde Park. This was the age of revolution and crowds were viewed with suspicion by the authorities. But this crowd carried no banners and chanted no slogans; it was wholly peaceable – expectant, jubilant and full of curiosity.

All Regency society was there in the park in carriages and phaetons, top hats and high collars, knee-breeches and cravats, for this was also the age of Beau Brummel and Regency bucks. Hyde Park was looking innocent in the morning sunshine, but it none-the-less had scaring and sinister connotations for some of these dandified aristocrats; for it was here, on the well-scythed grass and under the ancient oak trees, that they were prone to meet each other to settle matters of honour by duels. The Duke of York himself – now once more Commander-in-Chief of the army – had fought such a duel a few years earlier, and several army officers had survived the dangers of the Peninsular War only to fall victim to a duelling pistol's bullet here in the park at some chilly early morning rendezvous.

Low life was represented here as well, though at a greater distance from the centre of attraction: costers and whelk vendors, girls of dubious virtue selling dubiously fresh posies, Spaniards with dancing bears, and jugglers who were not above a little pick-pocketing ... all were there.

The Prince Regent himself was there, corpulent, puffy-faced and corseted into the uniform of an Hussar officer. With him were his guests, the greatest crowned heads of Europe: Alexander I, Tsar of All the Russias, prancing by in his white and gold coat with his standard bearer carrying aloft the double-headed eagle of the Romanovs; Frederick William III, King of Prussia, trotting past the assembled crowd in blue and scarlet with his heraldic single-headed eagle on a blue and white background carried in front of him by a cuirassier on a white charger. The Duke of Wellington, recipient of the highest decorations of most of the Allied Powers, was hurrying over from Paris to join belatedly in the celebrations.

For this was the great Victory Parade to celebrate the defeat of Napoleon and his exile to Elba. More than 15,000 troops had been camped in the park the night before; most were British, and represented a cross-section of those regiments who had chased the French armies out of Portugal and Spain, and finally across the Pyrenees and into France itself. There were Horse Guards in their gleaming helmets (specially designed by the Prince Regent to impress the Tsar); there were Highlanders in garish tartan kilts; there were new-fangled Riflemen in

Tsar Alexander I and his Cossack coachman.

their sombre green tunics. The continental contingents were smaller, but equally glamorous, mostly consisting of equerries, staff-officers and body-guards to their respective sovereigns. Everywhere there was bustle, bugling, bowing and doffing of hats.

But among both the grandees and the plebs there was one focus of special curiosity and attention. On the fringe of the military gathering, and waiting their turn to ride past the sovereigns, was a small cluster of bizarre horsemen who seemed to have little in common with the gorgeous panoply of soldiery that stretched out across the green swath of the park. Their leader was a sixty-three-year-old veteran of swarthy appearance and unfashionable moustaches. He rode his mount in a loosely relaxed manner, very different from the *haute école* techniques of the cavalry maneges of Western Europe. His followers wore shaggy fur hats, high soft-leather boots, cross-belts of cartridge bandoliers, and over their shoulders – even on this warm summer's day – hung long, heavily-lined cloaks. They carried curved sabres or tall lances. Their mounts were smaller than those of the other cavalry on parade, and less highly groomed, with their manes flowing freely. Their encampment in the park had not been part of the serried lines of white bell-tents in which the Guards, regular cavalry and line regiments had been billeted, but had been an untidy cluster of bivouacs around an open fire on which they had roasted a sheep of questionable provenance. They were gawped at by soldiery and civilians alike, for they were something that had never been seen in the West before: they were Cossacks.

Of course their reputation had gone before them. And it was a mixed reputation. These were the untamed horsemen who had tormented and harassed Napoleon's *Grande Armée* across the snows of the Russian steppes from Moscow to Warsaw, and then onwards across central Europe to the gates of Paris itself. They were said to need almost no rations, plundering what they required from friend and foe alike. The French believed that they barbecued and ate children. On campaign, they declined to sleep in ordinary billets, preferring to camp under the stars. Private property had a way of evaporating in their wake: the whole contents of palaces, herds of cattle, complete altar pieces from non-Orthodox churches ... all these found their way along a trail of Cossack encampments that led from the front line to the settlements on the banks of the Don or Dnieper rivers deep in the heartland of Russia.

The night before the parade, the Cossack contingent had strayed from their bivouacs to witness a spectacle which had greatly excited them. A prize-ring had been set up in a quiet corner of the park. Some of the foremost pugilists of the day had been among the participants and spectators: 'Gentleman Jackson', Hen Pearce known as 'the Game Chicken', and the great John Gully himself, who had knocked out Pearce a few years earlier and was shortly to become a Member of Parliament and the owner of a Derby winner, were said to be sighted among the crowd. The Cossack troopers had wanted to join in what they saw as the makings of a promising brawl; they had only been restrained by the pugilists' seconds and the 'bottle-carriers', who had thrown them out of the ring as quickly as they tried to climb in to join the fun. Clearly these wild horsemen were sporting figures whom it would be good to have on one's side in any affray.

There had been cartoons of Cossacks in the London press already. James Gillray had depicted an uncouth Tartar-like figure using his vast fur hat as a candle extinguisher to place over the diminutive figure of a frightened Napoleon scurrying out of Russia. They were variously considered as bogiemen or freedom fighters. Napoleon had called them 'a disgrace to the human species' and his troops had referred to them as 'the vultures of the battlefield' because of their reputation for taking no prisoners and for robbing the dead and dying. Even Walter Scott had noted while he was in Paris earlier in the year that the Cossacks' reputation for being quick-tempered and light-fingered had resulted in the term Cossack becoming synonymous in that city with trouble-making. But London was not Paris, and here among their allies they seemed congenial enough.

London had sighted its first Cossack the previous year, when a private trooper from a Don regiment had been sent to deliver despatches. Although not particularly articulate in any language, the courier had managed to reply to a question as to whether he had himself killed any

The following page:
Cossacks encamped on the Champs-Élysées in
Paris after the defeat of Napoleon: they were
hated and feared by the population in France
and loved by the population in England.

French soldiers with the memorable response: 'Three officers, besides the fry'. This had endeared him to his English allies, and he was henceforth received as a hero. Ackermann made a famous print portraying him as a noble savage; the City of London lionized him at a luncheon and readily forgave his obvious embarrassment when confronted with conventional cutlery; and the Prince Regent himself presented him with a sabre whose velvet scabbard seemed slightly effete compared to his other accoutrements. Now for the great Victory Parade there were more such men to be seen in London from the same stable.

But most of all it was the Cossack's moustachioed leader, Hetman Count Platov, who intrigued the British public. His fame had already reached London before him, and Richard Evans (print maker of Spitalfields) published an equestrian portrait of him in the same series as he had portrayed all the principal Allied royalty and generals; he was depicted in a green frock-coat with plumes sprouting from his Astrakhan hat and flourishing a sabre as his horse reared up under him – an heroic figure indeed.

Platov had been soldiering from the age of thirteen and had risen steadily through the Cossack ranks by his courage, dash and loyalty to successive Tsars. By the age of forty he had fought on almost every front against Tartars, Turks and internal rebels; he had been severely wounded; he had won gallantry medals and a knighthood. It was however against Napoleon that Platov made his greatest contribution. As commander of the cavalry under Marshal Kutuzov (broadly the equivalent of Lord Uxbridge under Wellington) he led the Cossacks at the Battle of Borodino, being among the last to leave the field, and later orchestrated the Cossack guerrilla campaign against the retreating French armies. He was said to have offered the hand of his daughter to any Cossack who could capture Napoleon during the famous retreat, and one band of horsemen under his command came near to winning

Count Platov, Hetman of the Cossacks, led the harassment of Napoleon's Grande Armée on its retreat from Moscow, and was later greeted as a hero in London where this print was widely distributed.

this prize between them when they seized a gun from a French encampment without noticing a silent and scowling figure – his right hand tucked into the front of his greatcoat – standing only a few yards away in the entrance to his tent.

It was Hetman Platov and his men whom the British public wanted to see for the first time that June morning in Hyde Park. When eventually their turn came to gallop past the saluting stand, every neck was craned, every head was turned. A great cheer went up as they cantered past. They were the heroes of the hour on a day given over to heroes. Perhaps only the Duke of Wellington when he was to see them a few days later might have recalled his own dictum about a consignment of recruits sent to him: 'I don't know what effect they have on the enemy, but by God they frighten me!'

Eighty-nine years later a similar group of Cossacks slouched in their saddles in a very different climate and a very different park. It was the 9th of January 1905 and light snow, driven by a biting wind, was sweeping across the Alexander Gardens leading out of the vast open square in front of the Winter Palace in St Petersburg. Snow was packed in hard piles at the street corners and the horses' hooves slipped on patches of ice. It was the end of a long, cold day and nerves were taut: they had been there since dawn on that Sunday morning.

Rumours had been rife, but briefing and orders scarce or non-existent. Everyone was expecting trouble. The factory workers of the capital were on strike. A dissident priest – Father Gapon – had been fanning their discontents. Plans for a march on the Winter Palace had been widely put about; but it was to be a peaceful march, bearing a petition to Tsar Nicholas II – their 'Little Father'. Icons and portraits of the Tsar had been distributed among the strikers and their families and supporters. Father Gapon had personally notified the city authorities of the routes his marchers would take, and – although such marches were theoretically forbidden – there had been no order to desist.

On the Sunday morning everything had started as planned. The crowd had converged in five columns, from different sectors of the city, towards the Winter Palace. They had sung hymns as they marched, and the police had cleared the route as they usually did for religious processions. Gapon had been leading the column which approached through the Narva Arch and a mile and a half had been covered without any let or hindrance. The marchers confidently expected to be allowed to present their petition to the Tsar in person, being unaware that the Tsar had left the capital for his country retreat the previous day.

The authorities had had plenty of warning of what was coming but had done very little about it. The Minister of the Interior and the Prefect of Police in St Petersburg had leant heavily on the Grand Duke Vladimir, an uncle of the Tsar and the Commander-in-Chief of the St Petersburg Military District, who was known to treat all demonstrators as revolutionaries and to favour teaching them a sharp lesson. Orders had gone out for the arrest of Father Gapon well before the fatal Sunday, but no-one had implemented the orders. Nor had anyone tried to head the strikers off their march or warn them of the consequences. What should have been a police problem was allowed to become a military one, and the military preferred to prepare for trouble rather that to prevent it happening.

One preparatory action had been taken. It had been decided by the Grand Duke that General Prince Vassilchikov, who was in overall command of the Guards regiments, should throw a cordon loosely round the Winter Palace and stop the marchers at a safe distance. The first to reach the cordon was Father Gapon's column at the Narva Arch. When the order to halt was given, it was disregarded; possibly the sheer momentum of pressure from those behind made it hard for those in front to stop in their tracks. A squadron of Horse Guards was ordered to gallop into the oncoming civilians; when this proved only a temporary set-back to the demonstrators, the Irkutsk Rifle Regiment fired into the crowd, leaving at least ten dead on the ground and more than twice that number wounded. Meanwhile at the other points on the cordon round the Palace similar encounters were happening: the columns were being charged by cavalry and then fired into by infantry – and bodies were pil-ing up at the various check points.

So far most of the action against the demonstrators had been taken by the Tsar's household troops: the Horse Grenadier Guards, Peter-the-Great's Preobrazhensky Guards and the Chevalier Guards were Prince Vassilchikov's chosen instruments. In any case, most of the Cossack regiments – which formed the bulk of the Russian cavalry – were still far away in Siberia fighting in the Russo-Japanese War. But Vassilchikov had a second line of defence, immediately round the Winter Palace itself in the great open square and the adjoining Alexander Gardens. It was here he held his reserve including Cossack cavalry units. As the day marchers, swelled by disaffected students and members of the public who were curious to see what had happened or anxious to protest at the violence used against unarmed petitioners, began to filter through the Alexander Gardens towards the precincts of the Palace itself. Taunts were hurled at Guardsmen and Cossacks: Why were they not fighting in Siberia? Why were they lackeys of the landowners and factory bosses? An occasional over-bold and unwise youth tried to unseat a Cossack or a mounted policeman or to wound or scare the horses.

Eventually the patience of the officers wore thin, and the temper of the troops deteriorated. Shots were fired into the ragged groups of demon-strators. A few Cossacks rode in among them wielding their heavy whips and, when this did not instantly clear the ground, wielding their sharp sabres. When the Palace square and the Alexander Gardens had been cleared, the

Cossacks, with the help of police, dispersing one of the many strikers' gatherings in 1905

cavalrymen moved on to the Nevsky Prospekt – the main shopping street – and continued to break up or ride down any groups that looked menacing.

By nightfall the streets and squares and gardens were clear, but over 130 were officially recorded as dead or dying, and many more had shunned the public hospitals for fear of arrest and were nursing their wounds furtively at home. Liberal journalists were later to claim that the total casualties of the day amounted to almost 5,000 in all. The government casualties amounted to two policemen killed. The following day, Guards and Cossack officers were refused entry to the Merchants' Club as a protest against their part in the events of the previous day. In the Alexandra Theatre that evening some students got up in the first interval and declared that this was a time for mourning and not for entertainment; the audience agreed with them and, reaching for their furs and stoles, quit the theatre for the snowy, blood-spattered streets. 'Bloody Sunday' had stained the Tsar's reputation irrevocably; the first step in the Russian Revolution had been taken. 'Oh God, how sad...' wrote Nicholas II in his diary. It was to be more sad for him than he knew.

It was also sad for the Cossacks. As throughout the rest of 1905 they put down strikes and demonstrations in one city after another across Russia, as their *nagaika* whips or sabres cut a swath through their compatriots, so they came to be seen as the enemies of the people, as the savage instrument in the bloody hand of the Tsar. Never again would they be cheered by the populace in the parks of London or St Petersburg. Their role in Bloody Sunday had been minimal, but – as they followed up its aftermath elsewhere – it was the silhouette of a file of Cossacks across a snow-bound street that was to burn into the consciousness of the nation and provide a symbol of repression.

The welcome strangers in Hyde Park in 1814 had become the sinister outsiders in every park in Russia by 1914.

INTRODUCTION: WHO ARE THE COSSACKS?

Few people are indifferent to the concept of the Cossacks.

In Western Europe the romantic perception predominates. A vision of dexterous horsemen, decked in cartridge belts and fur hats, armed with sabres, and galloping over the dusty or snowy steppes of Russia springs to mind. Courage and bravado are seen as concomitants of independence of spirit. Shaggy elders and dark-haired maidens are visualized around a camp fire group of virile singers, dancers and carousers. All is Byronic and stimulating.

In other parts of Europe and Asia – particularly in Poland, the southern Caucasus and some of the Russian industrial cities – a more sombre picture prevails. The gallant cavalry appear more like fiends on horseback. The crack of Cossack knouts across the backs of peaceful demonstrators has replaced the seductive tones of the balalaika. Rapine and plunder are recalled more readily than dash and daring: drunkenness and lust more readily than good-cheer and charm. Far from being free independent souls, the Cossacks are seen as the brutal instrument of their paymasters – whether rebels, Tsars or Commissars.

History confirms both perceptions. The Cossacks have proved to be a weapon that can turn in the hand of the wielder. How this has happened is a theme of this book.

Whether descended from Tartar horsemen or runaway serfs, the Cossacks who settled on the Don and later the Dnieper, the Terek and the Ural rivers were early identified as a useful buffer between the Russian empire of Ivan the Terrible and his successors, and the intrusive Turks, Tartars, Chechens and others who intermittently harassed the frontiers of that empire.

They were a military caste whose service – though not always whose loyalty – was to be bought for concessions of land, limited independence and immunity from taxes and normal conscription. But like most military castes – be they Praetorian Guards or Janissaries – when they rebelled they threatened the very existence of the state that had called them into being. Successive Cossack rebels – Bogdan, Stenka Razin, Mazeppa, Pugachev – buffeted the Russian ship of state during the seventeenth and eighteenth centuries.

By the beginning of the nineteenth century the Tsars had effectively harnessed the Cossacks for their own purposes. Napoleon's Grand Army, in full retreat from Moscow in 1812, must have seen the encircling Cossack hordes – cutting down their stragglers and harassing their weary columns – as veritable horsemen from hell. Later in the century, the chain of forts across the Caucasus (the Cossack Line), that had for so long marked the southern boundary of the Tsar's domains, became the launching pad for a series of bloody campaigns to incorporate that wild and mountainous region into the rigid confines of an empire ruled and administered from St Petersburg.

As the nineteenth century progressed and during the first decades of the twentieth, discontent at this rigidity and at the outdated autocracy of the Tsars spread through Russia. Industrialization bred

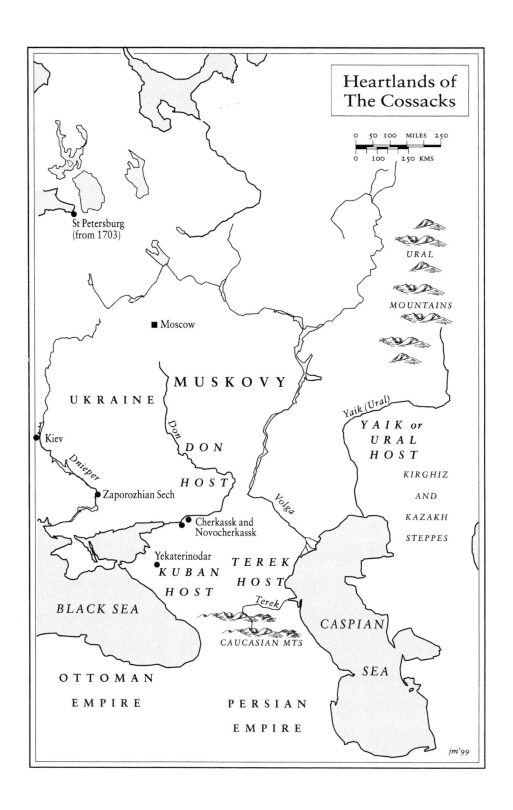

Heartlands of
The Cossacks

urban discontent; crowds increasingly frequently gathered in city squares in defiance of authority; Tsar after Tsar was exposed to the assassin's bullet or bomb. Now the Tsars found the Cossack regiments a rough and ready instrument of internal security. Whereas local troops and police might have had some compunction about charging unarmed civilians in the streets of their own home towns, the Cossacks – imported from the distant fringes of the empire and feeling themselves to be a distinctive military race (like the Gurkhas) – had no such compunction. Cossack whips and sabres were to lash into the disaffected proletariat as Cossack horses rode them down. There were Cossack Guards regiments in the capital, and the Tsarevitch (the Crown Prince) was to be their hereditary *ataman* or leader. The Cossack sword seemed firmly in the hand of the Tsars.

But at the Russian Revolution in 1917 it turned again. Whole regiments defected to the Bolsheviks and swelled the ranks of the Red Army. Others remained loyal to the *ancien régime* and joined the White Russian intervention forces which tried in vain to reverse the tide of revolution. The old mirage of an independent Cossack state in the Ukraine loomed again on the imagined horizon. Stalin saw the Cossacks as a dangerous aberration: potential separatists and tiresome exceptions to his scheme of collectivization. Cossack communities were dispersed or starved during the purges of the 1930s.

So it came about that when the Germans invaded Russia in 1941 the Cossacks were divided. Some rallied to the pennants of the Soviet cavalry – under the hugely-mustachioed Marshal Budenny – and endeavoured to harass the Panzer tanks as Platov's horsemen had harassed Napoleon's invading columns. Others harkened to the blandishments of Nazi propaganda, hinting at Cossack independence from Soviet domination. The retribution that followed at the end of the Second World War was terrible indeed and caused grief and contention

A romantic impression of Gogol's Cossack hero
Taras Bulba crossing the steppes in summer.

to those who were involved in it. The end of 'Cossackdom' was proclaimed and appeared to be a fact: a once-proud race had been reduced to an itinerant equestrian act in Western circuses.

But the Cossacks would not simply fade away and, with the crumbling of the Soviet Union in the last decade of the twentieth century, the Cossacks again raised their heads above the parapet. Boris Yeltsin issued a series of decrees in the early 1990s reinstating their special status and even restoring Cossack units within the armed forces. By the mid-1990s they were engaged once more in the traditional pursuit of fighting the obstreperous Chechens. The Cossacks it seemed were too vital a strand in the fabric of Russian life to be unravelled even by Communism.

And not only in Russian life, but in Russian literature, art and music too. Although during the early centuries of the Cossack settlements there was little beyond verbal tradition and occasional ballads to perpetuate their legends, by the nineteenth century the Cossacks had entered the mainstream of Russian creative art – as a subject if not as a creative force themselves. Pushkin and Lermontov, Gogol and Tolstoy had all romanticized the Cossacks; Sholokhov was later to immortalize their dilemma in the First World War and the Revolution in his *And Quiet Flows the Don*; Repin depicted their impudent spirit in his monumental and boisterous canvas *The Zaporozhian Cossacks writing a reply to the Turkish Sultan*; Mussorgsky and Shostakovich incorporated Cossack tunes or themes in their music.

The intemperate strain in the Cossacks, that was a positive feature when they were fighting, had its drawbacks in other aspects of life. Their Christianity, for instance, was of a distinctively militant variety. While the Ukrainian Cossacks were strictly Orthodox, those of the Don and the Volga were often Old Believers who adhered to their own practices and theology. But to all of them Christianity was a rallying cry against Islamic infidels such as the Turks, Tartars and Chechens, or against

non-Christian traders in their own midst such as the Jews. Indeed, anti-semitism was never far below the surface in a Cossack *stanitsa* or village.

As in a medieval town, life in the *stanitsa* would be dominated by the sound of bells. The wooded Orthodox churches would be flanked by crude bell-towers; the watch-towers would have clanging alarm bells to carry their warning to the nearest fort in the Cossack Line; in summer there would be bells on the cattle roaming the steppes, and in winter bells on the sledges gliding over the rivers. The sound of bells linked the frontier Cossacks with the soul of Mother Russia.

The Cossack community was also an equestrian society. Every man had his horse – usually a sturdy steppe pony – and when mobilized was expected to provide his own mount as well as arm himself. The giving of a fine horse was one of the ways in which Tolstoy's aristocratic hero in *The Cossacks* tries to ingratiate himself with the Cossack family with whom he lodges. Spectacular feats of horsemanship became a fea-

Traditional dances were always an important part of life in a Cossack stanitsa.

ture of all Cossack communities even in exile, where Cossack circuses were often the last and rather sad remnant of a Cossack way of life. But this way of life was not always quite what it seemed.

In theory the Cossack communities received certain set privileges in return for certain set obligations. Not being serfs, they were not tied to any particular landowner. Free grazing for their horses and cattle was available. Being a military caste descended from a nomadic people, they despised those who laboured in the fields at the plough or in the village at the workbench; and in return for their martial services they expected free deliveries of grain and other provisions. They were not taxed by the central government as others were, nor ruled by local governors and the normal hierarchy of petty administrators which was such a stifling feature of Russian rural life. They elected their own leaders and decided their own affairs. Their military units – Hosts – were officered by their own kind and not by outsiders from the aristocracy. They thought of themselves as free men who had chosen to offer their allegiance to the Tsar on their own terms.

In practice, almost from the beginning, things were very different: none of these privileges or obligations were absolute or consistent. From early times they were modified, abused, distorted or ignored in varying degrees at various times and in various places. Rich Cossacks enclosed what had previously been common land. The leaders of Cossack communities – the *atamans* or *hetmans* – were frequently appointed by the Tsar rather than elected from below. The traditional requirement of military service was unequally applied. Whereas in theory all Cossacks were liable for military service – often for as long as thirty years – in practice many of the richer or more influential youths would provide the horse, equipment and pay for some less-well-endowed relative to stand in for them. Increasingly the officers in Cossack regiments tended to be outsiders who were attached for service from line regiments of the Russian

army. Indeed, in the early nineteenth century there was a school of
thought in St Petersburg that considered Cossacks were by definition
unfit to be officers, and in some Cossack Hosts – such as the Terek –
Cossack officers could not rise above the rank of subaltern (in much the
same way as Gurkhas could not rise above junior commissioned rank in
the British Indian Army).

Another aspect of Cossack life which was not as straightforward at it
was often portrayed was the predominantly military nature of their society.
Although non-martial arts were despised in the early Cossack communities
(as is explained in the following chapter) gradually horse-breeding led the
way to animal husbandry and the latter to arable farming and the planting
of vineyards; gunsmiths and blacksmiths led the way to other more diverse
trades and manufactures. When this was so, the case for shipments of regular supplies from metropolitan Russia was largely discredited, but the dis-
continuance of such supplies was resented.

*The **krug** or circle
assembles at a Cossack
settlement to decide
on policy.*

Nor was the unity of the Cossacks ever as solid a feature as the outside world has tended to believe. The early settlements on the River Don – with their capital first at Cherkassk and then at Novocherkassk – were followed by other thriving communities on the Kuban river (north-west of the Caucasus) with its capital at Yekaterinodar (later call Krasnodar), on the Terek river (north-east of the Caucasus), on the Yaik (or Ural) river, on the Amur river (in the Far East of Siberia), on inaccessible islands on the Dnieper and elsewhere along the southern frontiers of Russia (see the map on page 27). Although there was much in common between all these communities, they had different characteristics and often different customs and costumes; only to outsiders did they all appear the same.

So although it may be possible to answer the question 'Who are the Cossacks?', the answer must be one hedged around with many qualifications and beset by many contradictions. And even when allowance is made for this, there remain unresolved enigmas. Are they a military caste firmly anchored within the Russian race; or are they a separate ethnic grouping who ought to be recognized by having an independent nationality? Are they historically a force for Orthodox solidarity and Russian expansion – as the exploits of Yermak in Siberia and the Terek Cossacks in the Caucasus suggest; or are they a force for disintegration and revolt – as the activities of Stenka Razin, Pugachev and the latter-day 'White' Cossacks suggest? Possibly most relevant of all, are they a spent force, a colourful series of chapters in the turbulent story of Russia but essentially an anachronism; or are they a vibrant and enduring strand in the Russian national persona?

This book does not attempt to give categorical answers to these questions, but at least it explores them against the background of five centuries of Russian history. And perhaps more importantly it tells the story of a great people and of the dramatic events which helped to form them.

1:
IVAN THE TERRIBLE
FINDS AN
UNLIKELY ALLY

Nature abhors a vacuum. Although not completely devoid of population, in the Middle Ages the vast region south and east of the Kingdom of Kiev – Kievan Rus – was effectively an empty quarter. It lay between the forests and scattered settlements of Muscovy to the north and the limitless plains and mountain ranges of Asia stretching away to the east. This vacuum was to be filled – or at least temporarily occupied – in a dramatic manner in 1240 AD. The hordes of Tartary swept through like a hurricane, ravaging and laying-low everything in their way. It was said that you could smell them before you could hear them, and you could hear them before you could see them. These Mongol or Tartar warriors (both names are accurate descriptions) clad in iron and leather, riding their steppe ponies and loosing off their quiverfuls of arrows, appeared to the citizens of Kievan Rus to be as deadly as a plague virus and as destructive as a swarm of locusts.

For the following two centuries the Mongols were to exercise their loose sway over the lower reaches of the Dnieper, Don and Volga rivers.

Some settled in Tartar khanates; some collected tribute for the Golden Horde (their main settled off-shoot) from the Muscovites; others roamed the empty plains and forest clearings, raiding settlements and caravans and carrying off prisoners to be sold in the slave markets of Central Asia.

Those who wished to lead a peaceful and secure life needed a measure of protection from these raiders. And on the principle that one should set a thief to catch a thief, it was found that Tartar gangs could be hired to protect their patrons from other Tartars. By the middle of the fifteenth century, a name for these protection gangs was emerging: 'quzzags' the Turks called them, and later 'Cosaques' or 'Cossacks' (a Tartar word for horsemen) became the accepted label.

Protection gradually became concentrated in two forms: escorts were hired by those who had to travel through these dangerous lands, and a chain of forts was set up to protect those who had the misfortune permanently to reside in this troubled region. The latter was a far cry from the eventual Cossack Line that was to form the southern frontier of much of the Tsar's domains; the early forts were no more than a string of wooden palisades which could give mutual support to each other against intruders. But already by the sixteenth century two distinct types of Cossack were identifiable: 'service Cossacks', who were prepared to act as mercenaries to defend their paymasters, and 'free Cossacks' who were a law unto themselves – or more often a lawlessness unto themselves.

By the second half of the sixteenth century – just as the Tudors were consolidating their grip on the strife-torn land of England – a unifying force was emerging in Russia. The Tsar Ivan IV, to be known to his own people as *Grozny* or 'the Dreaded' and to posterity as 'the Terrible', was setting his mind to extending and consolidating the bounds of Muscovy. He was a sinister figure: licentious and diabolically cruel, he was none-the-less an able administrator and shrewd ruler. His policy of expansion on the frontiers and terror at home was sustained by the use of various new military formations. He raised the regiments of *Streltsi*, or sharp-shooters, who were to play the key role in the capture of the Tartar stronghold of Kazan on the upper Volga (and who were to be a fickle factor in the stability of later reigns – notably that of Peter the Great); and he recruited the *Oprichniki*, the autonomous 'special forces' who policed the realm in their black uniforms, on their black horses, with severed dogs' heads hanging as grim talismans from the pommels of their saddles. The *Oprichniki* were the Tsar's instruments in the harassment and persecution of the Boyars – those over-mighty subjects whom Ivan IV was as intent on cutting down to size as Henry VII of England was the surviving warlords of the Wars of the Roses. Those who resisted the Tsar's reforms were liable (like the Archbishop of Novgorod) to be sewn into bear skins and hunted to death by packs of wolf-hounds.

Ivan the Terrible, who first used the Cossacks to help expand the frontiers of Russia.

There was one other new military formation which completed Ivan the Terrible's ranks. He mobilized the Service Cossacks to serve the state rather than the security requirements of individual landowners. Having captured Astrakhan from the Golden Horde in 1556, he now controlled the length of the Volga from Moscow to the Caspian Sea; for the first time this great waterway was an internal Russian river. To prevent counter-offensives and incursions into his new terrain, Ivan paid the Cossacks to act as Russians rather than Tartars and to be the first line of defence. Although there were still many bands of free Cossacks ranging the steppe, an increasing number of them – having accepted the Tsar's rouble and attendant privileges and homesteads – considered themselves to be a loyal frontier force. The poachers – or at least some of the poachers – had turned gamekeepers.

And the character of the Cossack bands was changing in other ways too. Whereas originally they had been mostly left-behind Tartars, now their ranks were swelled by renegades from Muscovy and the lands to the north. One of Ivan the Terrible's reforms had been the retrograde step of tying the peasants ever more closely to their landlords. Those who resented this, or who fell foul of the authorities in their own localities for other reasons, looked for a safe haven beyond the reach of the local gentry and militia. The vast region which the Cossacks had made their own – 'the Wild Steppe' as it was widely known – was a natural destination for such refugees from oppression or from justice.

The Wild Steppe, and its Cossack residents, provided the sort of anonymous protection associated with the Foreign Legion in nineteenth-century Europe: no questions were asked about the background or previous career of newcomers. Even more importantly, no demands for the return of renegades or runaways were entertained by the Cossacks. It was to become a recurring source of friction between the Tsar's government in Moscow (or later St Petersburg) and the Cossack settlements on the Don and elsewhere that those sent to seek out and recapture runaways were given short shrift in this wild country.

Although no-one was turned away from the Cossack community on account of previous misdemeanours, many were turned away because they were deemed too weak to survive and pull their weight in the frontier environment. Newcomers were expected to be agile horsemen, sturdy swordsmen and good shots. They also had to acknowledge the Christian faith; although doctrinal correctness and morality was certainly not a prerequisite, there was little room for Turks or Jews here.

It was frontier existence in every sense. Settled agriculture was both impractical and despised. Hunting and fishing were the recognised means of support in a land well-stocked with game and traversed by rivers teeming with fish; when natural supplies were inadequate, these were supplemented by raiding passing caravans or neighbouring communities. The line between poacher and gamekeeper was at best tenuous and at worst non-existent. In this hand-to-mouth society there was no room for family life: in its early decades, the Wild Steppe was a single-man's world. When the Cossack braves felt the need for women, they raided Tartar or Turkish settlements. Sometimes these raids miscarried, as one did when a party of Cossacks from the Urals trekked across the deserts of Central Asia to carry off women from the city of Khiva and were overtaken and slaughtered by the Khan of Khiva on their way home. But more generally the raids were successful, and gradually women and children began to be a feature of the more permanent Cossack settlements.

Even when this had happened, the women in a Cossack *stanitsa* were very different from their sisters in northern Russia and poles apart from the women to be found in a Turkish harem further south. Cossack women were renowned for their independence and spirit; they shared in the hardships of their menfolk and they shared also in the camaraderie of the camp. This remained the case from the sixteenth to the nineteenth centuries, and Tolstoy in his novel *The Cossacks* makes his hero fall in love with one such 'liberated' young woman.

Cossack women also learnt to be adept at First Aid and nursed their injured menfolk when the latter fell victims of fighting or riding accidents, or when they were bitten by the numerous venomous snakes which frequented the banks of the Terek river. As doctors were rarely found in *stanitsas* in the early centuries of Cossack settlements, there was heavy reliance on traditional herbal medicines. Similarly, as teachers were few, most Cossack boys' education was limited to field crafts and the passing-down of verbal history, and literacy grew slowly in the *stanitsas* – but probably less slowly than among the serfs on the rural estates further north.

A Cossack bride's wedding dress, preserved in the Hermitage Museum in St Petersburg.

As the Cossack communities increased in number and size, so they began to establish a hierarchy of their own. Even though Cossacks might be prepared to act as mercenaries for the Tsar or others, they recognized no outside authority over their own administration. They were not prepared to have Boyars or Governors imposed on them by Moscow. They preferred to elect their own leaders for a limited period of a year and hold them answerable to the community as a whole. Such leaders were called either *ataman* or *hetman*, and they were chosen at an assembly of the *stanitsa*. These assemblies were known as *krugs* or circles, and every male Cossack had a right to attend and make his voice heard. Once elected, the *ataman's* authority was absolute and indicated by a horse-tail banner which fluttered over his tent or was carried beside him in battle: on active service he could inflict the death penalty on any offender who threatened the safety of the group. If he abused his authority, the *ataman* risked not only failure to be re-elected but the anger of the *krug* which could result in a lynching or a summary execution. In most respects, the Cossack system was crudely democratic. Loot was generally divided equally between the campaigners and in cases of dispute the *ataman* would attempt – not always successfully – to intervene before a fight broke out. Penalties were harsh: a Cossack who murdered another could expect to be buried alive alongside the corpse of his victim.

Self-sufficient as these *stanitsas* tried to be, they could not altogether dispense with outside contact and supplies. Although meat, fish, hides and honey might be in abundance, and although horses might be bred and weapons captured, there were still external requirements. The Cossack women spun cloth and grew fruit and vegetables, but they could not produce salt or make boots. So gradually outsiders penetrated the *stanitsas* to trade and barter, to perform skilled crafts or to exchange the loot and plunder of the Cossack encampments for household goods. These traders were sometimes Russians from the north, sometimes

Troika racing across the steppe was a favourite Cossack winter sport.

Armenians from the Caucasus, and occasionally Greeks who had come by water through the Black Sea. As time passed, Jews – who had never been welcome among the Cossacks – also attempted to service the needs of the *stanitsas*, but they were only ever accepted reluctantly and if a quarrel broke out over payment they were frequently roughly handled.

The pattern of Cossack life established itself in similar form during the sixteenth century in several parts of southern Russia. The banks of the river Don were always the heartland, but from early times there were prospering communities on the Terek (in the Caucasus), on the Volga and on the Yaik (Ural) rivers.

On the River Dnieper there was a unique Cossack community. These were the Zaporozhians. They lived on a series of small islands below the rapids on the Dnieper which were virtually inaccessible and hence impregnable. Their initiation rites were even more severe than those of other Cossack communities, and involved swimming the river in full flood. They also were the most amphibious of the Cossacks and played a major role in most of the seaborne assaults in the Black Sea. Their boats were called 'seagulls' and were glorified river-craft, which had to be given extra buoyancy on the high seas by having bundles of reeds attached to their sides. Cumbersome as this made them look, they proved a match for larger galleys and sailing ships. Buccaneering became another facet of Cossack activity.

But it was on land that tactics developed furthest and fastest. The Cossacks were always irregular forces and they employed the techniques of ambush and surprise associated with such forces. Their ponies gave them great mobility on the steppes and it was as cavalry that they pre-ferred to operate. Scouting and escorting were specialities from an early date. But they also sometimes operated in larger units, and when they did so they tended to adopt an extended line of attack which would out-stretch the line of the defenders and would curve in on them at the flanks in a semi-encircling movement. Cossack cavalry were quick to spot weak points in their opponents' defensive lines and would concentrate their attacks on these until a breakthrough enabled them to pour through the lines of the defenders and wreak havoc in their rear. Speed and lack of rigid formation were their defining features. When crossing open coun-try on campaign, the Cossacks would have their baggage carts in two par-allel lines. If they encountered a larger hostile force, these baggage trains would close up at the front and behind, forming a crude circle or oblong of barricades which would be manned by the dismounted Cossacks. The tactic was similar to that employed by the Boers in southern Africa who formed their wagons into laagers, or the pioneers of the Oregon Trail who deployed the same formation against Red Indian attacks. The steppe had much in common with the wide open spaces of the Veldt or the Prairie; and as in those other open spaces, there was a premium on good marksmanship. A Cossack would learn to shoot from the saddle as soon as he could ride, and to ride as soon as he could walk.

With so many martial skills, the Cossacks were sought after as mercenaries not only by the successive Tsars in Russia but by successive Kings of Poland too. Even during the reign of Ivan the Terrible there were Ukrainian Cossacks who had been recruited by King Stephen Bathory of Poland. The Poles tried however to enforce registration on the Cossacks in a way which caused offence and was incompatible with the free and easy life of the runaway communities in the Wild Steppe; registration involved head-counts, and head-counts were unacceptable in a territory which prided itself on its floating population.

Both at home in their *stanitsa* and when away on campaign the Cossacks avoided hierarchies and privileges to a much greater extent than their more settled neighbours. Every man thought himself as good as another. But as the communities on the Don became entrenched, so gradually class distinctions grew up among them. Those who lived on the lower reaches of the Don did so in more comfort and security than the more recent immigrants who settled further north. Although grazing was communal and there were no enclosures, and although hunting and fishing were not restricted by private rights, some Cossacks rose in prosperity faster than others. By the time of Mazeppa (who is the subject of a later chapter) there were many graduations between the *Hetman* and the rank and file, although there would never be as many as in the rarefied social atmosphere of St Petersburg.

Another distinctive feature of Cossack life from an early stage was the costume of the Cossacks. This was essentially adapted for equestrian pursuits. The long baggy trousers, that owed something to Turkish influence, were tucked into high soft-leather boots; the shaggy fur hats were a reminder of their Mongol or Tartar origins; the long cloaks, usually made of felt or sheep-skin, served as blankets as well as top-coats; and – most distinctive of all – were the slanting lines of cartridge slots sewn on their tunics, which were to become the hallmark of even the most formal Cossack uniform. There were of course endless variants on this dress, and most owed something to local circumstances: the Terek Cossacks had many Caucasian features of dress, while the buccaneering Zaporozhians tended to be decked out in the oriental finery of whoever they had most recently despoiled.

Although life was hard in the Wild Steppe in the early years of Cossack settlement, it was never austere. Wine and song were a feature of the *stanitsa* even before women were a regular feature. The *gopak* – originally a Ukrainian dance – was early adopted by the Cossacks who would jump on tables and kick out their legs displaying the flexibility of their muscles as vividly as the flexibility of their soft-leather boots. Variants of the balalaika provided accompaniment to these revels. As of course did vodka. But however inclined to drunkenness the Cossack communities might be, a rigid rule of abstinence took over when they were on raids and campaigns, and an *ataman* would feel himself justified in shooting a drunken Cossack who was jeopardizing the safety of his fellows by noisy behaviour or erratic shooting.

But neither the community life that developed nor the emergence of some measure of domesticity could disguise the fact that the Cossacks were essentially a military phenomenon: the *voiska* or 'host' was a more significant unit than the *stanitsa*. And because they were so largely a male, military entity most frequently fighting the infidel in the form of Tartars or Turks, and at least nominally Christian, the Cossacks have sometimes been compared to the military orders of chivalry: the Knights

Cossacks played balalaikas and guitars when relaxing as early as the 17th century.

Templar or Knights Hospitaller. The comparison does not stand up.

Although a nominal Christianity was a requirement of admission to the Cossack communities, religion did not play any major part in the lives of the early settlers in the Wild Steppe. There was no church at Cherkassk – their main centre on the Don – until nearly a century after Ivan the Terrible's time. Nor was any distinctively Christian code of conduct practised. In fact while they more usually fought against 'infidels', there were many instances of them fighting in the company of Muslims against fellow Christians. Again, while they more generally fought for the Orthodox Russians, there were cases of them fighting for the Catholic Poles against Orthodox Christians. So neither in religion nor in denomination were they consistent.

What they did have in common with the Crusading Orders of Chivalry was that they were a military caste, answerable in all matters of day-to-day administration only to their own appointed leaders, and answerable in the last resort only to the Tsar. In this they had common ground with the Templars, who did not recognize the jurisdiction of local bishops but answered only to their own Grand Master and through him ultimately to the Pope. They also were storm-troopers who could be deployed on dare-devil or even suicidal missions. The Cossack assaults on the Turkish fortress of Azov had echoes of the Templars' assaults on Acre, when the latter were so jealous of their achievement in breaching the walls that they posted sentries to prevent their allies joining them and sharing the glory.

This then – the Cossack community of the Wild Steppe – was the third of the military formations which Ivan the Terrible hitched to the Tsar's would-be centralized regime during the second half of the sixteenth century. It was to prove more durable than either of the other two: the *Streltsi* or the *Oprichniki*. It was also to prove even harder to control than either of the others – but all that lay in the future and was a problem for Ivan's successors rather than for him.

2 :
FIRST STEPS
INTO SIBERIA

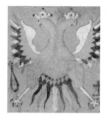

T HE MERCHANT-ADVENTURER FAMILY of Stroganov have made their
mark at various times and in various ways during the course of Russian
history over the past four centuries. They built palaces in Moscow,
Novgorod and St Petersburg, and they acquired titles: Baron, Count
and even Prince. They have been gamblers and notable hosts to Tsars
and foreign diplomats. One of them even invented a way of cooking beef
that has brought their name into the culinary vocabulary of Western
Europe.

But in 1558 they performed a service to the Russian state which –
in retrospect – probably outweighed all their other contributions. They
decided they should expand their estates on the upper reaches of the
Kama river, to the east of Moscow. They were entrepreneurs as well as
merchants and were looking for valuable commodities to market. Chief
among these were furs.

In sixteenth-century Europe, as the paintings of Holbein and others demonstrate, furs were not only a necessary adjunct to surviving the

rigorous winters in forests and inadequately heated castles, they were also (then as now) a significant status symbol. The fur of rabbits, dogs and cats might suffice for peasants and the petty-bourgeois of the burgeoning cities; but rarer pelts were in demand for the nobility and the wealthier merchants. Such pelts were to be found to a considerable extent within the Tsar's existing domains; indeed, Giles Fletcher, who represented Queen Elizabeth I of England as a merchant-ambassador to Tartary in 1588, recorded 'the native commodities of the country are ... first furres of all sorts'. However, the most sought-after and valuable furs – sable, ermine, white and black arctic fox, and certain sorts of bear-skin – were only to be found in the coldest climes and the remotest parts, and the Stroganovs identified the banks of the Kama and all points east and north as the most promising foraging grounds.

The problem confronting them was that, although they already owned extensive estates on the banks of the upper Kama, the region beyond – over the Ural mountains – was alien and hostile territory. Tartar khans with their bands of warriors – remnants of the Golden Horde – ranged these regions and did not take kindly to intrusion by hunters, trappers or traders. In particular, Kuchum, Khan of Sibir and a descendant of Genghis Khan, stood firm on the River Ob and its tributaries the Tobol, Tura and Irtysh. If the Stroganovs were to continue to protect their own estates from intrusion, they could not spare men and weapons to escort expeditions eastwards. Hired mercenaries appeared to be the answer, and indeed the Tsar encouraged them to think along these lines by granting them permission to raise their own militia.

The Stroganovs chose the right man. Yermak Timofeyevich already had a reputation as a free-booting Don Cossack who had built up, with reinforcements from absconding serfs and criminals on the run, a band of some 800 strong on the banks of his native Don. His youth had

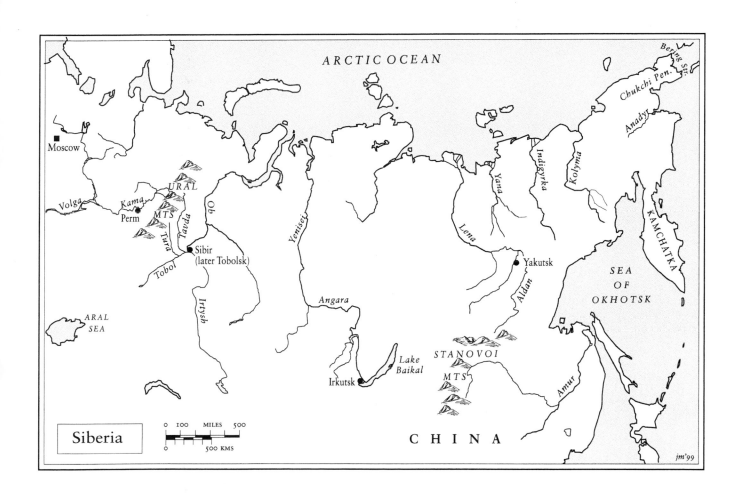

ARCTIC OCEAN

Bering Str.

Chukchi Pen.

Anadyr

Moscow

URAL

Volga

Kama

Perm

MTS

Tura

Tobol

Tavda

Ob

Sibir
(later Tobolsk)

Irtysh

Yenisei

Angara

Lena

Yana

Indigyrka

Kolyma

Aldan

Yakutsk

KAMCHATKA

SEA
OF
OKHOTSK

ARAL
SEA

Lake
Baikal

Irkutsk

STANOVOI

MTS

Amur

CHINA

jm'99

Siberia

0   100   MILES   500

0   500 KMS

been spent alternately in raiding caravans and wealthy travellers, and in acting as a hired arm of Muscovite authority when counter-measures against the neighbouring Tartars in the Wild Country were required. He had been both poacher and gamekeeper. Increasingly, as Ivan the Terrible's control spread, the opportunities for both activities diminished. Yermak had moved north with his band of followers to Perm, and it was here – in the region where the Stroganovs had been granted concessions to mine salt – that he came to the attention of that formidable family.

At first Yermak and his men were engaged by the Stroganovs on essentially defensive duties: preventing Tartar incursions. But hunger for furs, coupled with a curiosity to discover whether there were exploitable deposits of copper and other minerals beyond the Urals, soon persuaded the Muscovite settlers that a more offensive campaign was required. The risk of provoking reprisals from the Tartars – who not infrequently kidnapped Russian women and children – was not to be ignored, so the Tsar's permission for a 'forward' policy, which could exacerbate relations, was required and obtained.

In 1581 Yermak set out up a tributary of the Kama into the Urals accompanied by a force variously estimated as between 500 and 800 Cossacks. They were a hard-bitten bunch of warriors and no back-sliding or desertion was tolerated. Those who showed reluctance to press on were loaded with sandbags and tossed by Yermak into the river to 'strengthen the bond uniting his men'.

The Stroganov family had both provisioned and equipped the expedition to a much higher standard than that to which the Cossacks had been accustomed in their earlier days of casual raiding. In addition to the usual sabres and pikes, they were provided with arquebuses and ammunition. Also, like their near-contemporaries the Spanish conquistadors setting out for Mexico and Peru, they took with them an impres-

The Cossacks frequently took icons with them on campaigns. They preferred equestrian subjects, usually from the Novgorod school but sometimes of Greek origin.

sive array of holy banners and religious emblems (including icons) to give their campaign the flavour and appearance of a crusade against Islam and the heathen.

The first obstacle was the Ural range. Having left the Kama and its main tributaries behind them, they joined other smaller rivers and ended by penetrating the mountains in their flat-bottomed boats along rocky stream-beds. Sometimes they had to raise the water-level over a particular set of rapids by temporarily damming the stream with a sail, until they floated their craft past the hazard. At other times they resorted to portages. There were no maps or even travellers' tales to help them, as they were penetrating where no Russians – no Europeans of any description – had ever been before, since the occasional trading caravans which had crossed the steppes to the East had done so by other overland routes. Eventually they had to abandon their boats and march over the watershed carrying their weapons, their icons and their supplies.

On the eastern slopes of the Urals they again encountered navigable rivers. So they halted for long enough to construct fresh boats from the standing timber along their route. Now they were entering inhabited lands: the khanate of Sibir – Siberia in fact. The semi-nomadic Tartars exercised a loose sway over these regions, whose inhabitants – Voguls and others – paid them assorted tribute as protection money. Now the Cossacks were to encounter the Vogul tribesmen in the circumstances they most feared – sudden ambush.

At this, the first recorded instance of a Cossack force engaged in action with the authority of the Muscovite government on a completely new frontier of the Tsar's empire, what were to become the traditional roles were reversed. The sudden rush of mounted attackers, the flights of arrows shot into the air, the mobility and the surprise were all with the Cossacks' opponents. The fire-power and the discipline were all with the water-borne Cossacks. And it was the fire-power of the arquebuses which was decisive. Soon the Tartars and Voguls had scattered and fled, returning to report to their leader Kuchum that the intruders were armed with miraculous weapons sounding like thunder and penetrating any armour. They appeared to have supernatural advantages, just as convincingly as the Spanish conquistadors had over the Incas of Peru.

But despite his enemies' unfair advantages, Kuchum determined to resist. His next ambush was more carefully prepared in a gorge of the Tura river down which, with the winter's ice now long since melted, the Cossacks were rowing and sailing ever eastwards towards Sibir. Kuchum's men built an – apparently natural – barrier of brushwood across the river, and then concealed themselves at vantage points on the nearby banks so that they could fire their arrows at short range into the crowded Cossack boats as soon as these were immobilized.

It was fortunate for Yermak that his leading boat hit the barrier after dark and his men managed to disentangle themselves and withdraw, albeit under Tartar fire, relatively intact. The nature of the ambush had become apparent to Yermak and he determined to turn the tables on his opponents. He set his men also to cutting down brushwood, but instead of building a barricade with this he made dummy figures like scarecrows – dressing them in the clothes of his Cossacks – and put them in the boats, which were manned only by a skeleton crew of strong swimmers and allowed to drift back towards the Tartar ambush position.

At dawn the next day and while this manoeuvre was taking place, Yermak disembarked the bulk of his 500-strong force (some wearing what was left of their clothing and others virtually or completely naked – but all heavily armed) and led them silently along the banks of the Tura to take the ambushers in the rear and by surprise. This time the unsuspecting Tartars were completely routed by their under-dressed but heavily-armed opponents; they fled abandoning their casualties and left the route of advance along the Tura river open to Yermak.

The Cossacks pressed on until they came to the confluence of the Tavda and Tobol rivers where the Tartar forces were massing and waiting for a decisive confrontation. Yermak decided he had gone as far as he could with his meagre force and sent out reconnaissance parties to find out an alternative route back to Perm and the Russian side of the Urals. The prospect of another winter, either beleaguered in Tartar territory or freezing in the high Urals, was insupportable. The scouts returned however with bleak news: there was no viable alternative route of return.

Yermak decided that, since retreat was impossible, a bold advance on Kuchum's capital of Sibir was his only option. If he and his men perished, it would at least be a quick death in battle rather than slow starvation and frostbite in the Urals; and if he could – despite all odds – succeed in capturing Sibir, then he would have a comfortable and secure base for the winter months.

Beyond the confluence of the Tavda and Tobol rivers, the latter joins the Irtysh and it was here that Yermak was confronted with Kuchum's massed body of some 2,000 warriors. Neither side was in good shape for a battle. Yermak's Cossacks were exhausted, under-nourished and isolated. Kuchum's Tartar ranks included tribal levies who were less than fully integrated into the Tartar force, and their khan – Kuchum himself – was old and blind and had to be carried into the fray on a litter while his nephew took effective command.

The Cossacks had one unexpected boost to their morale. On the night before the engagement (according to the Remezov Chronicle) a vision was seen in the Cossack camp of a city with its church bells pealing above a pillar of fire. This was taken to be a clear indication that

Christ's improbable champion – Yermak – would triumph over the hordes of Mahomet and his representative Kuchum.

None of these handicaps or visions prevented the ensuing battle from being a long and fierce one. The banks of the river were piled with bodies as the hand-to-hand fight raged on intermittently for four days. The Cossacks had over a quarter of their total force killed, leaving little more than 300 to carry on the fight. But the Tartar depletions were greater because to their dead were added defectors from the Vogul and other tribes. Eventually the remnants of the Tartars withdrew carrying their bewildered and infirm khan with them. The way now lay open for the Cossacks to advance on Kuchum's capital of Sibir.

It turned out to be deserted, but it was hardly a rich spoil of war. Sibir was a palisaded encampment, more like a glorified stockade than a capital. There were no rich storehouses to be looted, but at least there was shelter and relative safety. Also, being installed at Sibir gave Yermak some local prestige and credibility; some of the tribal elements who had earlier paid tribute to Kuchum now brought gifts and offers of support to Yermak – the resident potentate.

But Sibir, though at first a safe haven, quickly became something of a prison camp to the Cossacks. When they ventured out in search of food and furs, they were subjected to sniping by the Tartars who still maintained a presence all around. Again, it was a reversal of what was to become the accepted Cossack role: they were the victims of guerrilla war rather that the perpetrators of it.

Eventually Yermak decided he must seek further support from home, that is from his Stroganov patrons. He dispatched one of his lieutenants – Ivan Koltso – to seek reinforcements. Koltso did not attempt the return journey by boat; the rivers were frozen, so he set off on skis and sledges by the so-called Wolf Road along the ice of the river beds to the Urals and on to Perm.

On his eventual arrival in Perm, Koltso did not receive the warm and congratulatory welcome he had expected and felt he deserved. The Stroganovs were in trouble with the Tsar. Although they had sought and obtained permission from Moscow to launch Yermak's expedition, this had had unwelcome repercussions. The Moslem Tartars – and particularly their tribal supporters the Voguls – had reverted to attacking Russian settlements along the eastern frontiers of the Tsar's domains. Children had been taken for ransom; wives had been taken for harems. The Tsar, forgetful of his own encouragement, blamed the Stroganovs for provoking this retaliation.

Maxim Stroganov for his part decided that Koltso had best be left to explain himself direct to Ivan the Terrible – a daunting prospect for the exhausted adventurer. Koltso prudently took with him to Moscow the bales of furs with which Yermak had entrusted him. Ivan the Terrible (like his contemporary Elizabeth I of England) was predisposed to forgive provocation of foreigners if it were profitable enough in terms of booty (his equivalent of Spanish gold being Siberian sable and arctic fox). Koltso was also able to reassure the Tsar that his Siberian neighbour was a less formidable adversary than had been supposed: was not his capital already in Russian hands?

Yermak's choice of Koltso as his envoy had been a shrewd one. He dissolved the Tsar's wrath and won his favour. He was soon dispatched back to Yermak loaded with provisions, ammunition and gifts, the last including a double-thickness suit of chain-mail armour for Yermak, embossed with the imperial double-headed eagle that was to endure until the Revolution of 1917 as the emblem of the Tsar. Reinforcements were also promised shortly.

When Koltso finally regained Yermak's headquarters at Sibir, he found that all had not gone well in his absence. Cossack sorties to fish and hunt in the environs of Sibir had fallen into Tartar

Yermak's Cossacks are ambushed by Tartars on a Siberian river in 1582: Christian zeal and superior firepower triumphed.

ambushes; on one occasion nineteen Cossacks out of a party of twenty had been slaughtered and their severed heads delivered to the gates of Sibir. Such incidents, coupled with hunger in the Cossack camp, had lowered morale: Yermak had had to resort once more to dropping attempted deserters into the rivers – each with their loaded sandbag attached.

Apart from the return of Koltso with his encouraging messages and gifts, there was however one other piece of good news: the capture – kidnap would perhaps be a more accurate word – of Kuchum's nephew and right-hand man – Mahmetkul. He had been snatched from a Tartar encampment and was now held by Yermak as a hostage.

Heartened by these two events, Yermak and his men set out on further exploration. They pursued the course of the Irtysh to the east as far as its junction with the Ishim river; doubling back to the north-west, they also explored the course of the Tavda river; and striking out due north they followed the Irtysh till it joined the Ob river, whose banks they also explored. Sibir had been made the centre for a whole web of further penetration and exploration of Western Siberia.

Since all these expeditions resulted in further areas of theoretical Russian domination, Yermak found his force greatly over-extended in its geographical commitments. Only 150 of his original Cossacks remained alive, and the reinforcements, when eventually they arrived from Moscow under command of Prince Bolkhovski, proved very disappointing. To start with, Bolkhovski's contingent of 350 Russians (not Cossacks) were utterly exhausted after their long and hungry march. They were alleged to have resorted to canabalism and to have eaten some of their fallen comrades *en route*, which upset even the hardened Cossacks among Yermak's survivors. They also arrived ill as well as weak, and Bolkhovski himself expired shortly after arrival. Their presence did little therefore either to raise morale or to supplement the fighting strength of Yermak's garrison.

Those Tartar tribes who were now nominally paying tribute to Yermak rather that to Kuchum were not slow to notice the enfeebled state of the Cossack invaders. Led by Karacha, a chief of the Ostyak tribe, they began to plot against Yermak. Having inveigled Koltso – Yermak's trusted lieutenant – into a trap, Karacha murdered him and led a general assault on the Cossack garrison at Sibir. Meanwhile, in the hope that it would please and impress the Tsar, Yermak had sent his hostage Mahmetkul to Moscow. Kuchum therefore felt his nephew's fate was remote from local events in Sibir and seems to have no longer been constrained by considerations of what would become of him. So Kuchum too started plotting against Yermak.

The plot he hatched was a cunning one. Yermak was known to harbour, among other ambitions, the desire to reinstate the trade routes between Moscow and the rich khanates of Central Asia: Samarkand, Bokhara, Merv and Khiva. In this he was furthering the legitimate aspirations of his master the Tsar. Kuchum knew of this interest of Yermak's in the caravan routes of the old Silk Road. He accordingly put about reports that a rich trading caravan from the Emirate of Bokhara would shortly be reaching the Irtysh river. Yermak fell for the bait and promptly set off with fifty of his best men to meet and escort the caravan on this crucial stage of its way to Moscow.

In the course of searching for the non-existent caravan, Yermak camped on a small island on the Irtysh river. Kuchum had been furtively following his party and monitoring his movements. Now he saw his chance. Some of Kuchum's men swam across to the island during the night, under cover of a heavy thunder storm, and found the Cossack guards far from alert: in fact, they managed to steal some arquebuses. When they reported back to Kuchum, showing their trophies as evidence of the lack of wakefulness in the Cossack camp, Kuchum decided to risk an attack.

The Tartars began swimming and paddling across to the island, their stealthy movements still under cover of heavy rain and rolls of thunder. Once enough of them had landed, they set about slitting the throats of the sleeping or somnolent Cossacks. By the time Yermak was roused, it was too late to rally his troops. Seeing that the position was

*A rare portrait of a 19th-century Cossack
fighting on foot rather than on horseback.*

desperate, he struggled into the heavy mail armour – with its rich embellishments – that the Tsar had so recently sent to him, and he fought his way to the shore in the hope of finding a small boat. Protected by his armour and lashing out at the Tartars he reached the water's edge, but no boat was to be found. With no alternative, he plunged into the waters of the Irtysh – that river on which he had performed so many feats of bravery – but was pulled under by the weight of the same armour that a few moments before had been his salvation.

Yermak was dead. There was a spate of legends and rumours about his body: first it was missing, then it was found intact, then it disappeared or was hidden. However that might be, without their living leader his remaining Cossacks decided to abandon Sibir and head for the Urals and home. Soon they were to return in greater strength, but the initial thrust was over. The first full-scale Cossack imperial venture had concluded. The first Cossack hero had found a place in the pantheon of glory. Statues of Yermak were to spring up on the Don and in Siberia. His effrontery and courage, endurance and single-mindedness were to be compared with those Spanish conquistadors only a few years away in time but half a world away in space.

In one respect Yermak's death was timely. Had he survived and been present in person to receive the reinforcements that were soon to be on the way, he might have become an over-mighty subject. Like Cortes breaking free from the Viceroy of Cuba who had sent him out, he might have felt strong enough eventually – if the local tribute from the tribes had resumed – to renounce his patrons the Stroganovs. He might even have flirted with the idea of a Cossack state in Siberia, independent of the Tsar in Moscow, just as the concept of such states was to haunt the Cossack communities in the Ukraine, the Don basin and elsewhere intermittently over the centuries. Yermak dead could be a Russian hero as well as a Cossack one; alive he might have been less dependable.

The further exploration and settlement of Siberia and the far east of Russia was also largely a Cossack achievement. It is possible to see the remarkably rapid progress of the Cossacks across more that 3,000 miles of this largest land-mass in the world (they had reached the Pacific at the Sea of Okhotsk by 1639) in two separate ways. On the one hand, it was one of the great adventures of world exploration, comparable to the voyages of Columbus or Vasco da Gama. On the other hand, it was at times a progression of slaughter, exploitation and pillage that left a trail of brutality nearly annihilating the sparse population of Siberia (a mere one inhabitant to every hundred square miles) and deeply shocking the more civilized population of neighbouring China as it encroached on the frontiers of that empire.

The landscape of Siberia is not – and was not then – uniform. Having crossed the Urals (the word means 'belt' in the Tartar language), the Cossacks found themselves first on the West Siberian plateau – a region running from the Arctic Ocean in the north to the Steppes of Kazakhstan 1,300 miles to the south, and from the Urals in the west to the River Yenisei 1,000 miles to the east. While the southern part of this region suffers from droughts, the northern part is largely a malarial swamp in summer and a wasteland of frozen marsh in winter. The rivers (including the Ob and the Irtysh on which Yermak campaigned) all flow northwards, flooding their banks and creating a desolation of lifeless lakes and treacherous bogs. Even the Tartars had by-passed this unpromising terrain. Where the tundra is drier, herds of reindeer roamed.

Beyond the Yenisei to the east, Siberia rolls on inexorably, and the traveller finds himself entering the *taiga*, that vast forest of cedar, pine, larch, birch and spruce of which – Chekhov was later to say – 'only the migrating birds know where it ends'. It is not a gentle forest for recreational walking: there are many hazards – forest fires, storms and floods, pestilential insects, and dangerous wild life. This wild life, which would have been more plentiful in the seventeenth century than today, included bears, badgers, otters, wolverines, pole-cats, spotted deer, a great variety of foxes, and – most frighteningly – wolves. These last would roam the *taiga* in alarmingly large packs and, even when they had moved on, riders would find it impossible to persuade their horses to cross the track where the wolf pack had passed. Further east still, the Siberian tiger – the largest variety in the world – would still stalk the steppes, raiding settlements and carrying off humans.

This was the unpromising terrain across which the Cossacks set out. The spur to their activity remained, as in the case of the Stroganovs and Yermak, what can best be called 'the fur rush'. To the intruders, the forested steppes of Siberia appeared as one vast game park where every mammal, from the smallest squirrel to the largest bear, was provided by nature with a pelt adequate for survival in temperatures often 30°C or even 50°C below freezing. As Giles Fletcher had gone on to say in his report to Queen Elizabeth I of England, 'God ... provideth a naturall remedie for them, to help the naturall inconuenience of their countrey by the cold of the Climat'.

Despite this 'inconvenience', and as a direct result of the Cossack activities in the years immediately following Yermak's death, furs became big business for Russia. The number of skins was a measure of the devastation being wrought: Tsar Fyodor, son of Ivan the Terrible, presented as a gift to the Holy Roman Emperor in 1595 over 400,000 pelts including many extremely rare sables. Already in 1605 it was calculated that eleven per cent of the total income of the Russian state was derived from fur.

The Cossacks did not normally hunt or trap the fur-bearing animals themselves: they preferred to cajole or intimidate the local inhabitants to supply the furs as tribute. Usually a proportion of the pelts

Bear hunting in the forest was a popular pastime in winter. The valuable skins were deemed worth the risks.

handed over would be retained as a perquisite of the Cossacks involved. Often they retained far more furs than they or their dependants could possibly use personally, and these – if they wished to conceal their illicit wealth from Moscow – they sold to caravans going southwards to Bokhara, Samarkand or the other emirates and khanates of Central Asia. Although for most of the year these southern oasis towns baked in hot desert climates, there were cold seasons and the furs served a practical as well as a prestige purpose – like in many Far Eastern countries today.

Personal cupidity therefore added to the demands of the state on the natives of Siberia.

In the years following Yermak's death, his Cossack successors continued his strategy of making advances up the line of the main rivers. They also established *ostrogs* (fortified trading posts) as they advanced. The first such was at Tobolsk, founded in 1587 near the junction of the Tobol and Irtysh rivers where the old Tartar capital had stood. These *ostrogs* were seldom left in peace by the locals. Tomsk, which began as one such *ostrog* on the flank of the Cossack advance before it became an established town, was attacked in 1609, 1614, 1630, 1654, 1674, 1680 and 1682. The Cossacks could seldom feel totally secure or relaxed even within their own enclaves. Despite – or possibly because of – this, their reputation for heavy drinking was formidable even by the standards of the place and time. Few *ostrogs* ever had a garrison of more than two hundred Cossacks at any one moment, and even when their exploring and colonizing activities were at their most intense, there were probably only a few thousand Cossacks in the whole of Siberia.

One of the first lines of advance was southwards along the Ob towards the emirates of Central Asia. From the eastern tributaries of the Ob it was a short overland portage to the western tributaries of the Yenisei river. Pursuing this river southwards through the very heart of Siberia, they linked up with the Angara river and discovered that vast lake of unfathomed depth – Baikal. The process of leap-frogging from river to river was continued. Another thrust further east exposed the explorers to yet another great Siberian river system: this time the Lena, first reached in 1628 by Vasily Bugor. The River Lena joined the River Aldan which in turn led them southwards to the Stanovoi mountains and the fringes of China. The Cossack *ataman*, Nan Moskvitin, having crossed the Stanovoi mountains, reached the Amur river and finally – in 1639 – the Sea of Okhotsk (joining the Pacific Ocean) to the north of Japan. It has been calculated that by this date the rate of Russian expansion into Siberia since Yermak first set out in 1581 had been almost 5,000 square miles a year.

The Amur river was clearly leading the Cossacks into country under Chinese influence, if not part of China itself. The Dauri tribesmen who inhabited its banks had hitherto enjoyed a measure of Chinese protection. But the intruders, despite the complications and risks involved, could not resist plundering and occupying the banks of the Amur. Here, for the first time in Siberia, they found waving corn and a more clement climate. Compared to their treks across the tundra and the *taiga*, this was a land of milk and honey. The complications and risks were to become apparent soon enough.

While all this riverine and overland activity was afoot, other Cossacks had been venturing their frail craft on the waters of the Arctic Ocean. In 1633 Ivan Perfiliv linked the mouth of the Lena river with the mouth of the Yana river some 400 miles further east. Five years later another Cossack – Ivan Rebrov – took the process a stage further and pressed along the Arctic coast for another 500 miles to the mouth of the Indigyrka river. From there, a fellow Cossack leap-frogged along the coast to the Kolyma river mouth. An *ostrog* was established some twelve days' sail up that river, and by 1647 it was recorded that there were nearly 400 Russians living on the banks of the Kolyma.

Eventually, in 1648, Semyon Ivanovich Dezhnyov, a Cossack collector of *yassack* (a tax collected in furs) sailed yet further east from the Kolyma river and rounded the Chukchi peninsula passing through the straits (later to be named after Bering) between Siberia and Alaska. The Pacific had been reached by sea as well as by land. Dezhnyov's ship became separated from that of his companion and he made a landfall near the mouth of the Anadyr river. He spent nearly ten years establishing a base there and exploring the region; walrus hunting (largely for the ivory tusks) was as profitable as fur trapping. The tragedy was that Dezhnyov's report, which proved conclusively that the Asian continent was neither linked by land to America nor to an Arctic land mass, was mislaid for over a hundred years in the archives of Yatutsk (an early instance of Russian bureaucratic inefficiency). So although the mystery of the continent's extremity had been solved by a Cossack in the early seventeenth century, it was not until Peter the Great sent the Danish sea-captain Vitus Bering to chart these waters nearly a century later that the truth became public knowledge.

Dezhnyov had behaved with a measure of consideration to those natives he had encountered on his journeys and voyages. But meanwhile great damage had been done to the good name of the Cossacks by others less scrupulous.

Peter Beketov, a Cossack sent out by the Tsar, was one such. While discovering the source of the Lena river and founding the *ostrog* of Yakutsk, Beketov was regularly collecting fur tax from the natives. But not content with this, he kidnapped them to sell as slaves on his own account.

Vasili Poyarkov was another such. One of his expeditions up the Aldan river in search of silver had been caught out by the oncome of winter and had resorted to cannibalism to survive, killing members of their own party for this purpose as well as eating captured Dauri tribesmen. When eventually Poyarkov moved on, he slaughtered so many of the Dauri tribesmen along the banks of the Amur river, and took so many into captivity as slaves, that even the Russian authorities in Yakutsk reacted with repugnance. On return he was arrested and sent back to Moscow to answer for his misdeeds. But this did not stop the rot.

Yerofei Khabarov led a party of 130 Cossacks from Yakutsk back to the Dauri lands in 1650, where he – like his predecessor – ravaged the countryside, setting fire to villages with their inhabitants still trapped within them. He boasted that 'With God's help ... we burned them ... we killed 661'. (In this engagement his own death roll was only four.) The Manchu Emperor of China was so incensed by these atrocities that in 1652 he sent an armed party to defend his subjects; but the Chinese posse was inadequate for the task and were themselves slaughtered by the Cossacks. It was the first of many Sino/Russian engagements on the Amur river. It was not until 1689 that a treaty defining the frontier was negotiated, and even then the Tsar's envoy required an escort of nearly a thousand Cossacks to ensure his safe return.

The Kamchatka peninsula at the eastern extremity of Siberia, with its volcanoes and roaming herds of reindeer, was also to be penetrated by Cossack overland expeditions from the north. This region too was to be the scene of further Cossack brutality. In 1697 Vladimir Atlasov forced many of the native hunters, fishermen and herdsmen to flee or kill their own wives and children rather than let them fall into Cossack hands. As with Poyarkov, his excesses dismayed his own masters and he too was arrested on return, but later freed to continue his campaign of rapine and personal enrichment. Atlasov's conduct was eventually too much even for his own Cossack rank and file, who turned on him and killed him.

Not surprisingly these recurring campaigns of brutality turned the whole of eastern Siberia into a region of prolonged conflict. Local walrus hunters, trappers and foresters turned their rough skills against the intruders, and the Cossacks themselves were ambushed, murdered and mutilated whenever they relaxed their defences. Even an official Russian government enquiry was critical of the way the government's own agents – the Cossacks – had got dragged into a semi-permanent state of warfare. As late as 1727 a Cossack *ataman* called Shetakov was murdered after a runaway reindeer pulling his sledge drew him unwillingly into a native encampment in Kamchatka. It was not until the last quarter of the eighteenth century that harmony was established in any lasting way.

If the Tsar and his government, first in Moscow and then in St Petersburg, were ashamed or embarrassed by the heavy-handed methods of their instruments of colonization, they had only themselves to blame. The Cossack bands that had been dispatched as explorers, fur collectors and prospectors were usually unpaid and expected to live off extortion; they included criminals on the run from justice and escaped serfs seeking their freedom; they were wild men on the make in a land where the climate, environment and every man's hand was against them. Many of those mentioned in this chapter were memorable explorers, but – like Stanley in Africa three centuries later – their conduct sullied their achievements: few of them deserved monuments of the type erected to their forebear Yermak.

3 :
BORIS GODUNOV
AND THE
TIME OF TROUBLES

'GOD HATH A GREAT PLAGUE in store for this people' wrote Jerome Horsey, the merchant-ambassador of England to Muscovy at the end of the sixteenth century. It was an accurate prophecy for the Russia which Ivan the Terrible had left behind him on his death in 1584. His brutalities had largely destroyed the Boyar class without putting anything in its place apart from the 'tyrannous practice that hath so troubled this country' – to quote again from Giles Fletcher.

As we have seen in recent times, the only thing worse than tyranny is often its sudden collapse and the vacuum that is left behind in its place. 'Without a Tsar, Russia is a widow, and the Russian people are orphans' ran an old proverb. This was the state of affairs when Tsar Fyodor, Ivan's son and successor, died a few years after Ivan himself. Fyodor had not been an effective Tsar: Sir Fitzroy Maclean summed him up neatly when he wrote in his *Holy Russia*, 'Though he was not, it appears, entirely indifferent to bear-baiting, young Tsar Fyodor's chief interests seem to have been bell-ringing and elaborate church ritual.'

Such arcane pursuits were hardly a substitute for the steely hand of Ivan the Terrible on the rudder of the ship of state. But Fyodor had one great asset which died with him: he was a hereditary and legitimate Tsar, though sadly he had no children and was the last of the Rurik line.

Fyodor had had a young half-brother – Prince Dmitri – who would have succeeded to the throne had be been still alive. But Dmitri had died seven years before at the age of nine in mysterious circumstances. He had been living with his mother at the small town of Uglich on the Volga when he had been discovered with his throat slit. His mother had no doubt the boy had been murdered by order of the ambitious and ruthless Boris Godunov, who had been one of Ivan the Terrible's henchmen and later Fyodor's right-hand man. A court of enquiry set up by Boris Godunov at the time had found that the unfortunate Dmitri must have slipped and cut his throat inadvertently with his own knife; it was even hinted that the child might have been epileptic.

Prince Dmitri, looking much older (in a 17th-century print) than the nine-year-old who was thought to be murdered by Boris Godunov.

In these circumstances, it was hardly a surprise when – on the death of Fyodor – Boris Godunov arranged to have himself elected Tsar. Boris was dogged by ill fortune from the start. An exceptionally severe autumn in 1601 led to widespread crop failures. Famine followed, and plague followed famine. Tsar Boris's efforts to distribute grain were frustrated by profiteering landlords and merchants. Muscovites starved and blamed their misfortunes on the absence of a hereditary tsar in succes-

sion to Ivan and Fyodor. In the towns employers discharged their workers, and in the countryside landlords expelled their tenants and peasants. The hungry and unemployed took to roaming the streets and the
river banks, plundering merchants, landowners and monastic houses;
castles were set on fire; the forests teemed with brigands; chaos spread
through the land. 'The Time of Troubles' had begun.

After the first three years of these troubles, a self-appointed sav-
iour arose. A figure claiming to be the infant Dmitri grown to manhood
emerged on the south-western borders of Russia. This figure – who may
or may not have been a runaway monk – claimed to have escaped the
murderous intentions of Boris Godunov. He quickly acquired a wide following among hungry peasants and disaffected Cossacks; more importantly, he received substantial backing from the King of Poland. Soon he
was marching on Moscow to oust Tsar Boris and 'restore the House of
Rurik'. His greatest asset was that the Russian people wanted to believe
in him: they thought that a descendant of the old line of tsars would
mean that Russia was no longer a widow, and that the hunger and lawlessness of the past three years would be at an end. In truth it was only
just beginning.

While Dmitri with his Poles and Cossacks advanced on Moscow
he had a stroke of luck. Tsar Boris, alarmed at his advance and disconcerted by the way in which his own supporters deserted the 'False
Dmitri', died of a sudden heart attack. The throne was vacant and Dmitri
with his Polish backers rapidly installed himself. The mother of the
infant Dmitri – a lady not slow to see where her advantage lay – arrived
from Uglich and promptly recognized the False Dmitri as her grown
son, conveniently forgetting the dead infant she had held in her arms
fourteen years before and whose murder she had laid to the charge of
Boris Godunov.

But Dmitri's asset of Polish backing was to be his undoing. The traditional Russian dislike and mistrust of all things Polish erupted when he had been on the throne for less that a year. A self-seeking and ambitious Boyar named Shuisky led a xenophobic mob into the Kremlin ostensibly to prevent the resident Poles from murdering Dmitri and the other Boyars. In the ensuing melee, Shuisky ensured that Dmitri was a fatal casualty – being hacked to pieces by the very mob who had come to 'rescue' him. Shuisky took his place on the throne but none could claim that he was a descendant of the Rurik dynasty, and he was to find it easier to grab the throne than to hold on to it.

Shuisky's first act was to have the body of Dmitri cremated and the ashes fired from a cannon in the direction of Poland, while indicating that the remaining Polish courtiers had better find their own way home before he assisted their departure in a like manner. But despite this and other actions designed to identify himself with grass-roots Russia, the Cossacks and others were unconvinced of Shuisky's credentials. There were also rumours that (the False) Dmitri was not dead after all, that it was someone else's ashes that had been blown from the cannon, and that he had survived just as he (the true Dmitri) had survived the incident of the slit throat at Uglich when a child. To try to scotch these rumours once and for all, Shuisky had the child Dmitri's body disinterred and brought back from Uglich to the Kremlin in Moscow where the infant was declared a Christian martyr and where miracles were reported to be performed around his coffin.

It was to no avail. Before long another – third – Dmitri had emerged, this time from the Ukraine in the person of a certain Mikhail Molchanov. He was at first a reluctant Pretender, partly because he looked nothing like the Dmitri he claimed to be, and partly because he was mindful that Pretenders tended to meet violent ends in Russia. But then something happened which made him set his reservations and fears aside: he was joined and acknowledged as Dmitri by a prominent

Cossack soldier-of-fortune called Ivan Bolotnikov. At a stroke, his new ally made him a serious contender.

Bolotnikov was a rascal in the traditional Cossack mould. Starting life as a serf, he had run away and joined the roving bands of Cossacks in the hinterland between Muscovy and the Crimea. He had been captured by Crimean Tartars on one of their forays and had been sold into slavery to the Turks, who – impressed with his physique – put him to work for a number of years as a helmsman in one of their galleys. His chance of escape came after a sea battle and he eventually crossed Europe from Venice to his native land via Poland, where he heard reports of a deposed Tsar seeking restitution. When he met Molchanov, the two men recognized that each might be useful to the other: Bolotnikov had found a patron and a cause in which to fight; Molchanov had found a seasoned soldier who was used to campaigning on the Russian steppes and disinclined to ask awkward questions.

By the mid-summer of 1606, Bolotnikov found himself at the head of an army of some 12,000 men committed to marching on Moscow and 'restoring' the Tsar Dmitri. The army was a prototype of many which were to be the scourges of successive Russian rulers: it was composed of dissidents, deserters from local garrisons, fugitive serfs, leftovers from the last revolt (in this case that of the Polish-sponsored Dmitri), and small landowners or minor nobility with little to lose. But the real teeth and muscle of the force was – as was to be the invariable pattern – the Cossack element.

At first everything went very well for Bolotnikov. A dozen towns fell quickly to his forces; the troops sent against him by Shuisky mostly came over to his side; success bred success and the revolt spread from the Ukraine into the heart of Muscovy; the population seemed to welcome a hereditary tsar (however dubious his credentials) rather than an upstart Boyar. The rebels advanced in two separate columns on Moscow, and Bolotnikov tried to win over the people of the capital by infiltrating 'cursed leaflets' (according to the Patriarch's letter to the Metropolitan of Moscow) inciting the poorer citizens to rise up and 'destroy the houses of the wealthy and wellborn, and take their wives and daughters for yourselves'. Shuisky was so alarmed at the copying and dissemination of these leaflets that he rounded up all the city's scribes and checked their handwriting against that of the leaflets. It seemed that Moscow like the outlying cities would fall.

But at the last moment one of Bolotnikov's two columns deserted en masse to Shuisky. The problem was that Bolotnikov had allowed his two columns each to represent a different aspect of the rebellion. His own column were Cossacks, workers and peasants; the other column (geographically and socially on the Right) represented the minor nobility and petty landowners – the 'service gentry' as they were known. This latter group became alarmed at Bolotnikov's 'cursed leaflets' and their incitement to a complete breakdown of good order and military discipline. Their leader decided that their interests would be better protected by Shuisky and his Boyars than by Bolotnikov and his motley band. When Bolotnikov tried to besiege Moscow and enter the city, a further defection by another group of service gentry left the initiative with Shuisky and the defenders of the Kremlin. Bolotnikov was forced to flee southwards while his captured supporters were rounded up and pushed under the ice of the frozen rivers – permanently to cool their hot-headed tendencies.

Bolotnikov halted his retreat at the city of Kaluga and, while he was besieged there by Shuisky's forces, yet another Pretender – this time claiming to be the non-existent son of the last dynastic tsar Fyodor – came forward further to complicate the scene. Bolotnikov escaped from Kaluga and made his next and final stand in Tula. Eventually, he too was betrayed and sent to Moscow for interrogation and torture; accounts differ as to his final fate, but it seems he was exiled to a remote settlement in the north of Russia where he was blinded by his captors and eventually drowned. His patron Molchanov – the second False Dmitri – was never to reach Moscow. But a Cossack had shaken the tsar's throne – an event which was to recur throughout the next two centuries of Russian history.

By 1612, the period formally known as the Time of Troubles was over with the election of a new tsar – Michael, the first of the House of Romanov. A tenuous link had been established between the Romanovs and the House of Rurik and the Russians, weary of a chapter in their history which can best be compared in English terms with the reigns of Stephen and Matilda 'when God and his angels slept', yearned for a period of peace. The period was not to be a long one, and once more it was a Cossack who was the central figure of the next great rising. It was a rising, at least in the first place, against the Poles who now dominated the Ukraine, rather than against Muscovy.

Engraving of Bogdan Khmelnitski.

Bogdan Khmelnitski was born in 1595, the son of an established Cossack family with military and landowning connections. For the first decades of his life, he was respectable enough, being educated by the Jesuits at Lvov and learning Polish in addition to Latin. His military experience was gained with the Zaporozhian Cossacks and he married a Cossack girl. But after the anti-Polish rising of 1637, things started to go wrong for him. His Cossack wife died and he took up with a woman who throughout her life seemed to bring trouble in her wake. He also quarrelled with the Polish authorities about the usual vexed questions of tax and land-tenure.

In 1647 his fortunes took a more desperate down-turn. A Polish official with whom he had fallen out raided his estate in his absence and made off with his mistress, killing his son and setting fire to his home in the process. Redress for a Cossack against such a Polish outrage proved impossible, so Bogdan decided to take the law – and much more – into his own hands. Turning to his old comrades in arms the Zaporozhian Cossacks, and burying the hatchet with his old antagonists the Tartars, he led a full-scale attack on the Polish administration, the Polish army of occupation and the Polish landowners. Even by the intemperate standards of the day (it was the period of the Thirty Years War in Germany) his campaign was infamous for its brutalities; nursing a personal grievance Bogdan encouraged atrocities against the Polish gentry and landowners who were burnt in their houses, flayed alive and torn limb from limb by horses; the Cossacks also took reprisals against the Polish priests on account of their not being Orthodox, and against the Jews on account of their not being Christians at all.

When the Poles reacted by sending a glittering army, led by the flower of the Polish nobility and attended by every campaign comfort, against him Bogdan managed to defeat it. He was now master of the Ukraine and in a strong position to press home his advantage by marching on Warsaw itself. He hesitated to do this and professed nominal loyalty to the King of Poland, but at the same time put out feelers towards the Tsar – Alexis the Gentle, the second of the Romanov Tsars. While the latter was procrastinating – he took over two years to respond – Bogdan had lost the support of most of his Tartar allies and was tired of negotiating with the Poles about the number of 'registered' Cossacks who could be allowed to enjoy privileges under any resumed Polish administration. Eventually in 1654, after many more ups and downs in his campaigns and negotiations, Bogdan and his Cossacks definitively threw in their lot with the Romanov Tsar and renounced the King of Poland. It was a

momentous decision, and although there would be many more rebellions, many flirtations with Swedes, Poles, Lithuanians, Germans and others, the lot of the Cossacks was from then onward to be linked with the destiny of the Romanovs.

But Hetman Bogdan Khmelnitski remains an enigmatic figure. His statue adorns the centre of Kiev, the Ukrainian capital. It has been revered in its time as a symbol of the unity of Russia and the Ukraine, and at other times as a memorial to Ukrainian and even Cossack nationalism. As with Tamerlane in Central Asia, he was a regional hero who was adopted as a national figure when it suited Moscow or St Petersburg to do so. But perhaps Bogdan himself was motivated more by hatred of what he feared – usually Polish arrogance – than by any considerations of high policy or national destiny. Like Bolotnikov, he was a horseman seeking firm ground in a quagmire of troubles.

A less formal portrait of Bogdan Khmelnitski, who in 1647 led a Cossack revolt against the Poles.

4 : COSSACK AGAINST TURK

To be a Cossack is to be a warrior, and to be a warrior requires an enemy. Over the centuries the Cossacks were to make enemies of almost everyone within their reach. Already by the early seventeenth century they had fought the Tartars and the Poles, the Swedes and the Lithuanians, the Moldavians and the Georgians. They were to go on to fight the Chechens and the Ossetians, the Uzbeks and the Kazakhs, the Persians and the Murids. They fought against the invaders of Russia from further afield – the French, the British (in the Crimean War) and the Germans; and when they were not fighting external enemies they rebelled and fought the Russians. To say they fought the Jews would not be strictly accurate, but they persecuted the Jews consistently and made enemies of them in perpetuity. But there was one nation and creed which they enjoyed fighting above all others and against which they pitted themselves with special zeal – the Infidel Turks.

There were geographical as well as religious and political reasons for this. The heart of the Cossack lands on the Don was cut off from the sea by the Turkish fortress at the mouth of the Don at Azov. They needed access to the sea for trade, and they also desired access to the sea – particularly the Black Sea – for piracy, raiding, plundering and other habitual Cossack outdoor activities.

It was not only the Don Cossacks who crossed swords with the Turks early in the seventeenth century. The Zaporozhian Cossacks in particular had a reputation for nautical piracy, being river folk themselves and much given to venturing down the Dnieper – from their island hide-aways – in their highly-manoeuvrable *chaika* ('seagull') craft, propelled by a score of oarsmen, to make Viking-like raids on the Turkish settlements around the Black Sea coast. In 1604 they had raided Trebizond, and in 1613 they raided the Turkish-controlled Crimea. In 1615 they even were so bold as to attack Constantinople itself from the sea. Against this background of coastal raids, there was also continual harassment of Turkish shipping in the Black Sea. *Chaikas* would slip through the tall grasses which flanked the mouth of the Dnieper and lie in wait for passing merchant ships, stealing up on them at night and stealing away again into shallow waters that defied pursuit. Discipline on these raids was good: it was said that the only time the Zaporozhians were sober was when they were engaged in a seaborne oper-ation. When at home in the *sech*, their island stronghold, the Zaporozhians displayed the personal loot which they had acquired during these piratical raids: the famous painting by Repin (referred to later in this chapter) shows them decked out in the silks and satins they had carried off as plunder, in baggy oriental pantaloons, in caftans and cummerbunds, and in turbans with curved Turkish scimitars. They believed in flaunting their prizes.

The Turks did not take all this lying down. They erected a heavy iron chain across the mouth of the Dnieper and they counter-attacked: in 1633 alone more than a hundred *chaikas* were sunk, more than a thou-sand Cossacks captured and sold into slavery on the Turkish galleys, and more than 2,000 Cossacks were killed outright.

But the biggest single frustration to the Cossacks remained the

The following page:
Azov Cossacks boarding a Turkish corsair
carrying Cherkassk women off the coast of the Black
Sea: the Cossacks were notorious pirates, but in this
case were probably rescuing their own people.

Turkish-manned fortress at Azov controlling the mouth of the Don. It was this that forced the Don Cossacks to run the gauntlet – usually unsuccessfully – every time they wanted access to the sea. And the fortress was a formidable one. It had a permanent garrison of over 4,000 Janissaries – the crack troops of the Sultan's army. Its walls were of legendary height and thickness, at least twenty-five feet high and more than twelve feet thick. Its design anticipated Vauban by having a dozen corner bastions from which the length of the walls was protected by enfiladed fire. There were fortresses within fortresses, the inner citadel being protected by two outer ones. There was a moat of a depth equal to the height of the walls around the whole complex. This was no frontier post that could be overrun by a sudden bold assault.

By 1637 there were a number of major Cossack settlements along the Don, accommodating some 5,000 Cossack warriors in all. This was hardly an adequate force to dislodge the Turkish garrison from Azov, but the Don Cossacks declared their intention of so doing and solicited support from elsewhere. The Zaporozhian Cossack enclaves on the lower Dnieper – not surprisingly in view of their long-standing hostilities with the Turks – sent a few thousand fighting men, and the Tsar in Moscow sent money, ammunition and supplies for a venture which he tacitly supported without wanting to be too closely identified with it.

Led by the Don Cossack *ataman*, the augmented Cossack army marched on Azov in the spring and invested the town. Inevitably they first tried the sudden bold assault which was the usual Cossack key to success, but equally inevitably it was repulsed with heavy loss of life. The engineers were now invited to take over from the cavalry and infantry. Trenches were dug around the perimeter and tunnels were excavated under the massive walls. By the middle of June the Cossacks were ready to try again.

This time a deafening explosion not only announced the attack but made the attack when it came much more effective than the previous one. The explosion had breached the twelve-foot-thick ramparts in one place and the Don Cossacks under their *ataman* poured into this breach, swimming over what remained of the moat and clambering over the smashed masonry of the walls. While this frontal attack was in full swing, the allied Cossack contingent from the Zaporozhian *sech* attacked from the rear. The latter did not have the advantage of a breach to assist entry, but they had constructed long ladders which in the general confusion they managed to place against the high walls and up which they swarmed. The Turks withdrew from the outer fortress to the inner one, and from there eventually to the innermost one of all. It took three days of pounding with battering rams and hand to hand fighting to overwhelm the hard core of the Janissaries, but at the end of that time Azov was in Cossack hands and the river Don was open to the Sea of Azov and thence to the Black Sea itself.

The new rulers of Azov intended to make their occupation permanent. They established a garrison as large as the one the Turks had deployed. They repaired the walls and dug out the blocked sections of moat. They also encouraged the return of business: foreigners – Levantines, Greeks and Persians – were persuaded to bring their goods to sell or barter in the narrow streets of Azov; and civilians from Muscovy were enticed to this southern extremity of greater Russia to settle as tradesmen and labourers (neither of which occupations appealed to the Cossacks). Azov became for a while the unofficial capital of the Don region.

But the Cossacks were grimly aware that a day of reckoning would come: the Sultan would not accept the permanent loss of even a minor jewel in his crown. For the present, the new masters of the city comforted themselves with two considerations. Firstly, the Sultan was too preoccupied with military adventures against the Persians and naval adventures against the Venetians to be able to spare the resources for a reconquest of Azov; and secondly, the Cossacks trusted that before the

Sultan would be ready, the Tsar would have taken over responsibility for the defence of a town which was as strategic for the inhabitants of the Don basin as Astrakhan was for the inhabitants of the Volga basin. Surely Tsar Michael would not let the Turks once more bottle up his Cossack subjects on the river Don?

Both the Cossacks' grounds for comfort were to prove illusory. A new Sultan found that his other preoccupations melted away, and the Tsar was not prepared to back the Cossacks and rupture his fragile relations with the Turkish Empire. Tsar Michael sent to the garrison at Azov more money and food, arms and ammunition, messages and moral support; but he did not send an army, and it was an army that was required to hold Azov against the veritable armada which the Turks now launched to recapture their lost city. In June 1641 some hundred and fifty war galleys appeared at the mouth of the Don, and the city was surrounded by the silken tents and bronze cannons of the Turkish Janissaries. A full-scale siege ensued.

Static defence was never the Cossacks' preferred stance in war. Attack and mobility were their strengths. But on this occasion they acquitted themselves memorably in an unwelcome role. They made innumerable sorties into the Turkish camp, and they reversed the process of burrowing under the walls to blow up Turkish ammunition and supplies. Their women joined in the fray, starting by helping to prepare the earth-works and ramparts, and ending – as casualties mounted – by taking over the muskets of their wounded or dead menfolk. It was two centuries since the Turks had pounded the walls of Constantinople and brought an end to the Byzantine Empire; during that period they had made notable advances in siege technology, and Azov – badly damaged by the Cossacks in their own attack four years earlier and only hastily repaired since then – was no longer an inviolable fortress. But still the Cossacks hung on.

Their salvation was no less deserved because it was totally unexpected. In the last days of September the garrison decided on a final sor-
tie: everything would be risked in a do or die raid. While they prepared
to sally out, they observed an unusual degree of activity in the Turkish
camp. Tents were being struck, wagons loaded, ships prepared for
embarkation. The Sultan's army was packing up and going home. The
Cossacks and Azov had survived.

But the victory was soon to turn to ashes. Those Cossacks who had
survived the siege were in no condition to repair the fortress and hold it
in perpetuity against future Turkish assaults. The only way the River
Don would remain open to the sea was if the Tsar and his Moscow-based
kingdom were to take over direct responsibility for Azov, and man it with
Russian troops at Russian expense, instead of leaving it to the Cossacks
to protect with their local resources. The *ataman* wrote a carefully worded
appeal to Tsar Michael less than a month after the Turks had withdrawn, and the Tsar responded by sending officials from his treasury
and his armoury to assess the extent of the commitment. While there can
be little doubt that Ivan the Terrible half a century earlier, with his
enthusiasm for expansion into Siberia and down the Volga, would have
accepted the challenge, Michael was a more cautious man. He estimated
the cost to the exchequer of repairing the walls and providing a permanent adequate garrison; and he estimated the diplomatic cost of taking
on a permanent irritant to the Turkish Sultan. He decided he could not
afford to indulge the Cossacks any further, and he instructed them 'on
pain of his displeasure' to abandon the city, destroy what was left of its
fortifications and withdraw to their former haunts further up-river.

All the effort and all the blood-letting appeared to have been in
vain. The Cossacks had no alternative but to withdraw, which they did
with great reluctance. Once more they became increasingly dependent
on outside protection and support in their homelands. The period of

Polish domination and subsequent Cossack rebellion (described in the latter part of the last chapter) was beginning; and this in turn was ultimately to lead to yet greater dependence on the Tsar and a greater measure of incorporation into Russia.

The evacuation of Azov did nothing to endear the Turks to the Cossacks, but their relationship was never simple. At one point in the 1660s one of the Cossack *hetmans* went so far as to become a nominal vassal of the Sultan and the latter briefly styled himself 'Protector of All the Cossacks'. It was not to last long.

The most intransigent of all the Cossack clans were the Zaporozhians. Tsar Alexis I (who had succeeded Michael as the second Romanov tsar) was less careful of his relations with the Sultan than his father had been, and he encouraged the Zaporozhians to join with his own troops in fighting the Crimean Tartars, who were under the protection of the Sultan, and indeed to raid Turkish settlements on the Black Sea coastline.

Predictably this incensed the Sultan who in 1663 sent three hundred of his troops to the *Sech* on the pretext that they were there to help defend it against Tartar incursions but who, in reality, were ordered to report to the Sultan on the goings-on of the Zaporozhians. Their reports were not reassuring to the Sultan: the Cossacks from the *Sech* were continuing to attack targets of opportunity – including Turkish ones – wherever they occurred.

The Sultan's next move was therefore to send a much larger force in secret to exterminate once and for all this nest of brigands and pirates. The force was made up of a mixture of disciplined Turkish Janissaries and undisciplined Tartar bands. They managed to surround the *Sech* without being detected by the Zaporozhians who, over-confident in the inviolability of their base, were sleeping off one of their habitual nights of carousing. However, one of the Zaporozhians, perhaps less inebriated than the rest, woke to see armed foreigners prowling within the confines of their encampment. He raised the alarm and the Zaporozhian Cossacks roused themselves from their drunken slumbers sufficiently effectively to turn the tables on the intruders. The Turks and Tartars were routed.

This incident would probably have receded into the forgotten annals of history had it not been for the aftermath. The Zaporozhians resented the attack as particularly underhand because it came shortly after one of the periodic offers by the Sultan to act as a protector to the Cossacks. Having scored a material success on the ground, they therefore decided (according to the somewhat doubtful legend) to score a propaganda success as well. They sent an open letter to the Sultan, abusing and reviling him in terms which – even by the standards of the time and place – were unusually picturesque:

Thou Turkish Devil and Soulmate of Satan! Who dares to call himself Lord of the Christians, but is not! Pot-scraper of Babylon! Ale-vendor of Jerusalem! Goatherd of Alexandria! Swineherd of Upper and Lower Egypt! Armenian Sow! Insolent Infidel! Go to Hell! Cossacks spit on your present claims or any you may invent in the future!

The composition of this outspoken letter was the subject of one of the Russian nineteenth-century artist Repin's most famous paintings. He shows a swarthy band of Cossacks, decked out in the spoils of earlier raids, grouped round a scribe and suggesting with vulgar gestures and expletives the wording of the letter. The painting has come to be revered as a monument to the defiant spirit of the Cossacks and, by extension, of the Russian people as a whole. Although far from Repin's finest work, it

The following page:
Repin's famous **The Zaporozhian Cossacks Writing a Reply to the Turkish Sultan.** *Its impudence appealed to Stalin, who regarded it as his favourite painting.*

was Stalin's favourite picture and it still draws crowds of admirers at the Russian Museum in St Petersburg.

After the Cossacks' abandonment of Azov in 1642, it reverted to Turkish occupation. By the time that Peter the Great was concentrating his attentions on the expansion of Russia's frontiers at the end of the seventeenth century, Azov had again become an impediment to access to the Black Sea. In fact, it was even harder to get past Azov than it had been at the beginning of the century, because the Turks had built two watch-tower forts a mile up-river from the city and stretched a heavy iron chain across the river between them to block any vessel that might try to run the gauntlet.

Peter, who was only twenty-three at the time and had not yet made his famous ship-building visit to England and Holland, was attracted to the idea of a campaign against Azov as a means of trying out his new regiments: the Preobrazhensky and the Semyonovsky Guards. But he recognized that these untried units would be much strengthened by the presence of veteran Cossacks alongside them. He also knew that any expedition against Azov would be popular with the Don Cossacks and help to harness them to Moscow (he had not yet founded St Petersburg). The presence of a large Russian army in these traditionally Cossack lands could also be counted upon to remind the inhabitants of the might and power of Muscovy.

Peter accordingly set out with two columns to eject the Turks from the mouth of the Dnieper and Don rivers. He attached himself to the column aimed at Azov, and – because of his youth and inexperience – declined to take formal command of the force but took on the character of 'Bombardier Peter Alexeev'.

Perhaps Peter's choice of an artillery rank as his *nom de guerre* was significant: the gunners were to play the main role in the attack for the first two months while an incessant bombardment ensued. But artillery has seldom solved military problems on its own, and when it was proved necessary to storm the watch-tower forts, it was the Cossacks who were summoned up to do the deed. It was virtually the only success of the campaign and Peter was able to see for himself the fighting qualities of his loosely-attached subjects and allies. Soon it became clear that the Russians were not going to succeed in dislodging the Turks from Azov as easily as Peter had hoped. Leaving strong Cossack garrisons in the watch-towers up-river, he withdrew the rest of his army to Moscow, suffering harassment by Tartar skirmishers on the way.

The next year he set off for Azov again. He had spent much of the intervening time constructing war galleys and other ships at Veronezh on the upper Don, and these now carried the Tsar and his troops south again. But as in the previous year, when it came to the fighting it was the Cossacks who were brought to the front. The first challenge was when it was discovered that the Turks too had brought a fleet to Azov. Peter decided that there were too many Turkish vessels to risk an attack, but the Cossacks thought otherwise and while the Turkish cargo ships were busy unloading supplies to enable the garrison of Azov to survive a long siege, they attacked and captured ten Turkish vessels, and so frightened the other Turkish captains that they set sail for the open sea and left the city unprovisioned.

With the enemy fleet gone, Peter was able to bring his own newly-constructed craft down the river past Azov and blockade the city from the sea. Just as the Turks had earlier built forts up-river of the town, so Peter now built them down-stream to prevent any further reinforcement. Having encircled the city, and unsuccessfully demanded a surrender by the Turks, Peter began simultaneously a massive bombardment and the shovelling of earth to make a ramp up to the walls. As before, the artillery bombardment did not achieve any results on its own. The Cossack element in Peter's army wearied of shovelling earth and as soon as the ramp

*Peter the Great,
painted by Sir
Godfrey Kneller
in 1698.*

was within leaping distance of the top of the ramparts two thousand of them launched their own unauthorized assault on the city.

The Cossacks counted on the support of the regular Russian troops – the famous *Streltsi* – once their bridgehead inside Azov was established. But the Cossack initiative was considered irresponsible and was not supported. Driven back by sheer weight of numbers, the Cossacks eventually held a single tower only on the perimeter of the city walls. The Russian Generals – Peter was still not in direct command – and the *Streltsi* were still hesitating to launch a frontal assault when, to everyone's surprise, a flag of truce was seen to flutter from the Turkish Pasha's headquarters. Peter's call to surrender had been accepted in the nick of time, and the Turks were allowed to withdraw unmolested and in good order. It was the Cossack contingent which had provoked the surrender and carried the day.

Encouraged by the capture of Azov, Peter the Great began serious ship-building and the establishment of a naval base on the Sea of Azov. He was able to set off on his protracted tour of the West – which included his time apprenticed to the Deptford Dockyard in London – with a reputation as a victorious commander. He knew to what a high degree he owed this reputation to his Cossack contingent. It was to effect his judgement later and to account in large measure for the importance he was to attach to his favourite Cossack – Mazeppa (as will be shown in a later chapter). The Turks too were reminded that the Cossacks were an enemy worthy of respect – a lesson they were to forget at their peril over subsequent centuries.

5:
STENKA RAZIN—
THE VOLGA PIRATE

Stenka Razin, the seventeenth-century folk hero of Russia, was many things to many men: soldier, bandit, freedom fighter, champion of the poor, and scourge of the Sultan. But he is best remembered for his years in the 1660s as a pirate on the Volga river, and it is that chapter of his life that has given rise to the drinking-songs and the apocryphal stories that contribute to the on-going legend of Stenka Razin. The legend draws strength from the Volga, because the river is itself an integral part of Russian history and self-awareness.

It has often been said that whoever controls the Volga from Yaroslavl (near Moscow) to Astrakhan (on the Caspian Sea) effectively controls European Russia, and it is no coincidence that the first person to do so was Ivan the Terrible. Teeming with fish, most notably sturgeon, the Volga was traditionally the source of that most Russian of delicacies – caviar. The banks abound in game: bear, elk and deer stalk the forests and wolves prowl among the silver birches. When spring comes and the frozen stretches of the river begin to melt, lone wolves could often be seen, stranded on ever-shrinking slabs of ice, being whirled downstream and howling to the skies. Clustered along its banks lie sacred monasteries, ancient wooden churches and historic towns like Uglich, where the child Dmitri was murdered, supposedly on the orders of Boris Godunov. The Volga has always been a favourite theme in Russian art, and Repin's famous nineteenth-century painting of *Barge-haulers on the Volga* was to become one of the inspirational icons of the Bolshevik revolution. In the twentieth century the conquering might of the Third Reich was to be decisively repulsed on the banks of the Volga at Stalingrad. The Volga was part of Stenka Razin's mystique and he was to become part of the Volga's national heritage.

But it was neither as a rebel nor in connection with the Volga that Razin first made his appearance in Russian history in 1658. He was a Don Cossack and as such had been sent as part of a delegation from Cherkassk, the Cossack capital on the Don, to Moscow to obtain weapons to protect their town against marauders from the steppes. His mission was successful and he returned to the Don with substantial armoury, including several cannon, and a fighting fund. Another diplomatic mission followed, this time to the Kalmyk tribesmen who had been encroaching on Cossack settlements, but who were persuaded by Razin to desist, and to join the Cossacks in attacking Tartar settlements near the Sea of Azov. Razin also undertook military assignments. He intercepted a Tartar raiding party who were bringing livestock, slaves and booty back from the Ukraine to the Crimea; when he arrived home with several thousand horses and several hundred freed slaves, he was greeted as a hero and potential Cossack *ataman*.

His career was not to go smoothly. What appears to have turned Razin against Tsarist authority in the middle of the seventeenth century was the same traumatic event as turned the young Lenin against Tsarist authority at the end of the nineteenth century: the execution of his brother. Stenka Razin's brother Ivan had been a loyal member of a Don

Cossack regiment, but when his request for home leave was denied, he took the law into his own hands and – in the best Cossack tradition – saddled his horse and rode off across the steppe towards his *stanitsa*. Unfortunately he was tracked down, captured and hanged as a deserter.

For his brother Stenka Razin, Ivan's fate was not only emotive in itself but it was symptomatic of a widespread system of repression and injustice which formed a deeper and more permanent reason for Stenka Razin kicking over the traces. With the Time of Troubles behind them, the Russians were expanding into other parts of Asia and Eastern Europe. All this military activity required resources which, in turn, depended on stable agricultural production. Mobility of labour worked against such stability, and successive Tsars therefore tried to anchor the peasants to the land. The peasants found they had lost the right to offer their labour elsewhere and became serfs tied to a particular estate or a particular landowner. If they moved away, they were pursued and brought back. The safe havens were becoming fewer all the time.

But the main safe haven was still the wild country of the Cossacks, particularly the banks of the Don. Once a serf, or a family, or even a whole village full of peasants, could reach the lands of the Don they were immune from pursuit and capture. Such refugees were – by definition – anti-authoritarian. They turned angrily on their leaders – the local *ataman* or *hetman* – if search parties were allowed to operate in Cossack country, and they resisted fiercely any proposal that runaway serfs should be returned to their owners for punishment and a life of servile labour in response to pressure from the Tsarist authorities. They were prepared to serve the Tsars as mercenary soldiers of fortune, but not as policemen. This expanding immigrant element on the Don did not go unnoticed by Stenka Razin while he was still mourning his brother.

Razin still wanted to be a Cossack *ataman*, but he now saw more prospect of real power as an independent leader of the disaffected immi-

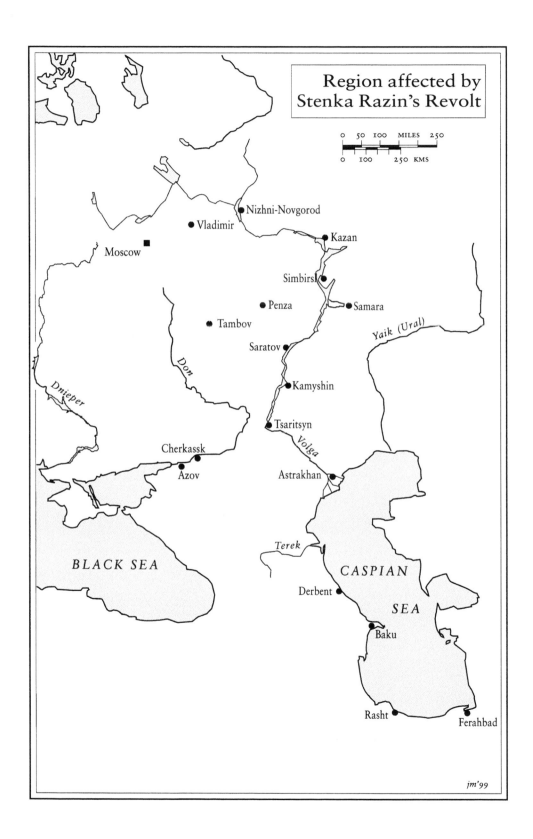

Region affected by
Stenka Razin's Revolt

jm'99

grant Cossacks, who were hungry because of the lack of land grants and frightened because of the prospect of being returned as captured runaway serfs to Muscovy, than as an official leader approved by Moscow. His personal bitterness lent colour to his ambitious calculations.

A like-minded recalcitrant Cossack – one Vasili Us – had already in 1666 led a marauding band of Cossacks and peasants into the Muscovite provinces north of the Don to within four days' march of Moscow itself. He had been forced to retreat by the deployment of Russian troops, but not before Razin had noted how readily the rebel ranks had been swelled by the discontented.

The following year Razin gathered together a force of some 700 Don Cossacks and equipped a fleet of sea-going barges and smaller craft. He would have liked to have sailed down the Don and raided Turkish shipping on the Black Sea and Turkish settlements on the Black Sea coast. But the Sultan had tired of the ease with which the fractious Cossacks had interfered with his ships and his coastline; this was the period when he had set up the two well-fortified towers either side of the River Don where it passed into Turkish territory at Azov and had fixed his mighty iron chain across the river near its mouth effectively preventing free passage by Cossack boats into the Sea of Azov and the inter-connected Black Sea.

If Razin was to take his water-borne force on a raiding expedition to restore their fortunes he could not use the Don as his waterway. Consequently he decided to effect a relatively short portage between the rivers Don and Volga at their closest point. The fact that most of the ground between the rivers – some forty miles – was snow-covered made it easier to drag and slide the boats than to roll them on wheels. When they reached the Volga – near to the Russian garrison town of Tsaritsyn – they managed (according to some accounts) to embark them south of the town and beyond the reach of the government troops, or (according to other accounts) to intimidate the garrison commander into letting them pass. The other smaller garrison towns on the lower Volga decided that discretion – or negligence – was the better part of valour ,and allowed the little flotilla to float past them unchallenged. Razin none-the-less made clear his disdain for Tsarist authority by seizing a convoy of cargo boats – most of them the personal property of the Tsar and the Patriarch – and recruiting the escort into his own force. The Tsarist officers of the escort were not given the chance to become turncoats: they were arbitrarily strung up from the rigging of their own ships.

With his ranks thus augmented, Razin pressed on downstream towards Astrakhan. Fortunately for him, at its mouth the Volga breaks into a labyrinth of different channels, and it proved possible to bypass the garrison at Astrakhan and reach the sea by selecting a passage which gave the city a wide berth.

But beyond Astrakhan the sea was of course not the Black Sea dominated by the Ottoman Sultan but the Caspian Sea dominated by the Shah of Persia. Razin did not allow this change of target to disconcert him. His first move on reaching the Caspian was to sail eastwards towards the mouth of the Yaik (Ural) river in the hope of recruiting Yaik Cossacks into his ranks. He not only succeeded in this, but his reputation as a free Cossack leader was spreading in the regions he had left behind him, and reinforcements caught up with him from his own Don homeland as well as from the Cossack communities on the Terek river (in the Caucasus) and from the Zaporozhian island strongholds (on the lower Dnieper). Razin's piratical force was now some 20,000 strong.

His first thought was that he could exist by attacking Persian and other shipping on the Caspian. He sailed westward again and established a shore base on a small island near the mouth of the Terek river which was strategically well-placed to intercept cargo vessels heading for the mouth of the Volga and the interior of Russia. At first he had some

successes, but it soon became apparent that with so many mouths to feed
he could not count on an adequate supply of shipping to intercept. Raids
on Persian coastal towns were going to be necessary.

Razin's first target was Derbent, a prosperous trading town further down the western coastline of the Caspian. The Cossacks swept in
from the sea (in the same way that British privateers like Captain
Morgan were doing in the same years on the other side of the world
against Spanish settlements in the Caribbean) and took the inhabitants
and their defences completely by surprise. In hand to hand fighting in
the streets Razin's Cossacks indiscriminately slaughtered defenders and
defenceless alike. Booty was piled onto their boats and they took to the
sea again and disappeared over the horizon as quickly as they had come.
It had all seemed so easy to Razin that he decided to repeat the operation at other Persian ports further south. Soon the whole coastline had
been laid bare and the Cossacks' boats – the sea-going barges had been
augmented by sleeker *chaikas* – were laden to the gunwales with plunder.

Razin now thought that, with his accumulated wealth, he could
return to his native banks of the Don and establish an independent free
Cossack state with himself at its head. But he had reckoned without the
reaction of the Tsar Alexis and the hierarchy in Moscow. He soon learnt
that formidable preparations were being made on the Volga and elsewhere to bar his return and that, even if he could fight his way back to
the Don, a disciplined army would be waiting to engage his motley crew.

Never lacking for impudence, Razin now decided that if Russia
was too hot to hold him he must mend his fences with the Shah of Persia
and settle there. Blithely overlooking the fact that he had already sacked
several Persian towns and villages and slaughtered their inhabitants, he
sent emissaries to the Shah at Isfahan. The envoys rode south to the
Persian capital and – having been granted an audience – pitched an
unlikely story to the Shah. They claimed that their violent and predatory

Cossacks embarked on frail craft, buoyed
up by reeds and enlivened by balalaika
music, on the Black and Caspian Seas when
engaged on missions of piracy.

behaviour had been forced on them by the 'inhospitality' of the governors and citizens of the towns and villages where they had put ashore. They now offered to put their sabres at the service of the Shah in return for sanctuary and a grant of land on which to settle. The Shah was astounded and at first non-plussed by this improbable suggestion. He played for time and sent his own emissaries to Tsar Alexis enquiring about the background and credentials of Stenka Razin and his Cossacks. He received a prompt and clear reply: Razin and his followers were runaway serfs turned pirates who warranted no consideration and should be arbitrarily punished. If the Shah harboured them, he must expect them to turn against him as they had against the Tsar.

The Shah now reacted with vigour. Some accounts say that he threw the Cossack envoys (whose table-manners had already given offence to the sophisticated Persian courtiers) into a noisome gaol, and other accounts report that he sent them back with a robustly negative answer to Razin; possibly he did one thing with some of them and another with others. Be that as it may, he ordered the Khan of Rasht, who commanded the Persian garrisons on the southern shores of the Caspian, to cut down the marauding Cossacks in their camp. The Khan waited until the Cossacks were having one of their frequent drinking bouts and then launched an attack while many of the intruders – including Razin himself – were helplessly inebriated. In the surprise assault, two or three hundred Cossacks were killed before Razin and the remainder of his befuddled force fought their way through to their boats and sought safety again on the waters of the Caspian.

Razin was once more obliged to plunder to survive. He crossed the Caspian to the port of Ferahabad, which was apparently far enough away for its citizens to be unaware of the danger represented by a visitation from the Cossack fleet. The visitors began by trading peacefully enough, and only after a week when cupidity had further lulled the denizens of

Ferahabad into complacency did the Cossacks turn on their hosts and start slaughtering them and sacking the town. The mosques, mansions and warehouses of Ferahabad disgorged rich pickings for the intruders.

But this pattern of surprise raids and looting could not go on. The Shah sent a sizeable army and a fleet to hunt down and destroy the Cossacks. They caught up with Razin near Baku on the western shore of the Caspian and a sea battle ensued. The Persian admiral chained his ships together and attempted to drag the smaller Cossack boats into a lethal corral where they could be fired down upon by the taller surrounding ships. But a lucky Cossack shot found the powder kegs on the Persian flagship and when this vessel blew up it dragged those chained to it to the bottom. Casualties had been heavy on both sides, but in strictly naval terms it was a victory to the Cossacks because they sank more ships than the Persians did of theirs. However, in political and strategic terms the victory lay with the Persians as the Cossacks could afford their losses less easily than their home-based opponents. Razin's numbers had already fallen since the Caspian campaign began, and now there were only some twelve hundred Cossacks left alive after the battle and many of these were unfit to fight again. They decided to head for home despite the perils.

Their luck held out. Although the Tsar would have liked to have captured Razin and stamped out his following, he was distracted by the problems of keeping law and order elsewhere in his domains – not least on the Don. He consequently allowed Governor Prozorovski in Astrakhan to offer an amnesty to Razin and his band of tired warriors on condition they travelled home without causing further trouble. Instead of arresting Razin, the Governor therefore 'escorted' him to Astrakhan where the populace gave Razin a rousing welcome. An artillery salute intended for the Governor was interpreted as one for Razin. The Cossacks – still opulently decked out with the proceeds of their Persian looting – were treated everywhere as honoured guests and valued customers. Demands by the Governor to hand over the Cossacks who had been deserters or escaped serfs were truculently rejected. Similarly, demands that they should hand over their arms were disregarded. Public opinion in Astrakhan had swung dangerously in favour of Razin, and the Governor dared not press his demands.

Astrakhan at this date was not only an important sea and river port but was a great trading entrepot and terminal of caravan routes. With its towers, churches and mansions, it was a bustling and prosperous city. Razin stayed for many weeks within the comfort of its walls. He and his followers eventually set sail in September 1669 up to Volga. What had been envisaged by the Tsar as a licensed retreat under amnesty to their homelands on the Don became in fact a triumphal progress through southern Russia. Parties of troops designated to escort the troublemakers defected to them. Peasants who had no Cossack connections joined their ranks. Casual piracy was mingled with social crusading as trading boats were plundered and corrupt officials threatened and manhandled. Tax collectors' doors were battered down and officious government agents tossed into the waters of the Volga.

Once again the Cossacks effected the portage of their boats between the Volga and the Don rivers, and Razin's force – now swollen to several times its size on leaving Astrakhan – finally came to rest on a riverine island just north of the Don Cossack capital of Cherkassk. Although recruits continued to flock in, Razin was still only the headman of a fortified village of some five thousand motley men-at-arms.

It was in early 1670 that Razin began to look to wider horizons. Hitherto he had been essentially an itinerant local pirate: now he was to become a revolutionary leader on a national scale. When the Tsar – sensing deep trouble – sent an emissary called Yevdokimov to Cherkassk to offer a mixture of inducements and threats to the loyal Cossack community, Razin intercepted him; Yevdokimov was beaten up, thrown into the

Volga and left to drown. The gauntlet had been thrown down once too often; there could be no more rapprochements with Moscow; Razin was now a public enemy of the sate.

But the state was so unpopular in southern Russia that to be its enemy was to be a rallying point for men of all kinds. Unpaid soldiers came over to him. Over-taxed smallholders saw in him a respite from their troubles. Old Believers, disgruntled at the tampering of a reforming Patriarch with the traditional rituals of the Russian Orthodox Church, overlooked Razin's own lack of religious conviction and swelled his ranks. Tribesmen from the wilder fringes of the empire – Tartars, Bashkirs, Kalmyks and others – brought their ramshackle weapons to the service of his cause. And still the tide of runaway serfs and Cossack adventurers kept flowing in. All who wanted freedom from tyranny and the hope of a brave new world saw Razin as their rallying point.

Razin decided to retrace his steps back to the Volga, but no longer as a daring fugitive slipping past defended towns but as a 'liberator' of those same towns. Tsaritsyn (the future Stalingrad), which he had been glad to avoid in 1667, now opened its gates to him. Its governor joined the growing number of corpses floating down the Volga. Other lesser towns on the Volga were also captured, frequently by the ruse of using deserters from the Tsar's army to pose as reinforcements for the beleaguered garrisons; once the former Tsarist troops had been admitted within the walls, they opened the gates to the Cossack horde.

Razin's next major target was the city of Astrakhan itself where he had rested the previous year after his Caspian adventures. The same governor – Prozorovski - who had escorted Razin to the city in 1669 was still in command of the garrison. This time he determined to resist the Cossacks by every means at his disposal: he even used his own private funds to settle the arrears of the soldiers' pay in the hope of securing their loyalty. Envoys from Razin were summarily executed. The gates of the city were bricked up. Foreigners were evacuated – or fled of their own volition. Church bells summoned the younger citizens to arms and the older ones to prayer.

But it was all to no avail. Too many of the rank and file were on Razin's side. Deserters betrayed details of the defences, while others actively helped the Cossacks to scale the walls at night. By the time Prozorovski knew that an attack had begun, the city was infested with Cossack gangs, and those who should have been organizing the defences were seeking sanctuary in the cathedral. Prozorovski himself, having been wounded in the fighting, eventually joined the sanctuary seekers. It did him little good. By the next morning he had been taken up to the top of the cathedral bell-tower and thrown over the parapet. Most of his officers suffered similar or worse fates, his son being swung like a pendulum against the city walls.

Razin was now master of a considerable tract of country on the lower reaches of the Volga. He felt the time was ripe to move northwards into the heart of Russia and thereafter towards Moscow itself. A veritable fleet – no longer a stealthy flotilla – sailed up the Volga, accompanied by thousands of Cossack and assorted cavalrymen on the banks. Towns such as Kamyshin, Saratov and Samara (later to become Kuibyshev and the seat of the Soviet Government when evacuated from Moscow during the Second World War) fell to Razin almost without a struggle as the entire population rallied to the rebel cause. And the revolt did not limit itself to the banks of the Volga. Several hundred miles further west towns like Penza and Tambov also tumbled. Stenka Razin's brother Frolka was sent back to the Don to pursue a parallel campaign there. Over a quarter of a million had joined a rising that had grown from the thousand-odd survivors of the Caspian campaign. It seemed unstoppable.

The rebel army – still something of a rabble apart from its Cossack backbone – was now within twelve miles of the capital, and the Tsar was shaking in the Kremlin as the people in the streets talked with increasing fascination rather than terror of the advancing mob. The key to Razin's success had always been that the troops sent against him and the garrisons he confronted had – when it came to a show-down – preferred to come over to him than to sustain their resistance. His capacity to defeat seasoned and determined regular soldiers had never been put to the test.

At Simbirsk it was to be put to that test. This town on the upper Volga was in many ways the key to Kazan, Nizhni-Novgorod, Vladimir and Moscow. At first everything seemed to be going as usual. The citizens opened the gates of their city to Razin's men, but they could not open the gates of the citadel. Here the governor and some loyal regiments barricaded themselves in and prepared to face assault and siege. The assault was savage and the siege protracted. But this time help was on the way to relieve the garrison. A few thousand *streltsi* (regular and disciplined musketeers) were sent under Prince Baryatynski to confront Razin's amorphous mob of half-armed peasantry.

The ensuing battle was decisive for the same reasons as – exactly seventy-five years later and at the other extremity of Europe – the Battle of Culloden was decisive. Wild and well-motivated tribesmen were no match for solid phalanxes of uniformed musketeers. Charges were sent reeling back; rebel casualties were awesomely heavy; the rebel leaders (including Razin himself who was rescued by his Cossack bodyguard) were wounded. When the dust of battle cleared Razin retreated to his camp outside the citadel of Simbirsk and, when that camp in turn was attacked by Baryatynski, Razin was found to have taken off with an escort of fast-riding Cossacks. Other rebel bands were routed further west. The whole movement was in disarray and its momentum broken.

There was to be no come-back for Razin. He was denounced by Church and state and hunted down remorselessly. Eventually it was Cossacks loyal to the Tsar who ran him to ground and brought him back in fetters to Cherkassk. From there he was quickly despatched to

Moscow together with his brother Frolka where he was paraded still in fetters on an open cart through the streets, with Frolka tethered like a dog behind. There was no formal trial; perhaps the authorities thought it might provoke a popular reaction in Razin's favour. Instead he was led out to execution a few days later and died bravely after enduring the worst tortures the executioner could inflict upon him. His followers, and indeed many others who had the misfortune to reside in the region where the revolt had taken hold, were subjected to punitive retribution by the authorities. The Bloody Assizes which Judge Jeffreys was to impose in the west of England a few years later pale into insignificance beside the scale of the hangings, knoutings and mutilations that stained the banks of the Volga in 1671 and 1672 and left a permanent scar on the Russian consciousness. King Charles II of England sent a message of congratulation to Tsar Alexis: rebellions, as he well remembered from his youth, were a nasty business and best dealt with firmly.

Stenka Razin and his brother Frolka being led to execution in Moscow after the collapse of his uprising.

And so the saga of Stenka Razin might have ended. But there were lessons to be learnt and repercussions for the future. Subsequent rebels – and there were to be many, most notably Pugachev – were to note that Razin exploited the peasants' affection for Tsar and Church even while he did his best to overthrow or undermine these institutions. Razin had maintained the fiction that he was not rebelling against the Tsar but against the exploitation of the boyar barons. He even dressed up a young Circassian prisoner in silken finery and took him with his fleet up the Volga on a barge covered with red velvet, presenting him as the Tsarevich Alexis Alekseevich, although the heir apparent to the throne had died some months before. Similarly he had another barge decked out in black velvet in which he had an impostor pretending to be the exiled Patriarch Nikon, whose credentials as an enemy of the boyars outweighed his unpopularity as a reforming prelate. These appeals to Russian Orthodox sentiment by the agnostic Razin were to be emulated by the atheist Stalin when he played the Orthodox-Nationalist card and opened the churches in the face of the Nazi invasion in 1941.

Another lesson which was noted but not always heeded was Razin's mistake in not striking against Moscow when his momentum and surprise were at their greatest. By turning south down the Volga to Astrakhan (where he had old scores to settle) before he turned north towards Moscow he gave the government forces time to rally and organize against him. The bold tactician should have been a bolder strategist.

The Tsar Alexis, the father of Peter the Great who came into the line of succession after the death of his elder brothers, also had much to contemplate after the revolt. He had been saved by his regular troops and viewed this as a vindication of the policy of building up a standing army; in the years that followed he was to increase this from 50,000 men to over 100,000. He had also noted that his *streltsi* musketeers in the Volga garrison towns had proved unreliable. Efforts were made to ensure more regular pay and to curb their excesses, but it was not until after the infamous revolt of the *streltsi* at the outset of Peter the Great's reign that discipline was finally imposed on these turbulent troops.

But perhaps the most abiding lesson learnt by the Tsar was that the Don Cossacks had to be brought under tighter control and harnessed more explicitly to the Russian state. Before the end of 1671 envoys had been sent from Moscow to Cherkassk to administer an oath of allegiance to the Tsar. No longer was it acceptable to claim that 'the Tsar rules in Moscow but the Cossacks rule on the Don'. Although subsequent rebels were to dispute or challenge this, the ironic result of Razin's attempt to secure greater independence for the Cossack communities was that his revolt ended by having the opposite result. The erosion of Cossack autonomy had taken a step which was to prove irreversible.

And yet, despite his miscalculations and the adverse reactions after his revolt, Stenka Razin did leave behind a legacy which was to prove an indestructible part not only of Russian folk-lore but of the Russian character itself. He was to be remembered, like Robin Hood, as a figure who robbed the rich to give to the poor, as a John Hampden figure who resisted taxation from the central government, as a William Wallace figure who struggled for independence and faced torture and death with equanimity, as a Falstaffian figure who could drink anyone under the table. His grossest excesses – he threw his mistress into the Volga because he could not take her on campaign – were romanticized. Henceforth – for better and worse – there was to be a little of Stenka Razin in every Russian and a lot in every Cossack.

6:
MAZEPPA AND
PETER THE GREAT

IVAN STEPANOVICH Mazeppa was a Cossack leader of a very different and more sophisticated sort than Yermak or Stenka Razin. He was born in 1645 into a family of minor nobility in Podolia, a part of the Ukraine west of the Dnieper river and then under Polish sovereignty. Although he and his family were Orthodox in religion, he was educated by the Jesuits and not only learnt to speak Polish, Russian and German but Latin as well. His intelligence was matched by his good looks, and he was selected to serve as a page at the court of the Polish king – Jan Casimir. He appeared to have a privileged and golden future ahead of him.

But like many of his race and background, Mazeppa had a quick temper, which was sorely tried by the continual taunts of his Polish and Catholic fellow pages at the court. To them he appeared unfashionable if not uncouth, both in religious convictions and in manners. Mazeppa's temperament was not one to take insults lightly: on one occasion he was so provoked that he drew his sword on his persecutor. This lapse of good conduct was considered as a threat to security deemed to constitute a capital offence within the precincts of the royal palace; it necessitated the personal intervention of King Jan Casimir – who appears to have had a fondness for the handsome and much-put-upon page boy – to have the sentence commuted to that of exile to his family's country estates.

It might have been thought that Mazeppa would have learnt his lesson and lived modestly and discreetly – at least for a while. But that was not his style. He was soon to be discovered in bed with the wife of one of the more important local noblemen, who thought the young man should be taught a lesson once and for all. He had Mazeppa stripped naked (or re-stripped as the case may be) and then tied to the back of a wild horse which was sent off to gallop through forests and thickets. By the time the excited animal had exhausted itself, the formerly handsome youth was so torn, lacerated and scarred that it was said his own family could not recognize him. He was also deeply humiliated by the ordeal, and could no longer contemplate a return to the Polish court or even to aristocratic local society.

Mazeppa's family had always had some Cossack blood, and now that he was rejected by more elevated society, he threw in his lot with the Cossacks in his native region of the Ukraine. Disgruntled and rebellious, he was a natural recruit to the Cossack bands. Here too his abilities were quickly recognized. His mastery of languages and quick intelligence made him a useful aide to the *hetman*, and before long he was selected to serve as an emissary from the Cossacks on the Polish side of the Dnieper to those on the Russian side. His diplomatic talents having been proved, he was sent on a mission further afield – to Constantinople.

It was on his way back from that mission that his fortunes took an unexpected turn. He fell into the hands of the Zaporozhian Cossacks, the wild fraternity who inhabited a cluster of islands on the lower reaches of the Dnieper. The Zaporozhians were – at this juncture – fanatically loyal to Tsar Alexis in Moscow; and they thought that Mazeppa's mission

smacked of treachery. Why should he be talking to the Turks? They
accordingly despatched him as a prisoner to Moscow for questioning.

We do not know quite how Mazeppa explained himself and his
irregular mission – a mission to the Tsar's potential enemies on the
fringes of Russia – but we do know that he acquitted himself so fluently
and convincingly in front of the Tsar's chief minister – Artemon Matveev
– that the latter saw in him a ready instrument for Tsarist control of the
Ukraine. He was no longer subjected to heavy-handed interrogation, but
was granted an audience with Alexis himself. The Tsar thought he had
found a trusty protégé in the youthful Mazeppa and sent him back with
a brief to watch over imperial interests in the distant and potentially-dis-
affected Ukraine.

Mazeppa determined not to risk his luck again. From this point
onward he began to demonstrate a remarkable ability to keep in with the
ruling factions and personalities in Moscow. Having already won the
regard of Matveev and Tsar Alexis, he managed to ingratiate himself with
the new rising star on the Muscovite horizon – Prince Vasily Golitsyn.

On the face of it Golitsyn was everything Mazeppa was not: a
product of one of the great aristocratic families of Russia, he sported a
neatly-pointed Van Dyke beard, and had a taste for all things Western
European. His opulent palace was a show-case for Renaissance paintings, Gobelin tapestries, Venetian mirrors and Louis XIV furniture.
His residence also abounded with foreign guests at a time – before the
foundation of St Petersburg – when Russia was still essentially an inward-
looking Asiatic power. He was to become Keeper of the Great Seal for
the Regent Sophia (during the childhood of Peter the Great) and eventually her lover also.

Golitsyn recognized in Mazeppa an ally, albeit an unlikely one.
Even if socially and temperamentally the two men were poles apart, they
shared a classical education and a thrusting ambition. When Golitsyn

The following page:
A scene from the early life of Mazeppa, the
Cossack leader who was bound to the back of
a wild horse as punishment for seducing a
Polish courtier's wife.

was despatched on a campaign against the Tartars in the Crimea in 1687 he enlisted the Ukrainian Cossacks to reinforce his army. And when the campaign proved to have been a total flop, despite Golitsyn's efforts to present it otherwise, Golitsyn blamed the *hetman* of the Cossacks – Samoyovich – for his half-hearted support. Samoyovich was stripped of his title of *hetman* and Golitsyn persuaded the Regent Sophia that Mazeppa was the right person to succeed him in that key position.

So it came about that in 1688 at the age of forty-three Mazeppa became *hetman*, a post he was to hold with increasing power and effect for two decades. His first venture as *hetman* was not a glorious one: he took 16,000 Cossacks to support his patron Golitsyn in a second campaign against the Turkish-backed Tartars in the Crimea. The reason for the war was – in large measure – to stop the continual kidnapping and capturing of Russians, particularly children, for sale as slaves in the harems and galleys of the Orient. Once more the campaign failed: by the time Golitsyn had reached the Crimea, the Tartars had built a four-mile-long earthworks right across the isthmus and the Russian army was too exhausted to attempt a frontal assault. Golitsyn opened negotiations with the Tartars and tried to persuade them to give up their Russian prisoners. The Tartars blandly replied that most of the Russian captives had converted to Islam and were perfectly happy where they were. Despite his almost total lack of success, Golitsyn again returned to Moscow and persuaded the Regent Sophia that he was the hero of the hour.

One man only stood out against the self-deception being practised by Golitsyn and the Regent. Peter, the younger of the two joint-Tsar half-brothers (for whom Sophia was acting as Regent), was affronted by these setbacks to Russian arms. He refused to receive Golitsyn, and the incident led on to the eventual confrontation between Peter (to become Tsar Peter the Great) and Sophia (to become a prisoner in the Novodevichy Convent outside Moscow).

Left: A contemporary miniature of Peter the Great with the Imperial Eagle on the reverse. Such mementos were given to Mazeppa by the Tsar.

Below: The insignia of the order of St Andrew, founded by Peter the Great and awarded by him to the Cossack leader Mazeppa before the latter's betrayal of him.

Meanwhile all this was very confusing for Mazeppa who had returned to the Ukraine and was – as ever – anxious to back the right horse in the Muscovite race for power. Initially he got it wrong. Because he was a protégé of Prince Golitsyn and because he had been involved in the abortive campaign in the Crimea, he was inclined to back the Regent in her struggle with Peter. Indeed he had journeyed to Moscow from the Ukraine in June 1689 with the express purpose of aligning himself with Sophia. But before he had entered the Kremlin he had heard reports of boyars, nobles and *Streltsi* trekking out to the Troitsky Monastery in which Peter had taken refuge to escape from Sophia's forces. Mazeppa summed up the situation correctly, put his former allegiances behind him, and took the muddy road to Troitsky where he placed his sword and the devotion of his Cossacks at the service of the young Tsar. He was only just in time. Almost all the other secular and sacred leaders of

Russia had got there before him. But as so often Mazeppa managed with his charm and wit to convince Peter that he was henceforth his man.

This was the beginning of a long and warm relationship between the Tsar and the *hetman* of his Ukrainian Cossacks. Mazeppa campaigned with Peter and Sheremetev in the expeditions against Azov in 1695/6 and his Cossacks distinguished themselves under his leadership. Peter responded to Mazeppa's flamboyant manner, obvious courage and practical ability. This was a man he felt he could work with to create his new Russia. Mazeppa received the Order of St Andrew (the Russian equivalent of the Garter) from Peter, and was treated with honour and respect at the Russian court in a way which contrasted sharply with his rough handling in his youth at the Polish court.

But most of the time Mazeppa was back in his own Ukrainian Cossack capital of Baturin and despite, or possibly because of, his close relationship with Moscow and the Tsar his role was not an easy one. His own position – which he had used to acquire a large personal fortune – required the support of Moscow, as did the position of the landowning and established merchant classes in the Ukraine. The traditionally free-booting Cossacks however resented the interference and demands (taxes and recruits for the Russian army) which this support entailed. As always there was a powerful element in the Ukraine who wanted independence from Muscovite as well as Polish rule. Mazeppa had to straddle these two factions. If he offended Moscow, he would be replaced as *hetman*; if he offended the local Cossacks too much, the Ukraine would become ungovernable and Moscow would intervene militarily. At some moments he had to invite such intervention; in 1687 for instance he had to call for Russian troops to provide a guard over his own residence at Baturin because the local Cossacks thought he was leaning too far towards Moscow in eroding Cossack privileges and practices. But by and large Mazeppa performed his balancing act for over twenty years.

The invasion of Russia by King Charles XII of Sweden in 1708 precipitated a crisis for Mazeppa. Charles XII's military reputation was supreme in all Europe. He had trounced Tsar Peter and the Russian army at Narva in 1700 and since then no-one had been able to halt the course of this northern meteor. He was indeed – in Dr Johnson's words – 'a name at which the world grew pale'. His early progress into the heart of Russia – like Napoleon's and Hitler's after him – was spectacular. There was every reason to think that Charles XII and his army would defeat Peter the Great again.

The battle for the crossing of the River Dvina in 1701, at which the Swedish king's easy victory over Saxon and Russian troops encouraged him into his fatal invasion of Russia.

Mazeppa had always managed to shift his allegiance at the opportune moment. Such a moment appeared to be approaching once more. Were he to throw in his lot with Charles XII and were the Swedes to win, there seemed to Mazeppa to be a good chance that his new master might acquiesce in the formation of an independent Ukrainian Cossack state, with Mazeppa at its head as the founder of a hereditary line of *hetmans*. Indeed, Charles XII had made overtures to Mazeppa already, offering him the title of Prince and lands in Courland (between Prussia and the Baltic States).

Mazeppa decided to hedge his bets. He had entered into a clandestine correspondence with Charles XII even before the latter's invasion got under way. Now he embarked on treasonous offers of support for Charles, while at the same time renewing his protestations of unswerving loyalty to Peter. He was playing a dangerous game and he came perilously near to being exposed.

Like most successful self-made rulers and entrepreneurs, Mazeppa had his enemies. These now began to pick up shreds of evidence of his disloyalty and to speculate about it. Rumours reached the ear of Tsar Peter, but he disregarded them: Mazeppa was a trusted favourite and drinking companion, a Knight of St Andrew and a man who owed his position and fortune to the Tsar. Peter could not bring himself to think ill of him.

The Tsar's confidence was put to the test in early 1708. The judge-general of the Cossacks – a certain Kochubey – denounced Mazeppa as one consorting with his country's enemies. The reports quickly reached the Tsar. Enquiries were put in hand and the reason for Kochubey's venom against Mazeppa was revealed. It was a story that was wholly in character with Mazeppa and appealed to Peter's indulgent concept of his *hetman*. It transpired that Mazeppa at sixty-three had fallen in love – a not infrequent occurrence for him – with Kochubey's nubile young daughter Matrena. She was totally enraptured with the charms of her older and powerful admirer, and ran away from home to live with him. What then occurred was not altogether clear at the time and

The Swedish Invasion
of Russia 1708–9

O   50 100   MILES 250
O   100   250 KMS

SWEDISH

EMPIRE

St Petersburg

SWEDISH
ESTONIA
AND
LAVONIA

COURLAND

† TROITSKY
MONASTERY
● Moscow

ROUTE OF CHARLES XII

■ Warsaw

RUSSIA

POLAND

● Baturin

Kiev ● *Dnieper*

UKRAINE ✗ Poltava

Bug

OTTOMAN EMPIRE

● Zaporozhian Sech

● Azov

BLACK SEA

Constantinople

jm'99

Peter the Great, who first trusted Mazeppa and then was betrayed by the Cossack leader.

has become less so since. It seems that having seduced the girl Mazeppa sent her home to her parents. He claimed he did not want to cause a scandal by marrying someone, who might in age have been his grand-daughter, against the wishes of the Church and the Cossack elders; her father, on the other hand, claimed that having tired of her he had rejected her in humiliating circumstances. Whatever the truth, the incident explained – in the Tsar's view – Kochubey's slander of Mazeppa. Peter attributed the reports of treason to malice and – after a peremptory examination had failed to provide convincing proof of Mazeppa's treason – told Mazeppa to deal with Kochubey as he thought fit. Mazeppa – having been badly scared – decided not to risk Kochubey being in a position to repeat or substantiate his charges, and promptly had him decapitated. It did not endear Mazeppa to Matrena, but it effectively silenced his accuser and frightened off others who might have contemplated revealing evidence against him. Once more, Mazeppa's wits and ruthlessness had saved him.

But the moment of truth was approaching for Mazeppa: he could not get away with playing a double game for much longer. The Tsar, perhaps wanting to satisfy himself directly of Mazeppa's good faith, summoned the *hetman* to Moscow. Mazeppa played for time, took to his bed, declared himself to be at death's door and called for his father confessor. Peter was placated for the moment.

Meanwhile events on the ground had taken a new turn. In September 1708 Charles XII, having had his direct advance on Moscow stemmed, turned south and led his army into the Ukraine. Peter for his part was marching towards the Ukraine also to head off the Swedes. The Tsar was already calling for Mazeppa to lead his Cossacks, as soon as he had recovered, across the Dnieper to attack the Swedes in their rear. War was coming to Mazeppa's homeland and he could not stand by as a spectator.

What finally brought Mazeppa down from sitting on the fence was his own deception catching up with him. The Tsar, who had been concerned at hearing of Mazeppa's grave illness, and realizing that it would be disastrous if the Cossacks were to be left leaderless at this juncture, decided to send his trusted lieutenant – Prince Menshikov - to visit Mazeppa at Baturin and discuss with him possible successors as *hetman* in the event of Mazeppa's death. Menshikov was sent on his way with a formidable cavalry escort. Mazeppa was seriously alarmed at this news. Menshikov was Peter's closest confidant, a self-made man of great ability in peace and war; avaricious and ambitious, he had a reputation for never forgiving or forgetting a slight. He was no friend of Mazeppa's, resenting the latter's position at Peter's court, and possibly coveting the title of *hetman* for himself – probably because of its potential for acquiring gifts and bribes. Mazeppa might deceive Peter at long-range about his state of health; he could never deceive Menshikov on his doorstep. Indeed, Mazeppa thought that Menshikov might well already know the reason for his prevarication and be coming not as an interlocutor but as an executioner. Action was needed.

Prince Menshikov who, as Peter's cavalry commander, helped to destroy Charles XII of Sweden and Mazeppa.

Mazeppa then made the gravest error of his life. He gathered around him two thousand Cossack horsemen and set off to join Charles XII, instructing the remaining three thousand Cossacks at Baturin to hold the gates shut against Menshikov and wait for the arrival of Charles XII and his invading army.

It was not long before Menshikov arrived and was denied entry to Baturin. His enquiries among random Cossacks outside the walls of their capital revealed the worst: Mazeppa had defected with a sizeable force and Baturin was, in effect, waiting to provide the invaders with much-needed food, ammunition and shelter.

Unlike Mazeppa, Menshikov never doubted on which side his bread was buttered. He rode post-haste back to the Tsar's camp and told him the bad news. Peter's wrath was as awesome as might have been predicted. He not only indicted Mazeppa as a traitor to Russia and vowed temporal vengeance, but he denounced him as an instrument of Polish-Catholic subversion of the Orthodox faith (which was a surprising charge in view of Mazeppa's own past record and Charles XII's impeccably Protestant credentials) and ordered the Metropolitan of Kiev to excommunicate Mazeppa and place the curse of anathema upon him. From now on Mazeppa would be damned in the next world as well as throughout the length and breadth of Holy Russia.

At a more practical level, Peter ordered Menshikov to return to Baturin not only with his cavalry escort this time but with batteries of artillery to demolish the walls and gates if these remained closed to him. At the same time he despatched loyal dragoons to stop other bands of Cossacks – notably the unpredictable Zaporozhians – from joining forces with the defected Ukrainian Cossacks.

Menshikov's reputation as a hard man had not been gained for nothing. He rode back to Baturin at the head of his task force without a moment's delay and arrived before Charles XII had reached this potential sanctuary. Still the gates were barricaded in his face. Menshikov's demands for immediate entry were refused. He knew that a siege would be too protracted to be over before the Swedes arrived, so at dawn the next day – despite the limited extent of his force – he ordered a full-scale frontal assault on the walled town. Within two hours Menshikov was master of Baturin.

Ideally he would have liked to have taken over the town's supplies and fortifications and repulsed the Swedish army when it arrived. But time was too short to repair the walls, and the risk of the Cossack garrison managing to overpower the Russian task force or open the gates to the Swedes was too great. Menshikov saw only one practical solution. He blew up the town's defences and supply depots – walls, ammunition, stores and all – and put the garrison and their families to the sword. About a thousand of the nimbler Cossacks managed to saddle their horses and make off to safety across the steppes. Of the remaining 7,000 inhabitants, Menshikov spared none. After the slaughter had ended, he set fire to what remained of the town.

When Charles XII and Mazeppa arrived at Baturin a few days later, far from finding a welcoming stronghold provided with all the stores they lacked, they found a ghost town heavy with the smell of slaughter and the smoke of destruction. Already Mazeppa must have wondered whether he had not made the wrong decision. And worse was to come.

Turning his back on Baturin, Mazeppa did his best to guide Charles XII towards the region between Kiev and Kharkov, which was normally a land of rich grazing and loaded granaries, where he hoped the army could spread out and spend the winter months in shelter if not comfort before the next campaigning season began.

The once proud Swedish army was now a hungry and dispirited force, deep in the heart of a hostile country, with a disappointingly small contingent of Cossack supporters, and the worst weather for half a century about to clamp down on them. The temperature fell all over Europe during the winter of 1708-1709: in far-off Versailles and Venice wine froze in the cellars and the canals iced over; in England there was skating on the Thames, and in the Ukraine Swedish dragoons froze to death on their horses. Again and again, the Tsar's skirmishers would tempt the Swedes out of their billets and then evaporate into the snowy wastes, leaving the exposed intruders to suffer the full rigours of this exceptional winter.

Mazeppa himself taught the Swedish king how to fend off frostbite by rubbing snow on his face, feet and hands when these were at risk. But many among the Swedish army seemed – despite their own Nordic winters – not to know of this trick, and over 3,000 were reported to have frozen to death while many more were crippled by frostbite in their extremities.

When Spring eventually came, Mazeppa set about trying to persuade other Cossacks to defect to the Swedish ranks. The elusive Zaporozhian Cossacks were his immediate target and he prevailed on the leader of these Dnieper river pirates to come over with 6,000 of his men. Even more potentially valuable to Charles XII was the fleet of river boats which the Zaporozhians put at his disposal, and which he hoped to use to ferry reinforcements from Poland across the Dnieper to join his continued thrust into southern Russia.

As a price for this support, Charles had formally to agree not to make peace with the Tsar until the independence of the Ukraine and the Zaporozhian Cossack lands was guaranteed. Another price paid for being joined by these undisciplined Cossack elements was that they introduced their own loose women into the previously celibate Swedish ranks: Charles's army now had a tail of Zaporozhian harlots to slow down its progress and divert its energies.

Just as the Tsar had authorized Menshikov to lay waste the Ukrainian Cossack capital of Baturin, so now he sent other troops to destroy the Zaporozhian island retreats on the lower Dnieper. Again, no quarter was given and those of the garrison who were not killed were reserved for a more grisly traitor's death. Worse from the point of view of Charles XII was the fact that while raiding the islands the Tsar's troops burnt all the Zaporozhian boats and so denied the Swedes the chance of ferrying reinforcements across the river.

The decisive test of strength between Charles XII and Peter the Great was about to ensue. Only by a convincing victory could Charles extri-

King Charles XII of Sweden.

cate himself from his predicament – being stranded far from home in hostile surroundings with an ever-diminishing military capacity. The setting for the confrontation was to be the small Ukrainian garrison town of Poltava.

Peter had the advantage of superior numbers – over 40,000 Russians as against 25,000 surviving Swedes – and also of being in prepared positions. The Swedes also had one unexpected and debilitating handicap: their king and leader – Charles XII – had been shot through the foot by a musket ball while on reconnaissance and was so severely disabled that he could neither ride nor walk. Even the greatest commander of his time could not effectively control a battle from a recumbent position on a stretcher.

The story of the battle of Poltava has been told many times. It was truly one of the decisive battles of European history, in that had Charles XII defeated Peter the Great the whole process of Russia's emergence as a European power, to which Peter had committed himself, would have been retarded – probably by many decades and possibly by a century. Sweden would have not only continued to dominate the Baltic and its shores, but all Eastern Europe too. But it was not to be: the Swedish century of glory – from Gustavus Adolphus and his dramatic intervention in the Thirty Years War to Charles XII and his series of military successes – was over.

The involvement of Mazeppa and the Ukrainian and Zaporozhian Cossacks in the battle was minimal. Although the 6,000 irregular cavalry which they constituted could have been an invaluable asset to the sorely-reduced Swedish army, Charles XII's whole battle tactics depended on the tight discipline of his troops. The Swedish veterans manoeuvred on the battle-field with the precision of a parade-ground exercise. Charles calculated that the Cossacks would confuse rather than assist the measured advance of his columns. So he left them patrolling the fringes of the battlefield to prevent the Russian army escaping after – it was to be hoped – it had been shattered by the Swedish onslaught.

The battle started before dawn on the morning of 28 June 1709. Charles had himself carried on a litter by a platoon of Guardsmen, but ceded effective command to Marshal Rehnskjold. Unfortunately the Marshal had quarrelled with the other Swedish generals and in consequence did not take them into his confidence about the battle plans. Since the Cossacks were not involved, the detailed stages of the battle need not be recounted. The lack of co-ordination between the Swedish commanders resulted in a confused attack, and eventually the sheer weight of Russian numbers began to tell as they encircled the Swedish advance. The Swedish initiative was lost and not only was their Marshal captured, but the King himself – with all but three of his platoon of Guardsmen-stretcher-bearers killed – nearly fell into Russian hands. Eventually he was scooped up onto the saddle of a passing Swedish officer and – pouring blood from his foot – borne off the field back to the Swedish camp which had throughout been protected by the frustrated Cossacks.

Now that Charles XII and the remnant of his army were in full retreat, Mazeppa and his Cossacks were once more able to perform a more useful function than guarding the camp. They acted as guides as the army moved off southwards towards the Tartar lands that bordered the Turkish empire. When the army eventually reached the junction of the Vorskla river and the broad Dnieper they discovered that the Tsar's troops had burnt the bulk of the boats collected there by the Zaporozhian Cossacks and that only a tiny minority of the Swedes could cross the main river and continue their flight towards the Sultan's domains. The rest would have to stay and fight the Russians again with little prospect of survival. Already the Russian cavalry was in hot pursuit.

Charles XII, suffering more acutely than before from his foot wound which had reopened in the stress of the battle, declared he would stay with his army. But Count Lewenhaupt, who was now the senior surviving Swedish general, persuaded him that this would be a disservice to

Sweden, as if the king were to become a prisoner-of-war in Russia the whole nation would be humiliated and a cripplingly high ransom would be sure to be demanded. Also, it was argued that if Charles were safely installed in the Ottoman Empire he might persuade the Sultan to join with him in relaunching his campaign in Russia. Reluctantly Charles agreed to take his place in one of the boats.

The question then arose of who should go with him. Clearly Count Lewenhaupt had to stay to command the bulk of the army. Mazeppa and his Cossacks, on the other hand, had no desire to be left behind: they pleaded that they would be useful as guides and escorts through the Tartar territory between the Dnieper and Ottoman Empire, but more emphatically still they argued that if they were left behind and captured they would be treated as traitors and subjected to the worst horrors of the Tsar's torturers and executioners. This argument prevailed with Charles XII who had – like everyone who came in contact with him – grown fond of Mazeppa and had no wish to leave him to the mercies of his former sovereign and present enemy. So in the end the party who crossed the Dnieper to relative safety comprised about one thousand Swedes and two thousand Cossacks. Not all the latter needed room in the boats as many of the Cossacks used their traditional method of river-crossing: they swam their horses across and held onto their tails. One cargo which did have to go by boat was two large barrels full of gold ducats which had been with Mazeppa as his personal war chest ever since he left Baturin.

Once on the far bank, Mazeppa took effective charge of the operation. He sent the king ahead in a carriage (since he was further than ever from being able to walk or ride) and split the rest of the Swedes and Cossacks into separate columns to cross the steppe by different routes. As each column entered the tall grasses south of the Dnieper they disappeared from the view of possible pursuers and left a confused trail that would be difficult to follow.

After a week of scorching travel under a mid-summer sun, the various columns met up on the banks of the Bug river on 7 July. This was the frontier between the empires of the Tsar and the Sultan: once across the Bug the party would be beyond pursuit. But their troubles were not over until they had crossed this last river, and they had to wait and negotiate for boats and safe passage from the Sultan's representatives on the other side. Three long days were passed in bargaining and bribery.

Meanwhile there had of course been no news of Lewenhaupt and the main part of the defeated Swedish army left behind on the Dnieper. Had Charles XII known what had happened with them he would have been even more depressed. The night after the king had left his army, the ever-energetic Prince Menshikov at the head of a flying column of 6,000 Russian cavalry had caught up with the 14,000 Swedes left on the Dnieper's north bank. Menshikov's horsemen had appeared on the skyline overlooking the river valley, and the Swedes had no way of gauging their numbers. Lewenhaupt knew that the king was expecting him to march the army in a broad swing through the southern Ukraine to an ill-defined rendezvous with the royal party on the Black Sea. But this plan assumed that Lewenhaupt and his army had escaped the Tsar's net; now it seemed – from the looming presence of Menshikov's cavalry on the horizon – that they had not escaped. Menshikov for his part was quick to follow up his moral advantage by sending an envoy to offer honourable surrender terms to the Swedes. The latter, lacking the incisive leadership of the king who had always hitherto inspired them, prevaricated. Lewenhaupt consulted the other generals; the generals consulted the colonels; the colonels consulted their junior officers and the officers consulted their men. Never was the military adage 'he who hesitates is lost' more vividly illustrated. By the time the debate had become a general one, the will to fight had evaporated. By 11 a.m. on the morning after their king had left them, the Swedish army had surrendered to a force less than half its own size.

The following page:
Charles XII's body being carried back to Sweden.
In England, Dr Johnson wrote of him:
"He left a name, at which the world grew pale,
To point a moral, or adorn a tale."

Predictably, the Cossack element in the Swedish army did not lay down its arms so readily. They knew that for them, as traitors to the Tsar, the status of prisoners-of-war would not apply. All who could mounted their horses and slipped away across the steppes. Some of these were cut down or captured. Others failed to get away at all. All those Cossacks who fell into Menshikov's hands had good reason to wish they had not: most were knouted and mutilated before they were hanged.

None of this was known to Charles XII and Mazeppa as they waited on the banks of the Bug to pass over into the Ottoman Sultan's domains. But they were soon to have their own worries. Some six hundred Swedes and Cossacks were still on the north bank of the Bug waiting their turn in the Turkish boats that were ferrying them to safety when Menshikov's advance guard, having failed to follow their tracks through the pampas-grass but guessing they were heading for the Bug river and the Turkish frontier, caught up with them. The scenes of a week earlier on the Dnieper were now re-enacted on a smaller scale on the Bug. The Swedes surrendered; the Cossacks fought to the last man. But this time Charles XII and Mazeppa experienced the agony of seeing and hearing the final fatal encounter for themselves; the invalid king and the Cossack *hetman* on the far bank could do nothing to save their comrades. The time spent bartering for the boats had cost another six hundred men killed or captured.

The Sultan, feeling guilty no doubt at having kept his distinguished refugee waiting so long, welcomed Charles XII to his domains and installed him in a royal encampment in what is now Moldavia. (He was to detain him for one reason or another for three years by which time his hospitality had worn distinctly thin.) Mazeppa remained with the king but – already an elderly man – his health collapsed following the excitements and disappointments of the months before and after Poltava. He was aware that Peter the Great had vowed vengeance against him, and Peter was a vicious enemy: if he fell into his hands he could expect to be exhibited in a cage and utterly humiliated before his physical sufferings began. It did not help his morale when he learnt that Peter had sent a private emissary to Charles XII in his Turkish retreat offering to exchange the Swedish King's closest adviser and confidant – Count Piper – for Mazeppa. Charles had ruefully refused: he was not going to sacrifice the garrulous and still-charming old Cossack even for his dearest friend. But Peter remained determined to make an example of Mazeppa; his next move was to offer the Sultan 300,000 gold ducats for the repatriation of Mazeppa; but the Sultan also declined – albeit reluctantly – as he felt that the deal would have been a breach of the traditional hospitality owed to one seeking his protection.

All this must have been very alarming for Mazeppa. He would have remembered how, on the Azov campaign back in 1696, a Dane called Jensen who was employed at the Tsar's headquarters had defected to the Turks and Peter had made it a condition of the negotiated surrender of the Turkish Pasha that he should hand over the traitor alive to Peter. The unfortunate Jensen had then been paraded through the streets of Moscow trussed up like a chicken and surrounded by the instruments of torture whose rigours he was shortly to experience. And Jensen had not even been a Russian to start with.

But Mazeppa need not have worried on this score. On 22 September 1709, only ten weeks after they escaped from Menshikov's pursuit, the problem solved itself: Mazeppa died of natural causes and was buried with full Swedish military honours.

The heroes of Cossack folk tales have frequently inspired great writers. Mazeppa was one of the first to do so. Lord Byron, intrigued by references to him in the writings of Voltaire, became so beguiled by the legends surrounding the *hetman's* early life and the tragedy of his final months, that he wrote an epic poem imagining a scene in which the aged Mazeppa regales Charles XII in their fugitives' camp 'after dread Poltowa's day' with an account of his youthful scrape with the wife of the Polish nobleman and the runaway horse. The whole incident may well have been fabricated by Mazeppa in the first place and Byron adds some good twists of his own, such as the fact that Mazeppa's horse dies under him and the lacerated young Mazeppa is about to become carrion for the ravens when he is rescued by a beautiful Cossack girl and taken into the bosom of a Cossack family:

> Since I became the Cossack guest:
> They found me senseless on the plain –
> They bore me to the nearest hut –
> They brought me into life again –
> Me – one day o'er their realm to reign!

Mazeppa is portrayed as a romantic hero after Byron's own heart. In reality he was a far more scheming character than Byron suggests.

In fact he had much in common with his contemporary Simon Fraser, 11th Baron Lovat, who was executed for his part in Prince Charles Edward Stuart's Scottish uprising of 1745. The parallels are extraordinary: both men were classical scholars of repute; both had chequered sexual careers as young men; both were great clan chieftains; both were raconteurs who got themselves out of tight corners by displays of charm and wit; both carried barrels of gold coins with them on their final flight; both changed sides repeatedly, and both ended by backing the wrong horse.

But the story of Mazeppa was not just a personal tragedy. It illustrates a facet of the Ukrainian Cossacks which future rulers of Russia would ignore at their peril: however loyal such Cossacks might appear to be to their Tsar or their government, the urge to achieve an independent Cossack state would never be far below the surface. Stalin was to prove at least as ruthless as Peter the Great when this urge demonstrated itself in a 'betrayal of Holy Russia' in the face of a later foreign invader.

CATHERINE THE GREAT
AND PUGACHEV

I F ONE LOOKS AT ANY of the numerous portraits of Catherine the Great of Russia – notably Mikhail Shibanov's painting of her in her travelling clothes at the age of forty-four in 1770 – one is confronted with the features of a kindly, almost cosy, middle-aged lady who might well have been matron of a hospital or a girls' boarding school. There is no hint of the sexually predatory empress, nor of the intellectually ambitious correspondent of Voltaire, nor of the belligerent hammer of the Turks and Poles, nor of the scheming conniver in the murder of her husband and the disinheriting of her son. For Catherine was in reality one of the most aggressive of Tsars, in the direct line of spiritual descent from Ivan the Terrible and Peter the Great. But it was not her enemies within her own family, nor her foreign adversaries that nearly unseated her. It was a Don Cossack who fermented, more successfully than even Stenka Razin had done, the frustrations of the Cossacks and serfs and who came to threaten Moscow itself.

Catherine prided herself above all on two characteristics: she was a champion of all things Russian, and she was a liberal-thinker in advance of her period. The latter claim at least had rather shaky foundations.

Catherine was born Princess Sophia Augusta of Anhalt-Zerbst (a minor German principality) and married at the age of sixteen to the future Tsar Peter III (a grandson of Peter the Great). She was received into the Russian Orthodox Church and re-christened Catherine Alekseyevna. Although she might have been expected to hark back to her country of birth, in fact she embraced her new Russian role whole-heartedly and her Germanic origins came to be forgotten or overlooked by herself – though not always by her critics. It was her husband who was mesmerized by everything teutonic; he idolized Frederick the Great of Prussia and made an inglorious peace with Prussia just when Russia thought she was winning her conflict with that country; he even appeared at the Russian court decked out in Prussian decorations. By contrast, Catherine's fondness for things Russian, however lately acquired, appeared genuine enough.

She was to use this factor to her personal advantage. When her husband succeeded to the throne as Peter III in 1762 his pro-German tastes infuriated the nobility, the Orthodox clergy, the army and even his own personal regiments of Guards. He was weak-minded, inclined to drunkenness, and predisposed to divorce his queen in favour of an unpopular mistress. Catherine used all these factors to stir up sentiment against him; she was already living in a separate palace. Her resentment of her husband's mistress did not prevent her from taking a lover of her own (not her first) in the form of Count Grigori Orlov. He was a practi-cal choice, as he and his four brothers were all serving as officers in units of the Imperial Guards. When a plot was eventually hatched – only a matter of months after Peter's accession – the Orlov brothers played key roles. Catherine appeared in Guards uniform to the Orlovs' regiments; these swore allegiance to her as Empress; the Archbishop of Novgorod proclaimed her as Autocrat of All the Russias, and a formidable body of troops assembled in front of the Winter Palace in St Petersburg to march

Catherine the Great in a
travelling costume, 1770.

under her banner to overthrow her husband. The unfortunate Peter was put under arrest, moved to a country estate under Orlov control, and decreed dead of the colic a few days later. There seems little doubt he had been strangled by one of the Orlov brothers, almost certainly with Catherine's knowing encouragement. The fact she and Peter already had a son and heir was conveniently overlooked, and under these dubious circumstances her long reign as Catherine II began.

From the beginning, she wished to be thought of as an enlightened monarch. The first areas of activity to attract her attention were agriculture and property rights for the peasants. She initiated an essay competition on the latter theme, and Voltaire wrote from France with a contribution. She corresponded directly with the sage from the first years of her reign. She went on to focus her attention on the legal system, denounced torture in judicial proceedings and set her face against capital punishment. She even envisaged deputies coming from various sectors of society – including the Cossack hosts – with proposals for the better governance of the country. Russia was to be a model among European nations.

It was therefore with particular resentment that she found, from the earliest years of her reign, that there was continual unrest in the remote border regions. A whole succession of impostors claiming to be her husband Tsar Peter III put themselves forward and gathered local support. The upstarts were arrested, knouted, branded, had their noses split, and suffered other indignities and torments before being banished into exile. But still others cropped up. There were no less than ten false Peters in the first decade of Catherine's reign and nearly two dozen before the end. It was – she thought – a throwback to the era of the Time of Troubles. While she was adopting so many liberal attitudes, in theory if not in practice – the knouting continued – she was shocked by this 'ingratitude' among her subjects.

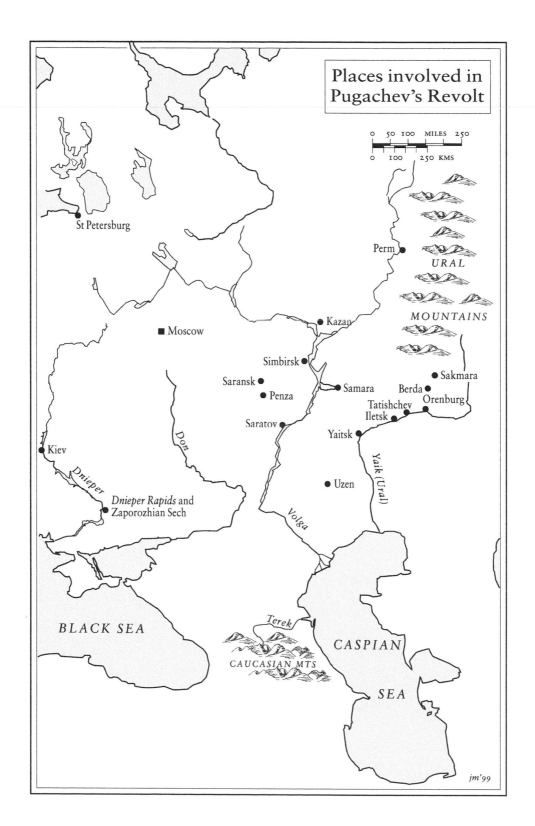

Places involved in Pugachev's Revolt

St Petersburg

Perm

URAL

MOUNTAINS

■ Moscow

Kazan

Simbirsk

Sakmara

Saransk

Samara

Berda

Penza

Orenburg

Tatishchev

Iletsk

Saratov

Yaitsk

Yaik (Ural)

Kiev

Uzen

Dnieper

Don

Dnieper Rapids and
Zaporozhian Sech

Volga

Terek

BLACK SEA

CASPIAN

CAUCASIAN MTS

SEA

jm'99

As so often, it was among the Cossacks that the trouble took root most seriously. There had been a flare up in 1771 among the Yaik (Ural) Cossacks, and then in 1773 – while Catherine's attention was focused on her foreign adventures against the Turks and the Poles – a dissident Don Cossack brought first the Yaik river valleys and then the whole Volga region into a state of open revolt.

Emelian Pugachev had already had a lengthy and chequered career before he came to prominence and the attention of the Tsar. Born in 1742, like most young Cossacks he had been called up for military service and sent to fight against Frederick the Great of Prussia. His first encounter with the enemy had a humiliating outcome for him: he had been put in charge of his colonel's horse and allowed it to escape, for which he was soundly whipped. The campaign over, he settled down to a peaceful enough life on the banks of the Don, combining agriculture with river-haulage, and occasionally having to rejoin the colours for brief periods of further military service. This was the pattern of Cossack life.

The pattern came to an abrupt end when Pugachev had to leave his wife and family and his burgeoning business for longer service overseas against the Turks. At first he did well, being commended for his bravery at the siege of Bender and promoted to the rank of cornet. But then he became ill and hired others to do his military service for him. Eventually, when his sick leave ran out he decided to abscond to the Zaporozhian *Sech* – that enclave of wild Cossacks outside the reach of the authorities. Further adventures, arrests and escapes followed in rapid succession. At the end of it all, Pugachev was an outlaw and on the run indefinitely.

Among those with whom the fugitive fell in were a group of Old Believers who had also suffered persecution. One of them, who had been a guardsman at St Petersburg, remarked to Pugachev that he was a spitting image of the supposedly-murdered Tsar Peter III whom he had

Catherine the Great of Russia who put down the revolt by Pugachev the Cossack rebel who claimed to be her dead husband.

frequently observed when on guard duty. At first Pugachev dismissed
the remark as an idle comment, but little by little the idea dawned on
him that – if he really resembled the Tsar so much – he might capitalize
on this to lead a revolt against Catherine in the same way as the False
Dmitri had challenged Boris Godunov nearly two centuries earlier.

All the ingredients for revolt were present. The Yaik Cossacks had
resented the way their own rising had been put down; the Don Cossacks
were restive and had nearly lynched General Cherepov – Catherine's
representative – when he had been sent to impose central authority on
them; the Old Believers were numerous, disgruntled and harassed; the
serfs had felt none of the benevolence which Catherine's liberal ideas
promised. Pugachev himself had come to the end of the line: his repeat-
ed desertions, escapes and attempts to reach safe-havens had left him a
marked man who could expect little mercy when next the authorities
caught up with him. In short, he felt he had nothing to lose by risking
all on a desperate venture.

On 17 September 1773 Pugachev issued an order of the day to his
supporters and putative supporters. Declaring himself as 'Emperor
Autocrat, the great Lord Peter Fedorovich of All the Russias' he called
on Cossacks, Kalmyks and Tartars to rise up with him and inherit their
rightful lands, pastures and rivers 'from the mountains to the sea'. He
promised them pay and weapons (which some of his more affluent supporters had undertaken to provide). The only trouble was that Pugachev
could not actually sign his stirring declaration because it transpired that
he was totally illiterate. But where so many wanted to believe that he was
indeed the rightful Tsar, and when it was recalled that Peter III had
absolved the gentry from their obligations of personal service and had
been expected to do the same for the peasantry shortly, no one thought
fit to question his credentials. Horsemen set out for the nearest town of
Yaitsk on the Yaik river with the reincarnated Tsar's pennants fluttering

A Cossack of the Urals as he would have
appeared at the time of Pugachev's revolt.

from their lances, and as they rode through the disaffected countryside scores of other horsemen joined them.

The first contact with the authorities was a triumph for Pugachev and a foretaste of what was to lie ahead. Colonel Simonov, Catherines's commandant in Yaitsk, sent out a detachment of 500 'loyal' Cossacks to confront half that number of rebels. When the two vanguards met, most of the loyalists abandoned their allegiance to Catherine and promptly joined the rebels. A few remained adamant in their allegiance and Pugachev, setting out as he meant to continue, unceremoniously hanged them as an example to others.

But if this encounter was to be become a pattern for many others, equally the turn of events when Pugachev reached Yaitsk itself was to be a pattern. Colonel Simonov declined to surrender his garrison compound, and Pugachev – rather than settle in to a siege – bypassed the obstacle and rode on to his next objective. This was Iletsk, where 300 more Cossacks rode out to join Pugachev and the church bells pealed out a welcome. Again, there were a few objectors whom Pugachev strung up without more ado. Continuing to press up the Yaik river valley, Pugachev overwhelmed Rassypnaya and then Ozernaya and Tatishchev; in each place more Yaik Cossacks came over to the rebels, and more garrison commanders were hung and their wives either hung with them or raped by the unruly band who grew in strength every day. They now numbered nearly 3,000.

Pugachev's next objective was the Russian regional military headquarters of Orenburg. This was a more formidable target than the small fortified towns and villages that had so far fallen to him. Orenburg also had a determined and courageous commander in the person of General Reinsdorp and a garrison of about the same size as the rebel force. Pugachev set up his own base at nearby Berda; he held court as a Tsar and offered inducements not only to Cossacks but to

Tartars, Kalmyks and Bashkirs; tribesmen and peasants flocked in from near and far and in a few weeks the numbers rose to nearly 10,000; a War College was established to act as a military staff for Pugachev; even disgruntled miners from the Ural pits threw down their tools and joined the rebels.

Despite his growing strength, Pugachev still did not dare to make a full-scale assault on Orenburg. Instead he did what guerrilla leaders

Bashkirs of the sort recruited by Pugachev for his revolt against Catherine the Great in the 18th century.

are best at; he ranged the countryside with his armed bands, surprising the estates of country landowners and outlying posts and leaving a trail of looting, arson, destruction and murder – including of priests – behind him. By this time – the end of 1773 – the revolt had spread to the Volga as well as the Yaik river basins, and rebel numbers were edging up to 25,000. There was talk of a march on Moscow, but Pugachev was uneasy about leaving the loyalist garrisons at Yaitsk and Orenburg in his rear. He failed to take the flood tide of events that could have led on to fortune.

Meanwhile, Catherine was becoming – not before time – seriously worried at the largest scale uprising so far recorded in Russian history. But the first force sent against Pugachev was wholly inadequate for the task. Colonel Chernyshev's troops were quickly overwhelmed, the officers being stripped naked and then hung while the men were forcibly recruited into the rebel ranks. Major-General Ker and a second task force fared little better, eventually retiring hurt from the encounter. Pugachev received spies from St Petersburg who reported that he had a following in the streets of the capital. He talked of pressing home his advantage, and of placing Catherine – like Peter the Great had placed Sophia – in a nunnery to repent of her sins. But despite all the talk, he still declined to move decisively.

Catherine now woke up to the fact that sending second rate military units under tired commanders was not good enough. In December 1773 she despatched General Bibikov to Kazan, 400 miles east of Moscow and at the north of the ever-widening region under Pugachev's control. He found everyone in despair: officials had abandoned their posts; landowners were cowering on their properties awaiting their fate; internal communications had collapsed. The General set about restoring some semblance of order and confidence: he organized the gentry into a local yeomanry, and he sent subordinate commanders out in all directions to stop the spread of the revolt and to attempt to hem in the rebels. He even sent a relief force under Major-General Golytsyn to the hard-pressed garrison commander at Orenburg.

The first pitched battle between Golytsyn and some 10,000 rebels under Pugachev's personal command took place on 22 March 1774. Although the rebel army was competently commanded, chose a good defensive position and resisted the Russian artillery bombardment better than might have been expected, the professional troops eventually broke them. A rout ensued, with the Russian cavalry cutting down nearly 3,000 on the battlefield and capturing or wounding as many again. It seemed a decisive encounter. Pugachev himself escaped from the field and fell back on Berda and then on Sakmara, finally disappearing with only a handful of supporters into the foothills of the Ural Mountains.

Meanwhile first Orenburg and then Yaitsk were relieved – only just in time. The garrisons had been reduced to eating cats and spinning out the last of their ammunition. It must have seemed to Catherine, reading the despatches from the south that reached her in St Petersburg, that the revolt was over. But her rejoicing was premature.

Partly because of his personal charisma and partly because of the very real grievances and disaffection among the tribesmen, serfs and miners, the revolt flared up again like a bush fire that had never been truly extinguished. Pugachev moved north, gathering support as he went, but also collecting a dogged Russian pursuer in the form of Colonel Mikhelson and his cavalry regiment supported by field artillery. Numerous encounters ensued, but always Pugachev managed to slip away. Sometimes he found fresh fortified villages to sack and more Russian garrison commanders to hang. Sometimes his men sacked churches, smashing icons and using vestments as saddle-cloths.

Having gone almost as far north as Perm (where Yermak had set out on his conquest of Siberia two centuries before) Pugachev turned

west and headed for the administrative centre of Kazan, where ironical-
ly a post-mortem enquiry was being held into the origins and character
of the revolt (Catherine was convinced there must be foreign intervention behind it and could not believe that her own subjects rebelled
against her of their own volition). Although the rebels sacked and set fire
to most of Kazan, they were still being harassed by the indefatigable
Colonel Mikhelson.

Finally, on 15 July 1774 Pugachev announced that he was setting
out from Kazan to capture Moscow, but Mikhelson got between the
rebels and their line of advance and, although his force was greatly infe-
rior in numbers to Pugachev's, he managed not only to halt their
progress but to convert their advance into a full-scale retreat. Once
repulsed, the rebels again disintegrated rapidly, and once more
Pugachev himself was left with a few hundred Cossack bodyguards to
flee as best he could.

But the flame of rebellion was still not dowsed. For the third time
Pugachev's force was reduced to a handful of followers, and for the third
time it picked up numbers as it moved through the exploited countryside. As he turned first west and then south from Kazan, it was once
more the Volga peasants who rallied to him and who were seduced with
promises of new rights and tax abolition. If only they would rise up and
destroy their landowners, there would be enough to go round for all to
be rich! The peasants would be honorary Cossacks! Three hundred gentry were hanged at Saransk; the Governor and all his family were burnt
alive in their residence at Pensa; the frightened garrison overpowered
their commanders and opened the gates to him at Saratov. It seemed
that the old story was repeating itself and that – while Pugachev lived –
the cancer of revolt could not be cured.

Any serious credibility as Tsar Peter III had long since deserted
Pugachev in the eyes of all but his most unsophisticated followers. In

Kazan, for instance, Pugachev's wife Sophia and children emerged from among the inhabitants, and instantly laid public claim to his support and affections. This was a considerable embarrassment because a few months earlier he had taken a new – much younger – Cossack bride and declared that she was his 'empress'. But never at a loss to talk his way out of difficulties, Pugachev declared that Sophia was the wife of 'his friend and loyal supporter Yemelyan Pugachev', and with a mixture of bribes and threats he prevented Sophia from causing too much trouble.

But however rapidly he moved on, and however many manor houses he might burn down, the persistent Colonel Mikhelson stayed on his tracks. So far Pugachev had raised support along the Yaik and Volga river banks; now he addressed himself to the settlements along his native Don. Here even the most unsophisticated became disillusioned about Pugachev's claims to be Peter III: there were just too many people who recognised him for himself. He shied away from the Don basin, and returned to regions where his face awakened no embarrassing memories.

Colonel Mikhelson, dogged as ever, also turned his back on the Don and once more headed back to the Volga. Towards the end of August 1774, Colonel Mikhelson's flying column finally caught up with the much larger but very ragged cavalcade of Pugachev's supporters. He engaged in battle immediately, and a combination of well-aimed artillery fire and disciplined cavalry charges scattered the rebels once more. This time Pugachev got away with some 400 Cossacks, but only half of them managed to find boats or swim themselves and their horses across the wide and fast-flowing Volga.

It was among the Old Believers – that harassed minority – that Pugachev felt most secure, and he headed for one of their settlements at Uzen. Little by little his party deserted him. Those few who remained around him were beginning to have thoughts of their own. A reward of nearly 30,000 roubles was on Pugachev's head, and whoever turned him

Pugachev, the Don Cossack who raised a major revolt against Catherine the Great, caged after his capture.

over to the authorities could be sure of a free pardon for himself. Pugachev kept his pistols loaded and in his belt; he was not a man to be easily taken by surprise. But taken by surprise he was. His long-standing Cossack companion Tvorogov and a couple of other trusted friends turned on him, tied him up and handed him over to the first senior Russian army officer they could find.

Pugachev was harangued, interrogated and put into a cage like an animal, for the onward journey first to Simbirsk and then to Moscow. After his false claims to be the Tsar and his savagery to the officers, landowners and gentry who had fallen into his hands over the past many months, it was hardly surprising that he himself was treated with little humanity by his captors. Unlike Stenka Razin, he did not display courage in adversity, but took every opportunity to blame others for his own crimes. To some extent this was made easier for him by Catherine the Great's continued conviction that there must have been some sinister foreign involvement orchestrating the revolt; she still could not accept that, in her 'enlightened' state of Russia, one local firebrand could turn whole tracts of the country against her. Commissions of enquiry were set up. Everyone in any way involved was rounded up, cross-questioned and – if they seemed to be with-holding anything – tortured. Every possible lead was followed up: could the Turks or the Poles have had a hand in formenting the rebellion?

At the end of the day, there was no hard evidence of any under-lying cause for the revolt except the hardship of the peasants' lives and the oppression of the landowners. Pugachev was brought to trial and, despite Catherine's much-vaunted aversion to capital punishment, was condemned with her approval to be publicly quartered while still alive and finally beheaded. The spectacle of executing, mutilating, branding and flogging lasted all of one Moscow winter's day. Even Pugachev's innocent children were despatched to a remote fortress where they were incarcerated for over fifty years. Retribution was not limited to the sav-age enforcement of justice: landowners and soldiery took a heavy toll of peasants in those areas where succour had been given to the rebels.

The fact that the Cossacks had throughout been at the heart of the revolt was forgotten, and the aftermath of the uprising also set a prece-dent – which was to be followed in later centuries – for attempting to har-ness or restrain the force of the Cossacks. The *Sech* – that watery hideout on the lower Dnieper – was largely cleared of Zaporozhian Cossacks; many of the Volga Cossacks were resettled in the Caucasus along the Terek river; the Yaik Cossacks were renamed the Ural Cossacks (the name of the river itself being changed) and their region dominated by an occupation force of troops from western Russia; only on the Don – the home of Pugachev but not the region from which he drew most of his support – did the Cossack life carry on relatively unmolested. But to the authorities it seemed that, as so often, the Cossacks were not to be trusted as law-abiding citizens: as under Bogdan, Stenka Razin, Mazeppa and many others, they had followed the wild urgings of a rebellious leader.

One bonus of the revolt was a memorable piece of literature. The poet Pushkin, having earlier written a history of the rebellion, published his novel *The Captain's Daughter* sixty years after the event. It is still a very readable, straight-forward adventure story, recounting how a young officer going to take up his first appointment on the barren steppe near Orenburg encounters and befriends a wayward ruffian who later turns out to be Pugachev. When his garrison town is attacked by Pugachev's rebels, the young hero has a series of adventures rescuing his commandant's daughter – with whom he has fallen in love – from the fate (rape or execution) that overtakes so many of the officers' women. In this he is hampered by the machinations of a treacherous officer who is also an admirer of the Captain's daughter and who has gone over to Pugachev, but he and his paramour are saved by Pugachev's recollection of his earlier kindness. Pugachev's apparent patronage of him goes badly against our hero when the revolt is over, as he comes under suspicion of having been one of the rebel's followers. But predictably all ends happily. The short novel has more insight into the feelings and social background of a young subaltern who is bored by a frontier posting than it does into the motivation of the rebels, but it certainly deserves a place – along with Tolstoy's eponymous novel about the Cossacks – on any shelf of background literature.

8 :
THE COSSACKS
AND NAPOLEON'S
INVASION OF RUSSIA

I<small>T WAS A</small> C<small>OSSACK OFFICER</small> who received the nearest thing Napoleon ever made to a declaration of war on the Russian empire of Tsar Alexander I. Advance cavalry units of the First Corps of the *Grande Armée* crossed the Niemen river on 24 June 1812, using the pontoon bridges rapidly assembled by Napoleon's sappers, and as they penetrated the lightly wooded territory on the eastern bank a lone Cossack officer emerged from the trees and rode towards them. He asked with cold courtesy what brought the foreigners into his country. 'To make war on you ... and liberate Poland!' was the brusque reply. The most disastrous of all Napoleon's campaigns had begun.

The fact that the Don and other Cossack communities rallied to the Tsar and the defence of Mother Russia, and that they were able and willing to provide an effective irregular cavalry, owed much to one man: General Count Platov. Born in 1751, Platov had left his comfortable Don Cossack home to join the army at the age of thirteen. By nineteen he had been commissioned, and very shortly afterwards he gained experience of active service in the Crimea and against marauding Tartars. He played an active part in putting down Pugachev's revolt and was raised to the rank of a Cossack Elder in consequence. By 1790, he was already a knight and a brigadier when he won the coveted Order of St George for his part under General Suvorov in the storming of the Turkish citadel of Ismail; it was on this occasion that the Cossacks had cut down their lances and fought as foot soldiers in the final assault. So courageous and loyal was Platov, that it was scarcely surprising that he was chosen by Tsar Paul to command the hare-brained expedition against Khiva and ultimately British India which set off – 22,000-strong – in 1801. The long march into Central Asia involved contending with snow, ice, deserts and hunger, and would almost certainly have ended in disaster had it not been for the death of Tsar Paul and the recall of the expedition. Platov was promoted by the new Tsar – Alexander I – to be *Ataman* of the Don Cossacks. This was the man who, at the moment of Napoleon's invasion in 1812, was commanding the Cavalry Corps which protected the northern flank of General Bagration's army. Almost half the Russian cavalry were Cossacks, and a very high proportion of those came from Platov's native Don region, so it was altogether appropriate that he should be in charge.

That Platov and his Cossacks were deployed to advantage throughout the period of the French invasion was largely because of the imagination of the supreme Russian commander – Marshal Kutuzov. This could not have been taken for granted. Kutuzov's background was diametrically different from Platov's: St Petersburg born and bred, he had held diplomatic as well as military posts. He had a reputation for eccentricity – boozing and snoozing through events that would have unnerved lesser commanders. Although Kutuzov felt that the Cossacks were an alien element in his army – mercenaries from the fringe of the

Tsar Alexander I presenting the leader of a Cossack band to Napoleon at Tilsit in 1807. Five years later, when Napoleon invaded Russia, he was to see a very different aspect of the Cossacks.

*A Don Cossack at
full charge.*

empire – he appreciated that these wild, bizarre horsemen terrified the French and could fulfil a number of specialized roles.

First among these roles was that of reconnaissance. Throughout the campaign, the Cossacks were to be the eyes and ears of the army (as they would later be in the Caucasus). They shadowed the *Grande Armée*'s advance across European Russia to the battlefield of Borodino and to Moscow. It was they who first discovered Napoleon's evacuation of Moscow, which Kutuzov initially disbelieved. It was they again who discovered the line of Napoleon's retreat, and later on it was Cossack patrols which intercepted Napoleon's correspondence with his wife and thus revealed to the Russian high command his long-term intentions.

Most dramatically of all, it was a party of Cossack scouts that nearly intercepted Napoleon and his Chief-of-Staff when they were themselves making a midnight reconnaissance near Ghorodnia; after that narrow squeak, Napoleon declared he had no intention of being taken alive by the Cossacks and ordered a phial of poison to be prepared which he carried on his person for the rest of the campaign.

Kutuzov was less sure of how best to deploy the Cossacks in pitched battle. On the field of Borodino, when at last Napoleon managed to bring his opponent into the open against him, Kutuzov kept the 7,000 Cossack horsemen out of the fray until nearly mid-day. Platov was fuming at this inactivity, and eventually obtained permission to charge the left flank of

Cossack troopers in parade dress at the time of the Napoleonic Wars.

the French line. When he did charge, the effect was shattering: the Italian and Croat contingents in Napoleon's army fell back in confusion and disarray, and had Platov been allowed to press on he might have cut through the squares of French infantry which next confronted him and reached the village of Borodino itself. But the antics of the wild and impetuous horsemen from the Don did not fit into Kutuzov's overall measured battle plan. They were restrained by orders from above, and only came into their own again when they formed the rearguard of the Russian army as it withdrew from what has generally been considered to have been a drawn battle. The Cossacks were the last to leave the field.

When Marshal Murat, Napoleon's second-in-command, pressed on from Borodino to occupy Moscow itself, he was met at the gates of the city by a detachment of Cossacks who had come to negotiate on instructions for the peaceful occupation of the city. It was a curious role for the ever-belligerent Cossacks. But Murat was flattered by their presence, as he rightly believed he had been something of a hero to the Cossacks ever since the Treaty of Tilsit on account of his sharing some of their characteristics: brilliant horsemanship, outstanding courage and eccentricity of uniform. He responded to the Cossack approaches by presenting their leader with his own jewel-encrusted gold pocket watch. Even after this strange ceremony, exchanges continued between Murat and the Cossacks who, acting on Kutuzov's orders, encouraged Murat both to think that the Russian army wanted an armistice, and to advance in the wrong direction – that is a direction different from that taken by Kutuzov.

Napoleon's occupation of Moscow after the Battle of Borodino proved a hollow triumph. The city had been deserted, and very soon after Napoleon's entry it was set on fire – almost certainly by the Russians themselves. Winter was approaching and Napoleon abandoned the city and began the long march home. It was during this famous retreat from Moscow that the Cossacks really came into their own.

Kutuzov's objective, which may well have been different from that of his master Tsar Alexander I, was not to defeat Napoleon in battle and rid Europe of an aggressor; it was the more modest objective of removing Napoleon and his *Grande Armée* from the soil of Holy Russia. To this end, more pitched battles were to be eschewed. Attrition was the order of the day. And for this purpose no better weapon could have been in Kutuzov's hand than the myriad squadrons of Count Platov's Cossacks.

They early showed that they were more at home in skirmishing that in accepting gold watches. Even before the French retreat began, some eighty French Hussars of the Guard were cut off and surrounded by a Cossack band and obliged to surrender – a most unnatural action for the proud and decorative Hussar Guards. As the general retreat got under way, the Cossacks pursued two parallel tactics: they harried the rearguard every step of the way, and they darted in and out attacking weak links in the main marching column of the *Grande Armée*. The retreat had started in October, but already it was too late in the season and soon the snow and frost were to become the Russians' best allies. Not for nothing did the Tsar's brother remark that the most reliable Russian Generals were General Janvier and General Février.

Stragglers fell easy victims to the Cossacks. They were stripped of their arms and gorgeous uniforms and left to die of exposure. Just occasionally, one was more fortunate: Captain Roeder who commanded Napoleon's Hessian Guards was found on the ground and spared because the Cossack trooper who would have stripped him mistook the ribbon of a Hessian order on his tunic for the Tsarist Order of Vladimir. Sentries struggling to keep alert or even alive through the long winter nights would be lassoed and dragged off for execution while their comrades slept. Some did not even need the attentions of the Cossacks to finish them off: every night French soldiers who had been too tired or badly wounded to get close to the camp fires at night would fail to survive the freezing temperatures and would be found the following day as scattered corpses round the periphery of abandoned camp sites.

But it was not only stragglers and the wounded who were to become victims of the Cossacks' harassment. Marshal Ney in command of the rearguard found his troops abandoning pay chests full of coins to speed their flight from Cossack patrols. When the French columns formed a solid mass to resist the Cossack efforts to cut off and isolate individual units, the Cossacks brought light artillery up on horse-drawn sledges and bombarded the columns from a safe distance. On one occasion after the retreating army had passed through Smolensk, the Cossacks swept down on a column and recaptured much of the loot from Moscow churches that was being carried off to France; on the same foray they managed to destroy a waggon loaded with maps on which the French had been relying to plot any variations on their course homeward. Gradually the veteran troops of the greatest army in Europe were reduced to carrying nothing but their personal weapons – and even these were being jettisoned by soldiers who no longer had the strength to shoulder their own muskets.

Arguably the worst deprivation that the *Grande Armée* suffered during the long retreat was the loss of their leader: the Emperor Napoleon himself decided to abandon his men and set off accompanied by his Master of the Horse on a fast sleigh with a tiny escort. He reckoned that his best chance of safety lay in speed and he persuaded himself that his empire needed him in Paris. He had had at least two narrow escapes: once on the occasion already recounted, and at another time when a party of Cossacks had broken into a French camp site and carried off some guns without noticing a squat figure in a greatcoat standing in the entrance to his tent.

The Cossacks were also to perpetrate one other much-resented insult to Napoleon. One of the Tsar's Generals, Count Wintzingerode,

A French artillery officer of Napoleon's invading army, which was severely harassed by the Cossacks in Russia in 1812.

*An officer of the **Chasseurs** in Napoleon's invading army: such splendid uniforms were looted by the Cossacks from those they cut down on the battlefield.*

was viewed by Napoleon as a personal enemy and as a traitor to his country. He had been born as a German in Württemberg which later became a French dependency but this did not prevent him from offering his military services to the Tsar of Russia. He therefore was among the Generals confronting the French invader, and he had the misfortune to be captured – allegedly in disguise and trying to subvert a French picket. When brought in front of Napoleon the latter exploded in fury and threatened to have Wintzingerode tried by court-martial and shot on the spot, but eventually relented to the extent of having his prisoner sent under close arrest to France. While on the journey, Wintzingerode's escort were ambushed by Cossacks who naturally released him and restored him to his position in the Tsarist army. It was just another provocation, and reinforced Napoleon's endorsement of his chief-of-staff's verdict that 'this rabble of Cossacks should be treated as we treated the Arabs of Egypt'. They were in Napoleon's own phrase 'a disgrace to the human species'.

In one respect the Cossacks certainly did behave disgracefully. They were inveterate looters. Their capture of French uniforms and their recapture of booty taken by the French from Moscow has already been reported and was understandable enough. But as the campaign went on, more and more loot fell into their hands not only from the invaders but from the countries of Western Europe across which the Russian armies were to pursue the French until they reached Paris itself. Silver plate, gilded statues, silks and brocades, cases of old brandy ... all found their way back from Poland, from Dresden, from Leipzig and from France itself via a well-established route and a series of transit stations reaching back to the banks of the Don.

Another activity which earned the Cossacks peculiar opprobrium in the eyes of the French was their support for the peasant bands who mutilated and massacred stragglers from the invading army. Often the atrocities committed by these civilian partisans were no more than retribution for awful deeds perpetrated by the French themselves; the Russian Colonel Davidov, who raised the first organised partisan unit, was reacting to the slaughter of Russian peasants on his family's estates near Borodino. But for the French, the partisans who materialized out of the white landscape to slit their throats and steal the boots from the corpses recalled all too vividly the nightmare of the Spanish guerrillas of the Peninsular War as immortalized in some of the more horrifying paintings of Goya.

If the Cossacks were the *bête noire* of the French, they were the favourite heroes of Napoleon's most intractable enemy – the British. Viewed from London, the Russian army consisted essentially of dashing Cossack squadrons galloping across snowbound steppes in defence of their native hearths. It was recognized in London that the Russians needed all the support they could get from their allies if they were to survive the onslaught of Napoleon's *Grande Armée*, and public subscriptions were raised to send relief aid to the suffering people of Russia. The Prince Regent subscribed £2,000 himself, and others chipped in with lesser amounts. (In retrospect, the whole operation had much in common with Mrs Churchill's Aid to Russia Fund in the Second World War.) The Russian Ambassador – Count Vorontsov – derived personal satisfaction from this public support, probably without realizing how much of it was due to a romanticized concept of the Cossacks.

But none of this compared with the adulation afforded to Count Platov and his Cossacks when they formed a contingent at the victory parade held in Hyde Park after the eventual collapse of Napoleon's regime and his exile to Elba. The welcome accorded to them has already been described in the Prologue to this book. Count Platov was made the guest of honour at a special performance at the Theatre Royal in Covent Garden and was treated with a respect which would more appropriately have been directed to Kutuzov; but there was no question of the latter coming to London; the old soldier's health – long weakened by age, exhaustion and drink – had finally collapsed and he had died as his troops pursued their enemy beyond those frontiers of Russia which were the western limits of his own ambitions. Kutuzov had at least lived long enough to see his country rid of the invader.

One person who was accorded even greater adulation than Count Platov was of course Tsar Alexander himself. As he rode in parades, attended gala dinners, received the plaudits of Oxford University and patronized the races at Ascot, he must have contrasted his welcome in England with the parsimonious greeting extended to him by King Louis

Cossack dancers as their British allies saw them during the Napoleonic Wars.

XVIII of France, who owed his restored throne in no small measure to the Tsar and his compatriots. Louis XVIII had notably declined to rise from his chair on first meeting the Tsar, and had allocated him such modest and uncomfortable apartments at his palace at Compiègne that the Tsar had left in a huff without staying there. The admiration of England for the Tsar and his Cossacks, and of Alexander and Platov for the hospitable and generous English, was therefore mutual.

As he ruminated on all this, the Tsar may well also have congratulated himself on having harnessed a national equestrian asset to the imperial carriage: the Cossacks, who had for so many of his predecessors constituted at best a thorn in their sides and at worst a dire threat to the dynasty, were it seemed transformed into an instrument for the defence of the realm, for the glorification of their country, and for the personal prestige of the Tsar of All the Russias. For the next century, Alexander's Romanov descendants were to see no reason to doubt or dispute this new verdict. Thanks in no small measure to Napoleon, the Cossacks had joined the Establishment.

9 :
THE CONQUEST
OF THE
CAUCASUS

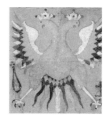

Of all the regions of Russia, the Caucasus has the most dramatic scenery and the most romantic story. This wild region between the Black Sea and the Caspian Sea includes the savage mountain ranges of Georgia and Ossetia and the fierce mountain peoples of Chechnia and Daghestan. Christians and Moslems have for centuries been uneasy neighbours here, and by the nineteenth century the region had long been an irritant on the southern flank of the Tsar's domains. This was the arena in which the Cossacks were to fight one of their longest and fiercest wars of attrition.

In December 1825 Tsar Alexander I, the self-styled conqueror of Napoleon and the patron of Count Platov, was reported to have died. There were rumours that he had in fact been smuggled to a monastery to spend the last years of his life as a religious recluse, and these rumours were given credence by the discovery – in the following century – that his coffin was empty. His heir should have been his next-eldest brother Constantine, but as the latter had renounced the throne, the next brother in line succeeded as Nicholas I. The new Tsar was a man of strong military enthusiasms. Having put down the Decembrist rising in the first days of his reign with personal courage and some brutality, he turned his attention for much of the rest of his long reign to the conquest and pacification of the Caucasus.

The process of subjugation had been begun in the previous century. Peter the Great had taken advantage of the Cossack communities on the Terek river to make incursions into the Caucasus and to establish the Cossack Line of forts between the two seas. Under Catherine the Great the process of expansion was resumed, but with only temporary and limited success: soon the Cossacks were back on the line of the Terek river.

In the reign of Alexander I – in the aftermath of fighting Napoleon – vigorous military plans were again put in hand: General Yermolov – a Russian hero of the Napoleonic wars – was sent as Commander-in-Chief to the Caucasus. One of his first decisions had been to reinforce the line of forts along the Terek river with a new and stronger chain of fortresses through the tribal areas themselves. The fortresses had immediately become the focus for guerrilla activity against the Russian garrisons, and Yermolov had seized this pretext to launch punitive campaigns: some of the remotest mountain fastnesses of Daghestan had been penetrated and massive reprisals taken. When the new fortress at Grozni came under Chechen sniper fire in 1818, Yermolov had resolved to teach the Chechens a lesson: he left a field gun apparently abandoned, but when the tribesmen descended to make off with it they found that all the surrounding Russian artillery had been trained on this one spot and 200 Chechens were killed and as many again wounded before they realized they had fallen into a trap. Yermolov was not a man to be trifled with.

The main instruments of this Russian advance into the Caucasus were to be the Cossacks. Although Cossack bands had worked for the Tsar and the Russian state in opening up Siberia in the seventeenth cen-

The Caucasus

Don

Volga

RUSSIA

CASPIAN

SEA

Pyatigorsk ●

Terek

OSSETIA

CHECHNIA

● Grozni

Dargo ●

Ghimri
●

● Akhulgo

DAGHESTAN

BLACK

Gounib
●

SEA

GEORGIA

Tsinandali ●

Alazani

Tiflis ●

TURKEY

0   50   MILES   150

0   50   100   150 KMS

PERSIA

jm'99

tury and in a few other specific campaigns in the Caucasus and else-where, most of their more lively activities until the nineteenth century had been concerned with causing trouble rather than preventing it: Stenka Razin, Mazeppa and Pugachev had been thorns in the side of government. Now the Cossacks were to build on their services under Platov against Napoleon by forming the spearhead of the Russian army in the Caucasus. The Cossack Line in the Caucasus was known as 'the advance guard of the advance guard'. It was manned mainly by the Terek or Grebentsky Cossacks who had settled there after a migration down the Don and the Volga to the Caspian in the fifteenth century. They were to find themselves pitched against peoples as tough and intransigent as themselves.

Our knowledge and understanding of the war in the Caucasus between the Cossacks and the Moslem tribes owes much to the fact that two great Russian writers made it a theme of their work. The poet Lermontov lived, wrote and died in the Caucasus in the early years of the nineteenth century. His story is a moving and a tragic one. He had started his military career as one of the smart young officers of the Life Guards Hussar Regiment of the Tsar, but following his writing some radical lines about the Tsar's court in his poem on the death of his fellow poet Pushkin, Nicholas I took umbrage and Lermontov was transferred to a less fashionable regiment and posted on active service to the Caucasus. This was not altogether unpleasing to the dashing young cavalry officer; he travelled and skirmished among the mountains and found in these places and events the material for his best work. After a short period he was reinstated and resumed his commission in the Life Guards. Leisurely soldiering in the capital left much spare time, and he turned his Caucasian adventures to good use in his first and only novel *A Hero of our Time*. It was at this period too that he wrote his enchanting *Cossack Cradle Song* which includes the lines:

A Grebentsky Cossack at home on the "Cossack Line" in the Caucasus in the 19th century: this was the life that Tolstoy experienced.

> Terek on his stones is fretting
>> With a troubled roar;
> Wild Chechen, his dagger whetting,
>> Crawls along the shore.
> But your father knows war's riot,
>> Knows what he must do.
> Sleep, my darling, sleep in quiet,
>> Bayushki-bayu*

But Lermontov did not stick to writing novels and lullabies; he fought a duel with the French Ambassador's son and was arrested. Once more he was disgraced and this time sent to an infantry regiment serving on the Caucasus war front. He was involved in the prolonged campaign against the Imam Shamyl of Daghestan and was to experience at first hand how – whenever there was action – 'Cossacks swarm like bees'. It was not long however before he was involved in another duel, this time with a fellow officer, and this time fatal to Lermontov. The poet of the Caucasus and the Cossacks was killed by a pistol bullet at Pyatigorsk in 1840, and the Tsar commented ungraciously, 'A dog's death for a dog'.

If it is to Lermontov that we owe a poetic vision of the fighting in the wars against Shamyl at this period, it is to Count Leo Tolstoy that we owe our knowledge and understanding of life in a Cossack fortified village in the Caucasus. He wrote his first novel about his own experiences in 1852 at one such settlement. Like many aristocratic and pampered officers in St Petersburg, he did a stint with a Cossack regiment on active service on the River Terek. For Tolstoy's fictional hero, his attachment to a Cossack unit was a voluntary escape from the debts and complications of fashionable life in the capital or in Moscow. His hero falls under the spell of the mountain scenery of the Caucasus and – in equal measure - under the spell of a handsome, healthy Cossack girl, who provided a contrast to the pale and sophisticated maidens whom he had known in the north.

*Translated by C.M. Bowra.

Tolstoy first developed that interest in military affairs
that was to become a strand in *War and Peace* when he was soldiering with the Cossacks. His descriptions of the fears and
excitements of guerrilla warfare with a Cossack unit engaged
against the Chechens would have been as relevant to the fighting in 1996 as it was in 1852: the tension alternating with bore-
dom, the terror alternating with elation, the frustration of fighting a people who (as Lermontov said of the Chechens) 'don't
seem to know when to die ... a people without the slightest idea
of propriety'.

Although the Caucasus had given trouble for long
enough, by the reign of Nicholas I and the period of Lermontov
and Tolstoy there was a problem for the Russians of unusual
magnitude. A tribal military leader had transmogrified himself
into a Moslem holy man: the Imam Shamyl (like Greenmantle
in the John Buchan novel) had acquired a spiritual domination
over the mountain peoples of Chechnia and Daghestan which –
coupled with a formidable flare as a guerrilla leader – threatened the whole Russian presence in the Caucasus.

Shamyl was born in around 1796 in the remote fortified
aul (a mountain village with more towers than houses) of Ghimri
in north-eastern Daghestan. When in 1832 the Russian commander in the Caucasus – Baron Rosen – culminated a punitive
campaign through Chechnia and Daghestan by a 10,000-strong
attack on the 500-strong garrison of Ghimri, Shamyl was one of
the only two men to escape alive. This he did by making his
horse leap over the heads of a line of Russian soldiers who were
about to open fire on him. He cut down three of them with his
sabre before a fourth ran him through with a bayonet; Shamyl
plucked the bayonet from his own chest, used it to despatch the

*The poet Lermontov (above), before his
disgrace, in the uniform of a Life Guards
Hussar, and (below) after his disgrace in
the uniform of the infantry regiment with
which he fought alongside the Cossacks in
the Caucasus.*

fourth Russian, and galloped off into the forests. By the time he had recuperated from his wound, he was already a legend among his Moslem followers – a cult already known as the Murids.

Although it was not until 1834 that Shamyl was formally elected as Imam, it did not take him long thereafter to present a more widespread challenge to the Russian forces in the Caucasus. By 1837 he was locked in conflict with a 5,000-strong army sent to destroy him or bring him to heel. The Russians had a special reason for wanting to settle the Murid question that year: Tsar Nicholas I had announced his intention of making a state visit to Tiflis, the capital of Georgia and the largest Russian town in the Caucasus, and receiving the capitulation of Shamyl. Nicholas was a frightening figure: his 'pewter gaze' terrified his subjects and even evoked an awed revulsion in Queen Victoria when he made a state visit to England. Every effort had to be made to resolve the Murid uprising before the arrival in the region of the Tsar.

It was decided that a meeting, under safe-conduct, should be arranged in a wild and remote mountain pass between Shamyl and General Kluke von Klugenau, the Russian field commander. Shamyl duly attended, escorted by two hundred Murids; while General Klugenau had just a dozen Cossacks with him. The meeting was not a success. The General, who was rather lame and always a crotchety character, arrived on his charger and found the process of dismounting and sitting on a cloak on the ground with a turbaned rebel to be uncomfortable and distasteful. It soon became clear no progress was being made, so the General got up

Tsar Nicholas I, whose 'pewter gaze' terrified his subjects as well as his enemies.

with some difficulty and offered his hand to Shamyl. At this point things went badly off the rails. Shamyl's aide grabbed his arm to stop the Imam contaminating himself by touching the General's hand, and the General was so affronted that he took a swipe at Shamyl's turban with his crutch stick. Now the fat was really in the fire, and both the Murids and the Cossacks reached for their weapons. The situation was saved by Shamyl's dexterity of hand and mind: he grabbed the General's stick and his aide's dagger simultaneously and ordered his escort to stand back. The General's aide for his part pulled his master away and the meeting ended with a bad grace but no bloodshed. On his return to his *aul*, Shamyl sat down and wrote a letter to Klugenau declining to meet the Tsar on his visit 'for I have often had experience of your treachery, and this all men know'. It was an unpromising curtain-raiser for the state visit.

The Imam Shamyl, with two of his sons, who harassed the Cossack Line in the Caucasus for more than twenty years.

Nicholas I was already on his way to Tiflis. He too arrived in a bad temper: he had been eaten by fleas at the Black Sea port where he had disembarked and a sight of Shamyl's letter did nothing to restore his equanimity. He soon found fresh causes for anger. The military administration of the Caucasus was, he decided, corrupt and inefficient. At a ceremonial parade he turned his pewter gaze on the unfortunate Prince Dadiani, Colonel of the Georgian Grenadiers, and personally ripped his epaulettes from his shoulders, thus reducing him to the ranks and driving him shortly thereafter to suicide. The long-planned state ball was a frosty occasion, and on his return to Moscow one of the Tsar's first actions was to dismiss Baron Rosen and resolve to press on with the rapid subjugation of Chechnia and Daghestan. More troops, largely Cossacks, were brought in and the campaign intensified.

Shamyl meanwhile consolidated his grip over the dissident tribes and established a new fortress retreat at Akhulgo, an *aul* built on a natural outcrop of rock six hundred feet above the River Koisou which surrounded it on three sides like a castle moat. So confident was he of the impregnable nature of his bastion that he allowed himself and 4,000 of his followers to be besieged there by the Russian army: he had lost the element of surprise which (as Sir Fitzroy Maclean – who knew about such matters at first hand – pointed out in his book *To Caucasus*) is such an essential element in guerrilla warfare.

Shamyl paid dearly for his mistake. Count Grabbe at the head of a formidable Russian force – 10,000 extra troops had been sent to Chechnia and Daghestan by the Tsar – arrived in June 1839 to besiege the *aul* and to flatten it with his artillery. He appeared to do the latter fairly easily, only to discover that the fortifications above ground were covering a warren of caves and trenches from which Shamyl and his defenders were able to carry on their resistance. Attempts to scale the cliff faces of the *aul* met with boulders, javelins and burning logs which were hurled down on the assailants (the Murids were frugal with their more conventional ammunition); 350 Russians perished on the first day of the attack and no foothold in Akhulgo had been gained.

Shamyl had a well for water and a good supply of food within the *aul* when the assault started. But the women and children (they could not be called 'non-combatants' because every woman and every child over the age of six was intent on using a dagger or a knife) were eating into the rations; also the stack of dead bodies that accumulated both without and within Akhulgo eventually poisoned the well water in addition to polluting the atmosphere. The Murids had to take to making precarious descents at night to the river to fetch in fresh water. Morale also suffered within the Murid camp: while warriors of both sexes were prepared to throw themselves to death over the precipices surrounding Akhulgo rather than surrender, they were not prepared to throw the bodies of their comrades over the edge of the *aul* or leave their dead unburied and as prey for the circling vultures. Burial within the *aul* became an impossibility, as every pile of rubble concealed a Murid sniper's post or was sheltering a Murid family.

In vain Count Grabbe sent for more guns, more scaling ladders, more ropes and more men. In July he launched a three-pronged attack. The new ladders and mountaineering equipment were put to good use, but the cliff ledge which the Russian staff officers had identified through their telescopes as a good spring-board for the final assault turned out to be swept by Murid fire and a veritable killing ground; almost 600 Russians were shot down on a rocky platform made all the more precarious by the blood so freely flowing over it. The other columns of the attack fared no better; a torrent of boulders from above, and an ambush by Murid women and children, flailing at the weary troops with whatever arms came to hand, resulted in further setbacks for the Russians.

Attack having failed, Count Grabbe decided to resort to a full-scale blockade and set about completely surrounding the *aul*, which he would have done earlier had it not been for the need to build bridges over the Koisou River, which surrounded Akhulgo, under heavy fire. By mid-August Shamyl was completely cut off from outside contact or supplies.

Recognizing that he was at last trapped, Shamyl reluctantly

agreed to negotiate. To guarantee the safety of his negotiators, Count Grabbe demanded as a temporary hostage Shamyl's eldest son – the eight-year-old Djemmal-Eddin. The boy was already known by sight to the Russian staff officers with their telescopes, as he habitually stood beside his father with his *kindjal* – a Caucasian curved dagger – in his hand. Shamyl agreed to part with his son for the period of the negotiations, and instructed the boy that he should bear himself with dignity and not use his dagger on his captors.

When Shamyl received an emissary of Count Grabbe the next day, the talks went little better than those earlier ones with General Klugenau: Shamyl insisted that if Akhulgo surrendered he should be allowed to live freely in Daghestan, while Grabbe insisted that his fate must be determined by the Tsar. What finally brought about a cessation of the talks was the admission by the Russians that young Djemmal-Eddin had already been despatched to St Petersburg, that in fact he was being treated as a permanent hostage rather that as a temporary guarantee of good faith. Shamyl responded to this admission of duplicity with a burst of gun fire into the Russian camp: negotiations were at an end. He vowed revenge.

Prince Djemmal-Eddin, the son of Shamyl, taken hostage by the Russians, in the uniform of the Tsarist cavalry officer.

Shamyl knew that Akhulgo could hold out no longer. He also knew that for resistance to continue in the Caucasus, and for there to be any chance of his son returning to his native land, one thing was necessary: his own survival. So the very next night he slipped away from the *aul* with his immediate family and one or two close lieutenants. When the Russians resumed their attack the following day they found organized resistance at an end, but desperate hand to hand fighting with the surviving Murids ensured that it was a bitter struggle to the end. Not until 29 August – eighty days after the siege began - was Akhulgo overwhelmed. And even then there was no sign of Shamyl or his body.

The escape had not been an easy one. Only the fact that it had been a dark night had enabled the party to climb down the cliff face from the *aul* without being observed by the hovering Cossack pickets forming the forward lookouts of the Russian force. One of Shamyl's party was Fatima, his first and favourite wife; she was eight months pregnant and – not surprisingly – could not keep up. One of Shamyl's lieutenants stayed behind to help her and eventually, after crossing a ravine by a fallen tree dizzily lodged high above a rushing torrent, she rejoined the others. The party hid in caves by day and moved at night. Even before they were clear of the cliff faces below Akhulgo, a Cossack picket had spotted them and opened fire, killing Shamyl's second wife and her baby son. The party pressed on, lashed some tree trunks together to form a raft, and floated straw dummies down the stream on it to draw the fire and attention of the Russians. This ruse worked well enough to enable

Murid followers of Shamyl fording a river in the Caucasus on their way to raid the Cossack Line.

Shamyl and his party to wade upstream unseen. But they were not through the cordon yet: they walked right into a further Cossack picket and another of Shamyl's lieutenants was killed while he himself was wounded and his younger son (Djemmal-Eddin's brother) was bayoneted through the thigh. Shamyl cut down the officer commanding the picket and, sweeping up his wounded son and the rest of the party, escaped again. There were more encounters, but always Shamyl faded away into the dark, wooded gullies of Chechnia. He was a fugitive without an army; but he was alive, and while he lived Muridism lived on.

The Tsar Nicholas I was told about these happenings while he busied himself with administration in far away St Petersburg. He was exultant and had a medal struck to commemorate the victory of Akhulgo; but already he realized the significance of Shamyl's escape; 'a pity', he minuted on the report, 'I fear more trouble to come'. But meanwhile he turned his ponderous attention to deciding what was to be done with the eight-year-old Djemmal-Eddin.

The unfortunate child had been trundling across a thousand miles of steppe and forest from the Caucasus to the capital. Accompanied by gruff but not unkindly officers, with whom he had no word of any common language, he had been bundled into a *tarantass* (an unsprung wheeled travelling-carriage) and despatched northwards. An escort of mounted Cossacks clattered beside the vehicle and some wolf-hounds (probably a present for a senior officer with a penchant for hunting) loped alongside also. At some stage, a more sensitive officer than the others had allowed the boy to keep his one possession – his *kindjal*; and the boy in his turn had heeded his father's injunction not to use this dagger on his captors. At times he snarled and wriggled like a wild cat, but mostly he had sat wide-eyed in the *tarantass*, and later in an upholstered carriage, as the marvels of Kharkov, Moscow and finally St Petersburg unfolded before him.

The Tsar, whose loathing for the impudent and troublesome Shamyl was tempered by some respect for his qualities as a guerrilla leader, received the boy in private audience with an interpreter. His pewter gaze was tempered for once with curiosity and compassion. Also possibly by considerations of self-interest: he may have calculated that a Moslem princeling who could be moulded to the Imperial design could have uses beyond that of a hostage. The Tsar spoke gently to the child, and placed him with one of his courtiers to be brought up as a member of the family. There was to be no question of returning him to the recalcitrant Shamyl.

The Tsar did not have to wait long to see the truth of his own prediction: more trouble was to come. Within less than a year Shamyl, aided by some tactless efforts by the Russian authorities to 'resettle' the Chechens as peasant farmers, had set the Caucasus ablaze again. Shamyl became an expert on jungle warfare: he lured the Russian troops into the forests of Chechnia and there ambushed and cut them down. The Russian forts along the Black Sea coast of the Caucasus were also systematically attacked and their garrisons slaughtered. St Petersburg suspected the hand of the British in encouraging and organizing these coastal activities; and indeed there was no doubt that individual British officers – such as the notorious Captain Bell – were arms-running and worse on behalf of Shamyl. There was no knowing where he would strike next. Taking advantage of a quarrel between the Russian commanders, Shamyl attacked the fortified encampment of Kazi-Koumoukh in Daghestan and carried off the Russian Resident and his complete Cossack bodyguard. Shamyl had captured a number of prominent Russians, but still no one who could be bartered for the release of his own son.

By now, not only the Tsar but the Russian commanders in the field recognized that Shamyl's escape from Akhulgo had been a disastrous lapse. Belatedly General Neidhardt, the local commander, offered to reward whoever would bring him Shamyl's head with its weight in gold. No one came up with anything, until a Tartar horseman rode into Neidhardt's headquarters with a letter: Shamyl regretted he could not reciprocate the General's offer, as he would not offer its weight in straw for Neidhardt's head!

It was not long before Neidhardt was replaced by a more active and impressive commander: Count Michael Vorontsov, although already sixty-three, was an officer of flair and quality. He was also a sybarite who believed in taking on campaign with him all the accoutrements of fashionable St Petersburg life: witty and aristocratic officers, thoroughbred horses, silver dressing cases, champagne and – of course – caviar. The Russian army in the Caucasus was becoming a very different force from the basically Cossack units, enhanced by outside officers and support arms, which had characterized the early years of the struggle.

As so often in the past, the Tsar had his own military agenda. He built up Vorontsov's command until this comprised more than twenty battalions of infantry, sixteen cavalry squadrons, four companies of sappers and forty-six pieces of artillery – in all some 18,000 men. In June 1845, he decided that the greater part of this army should be constituted into a massive task-force aimed at the heart of Shamyl's home base: the forest stronghold of Dargo in southern Chechnia.

Shamyl was prepared for the advance. He had enforced a scorched-earth policy on all the villages around: there was no food or shelter for the Russians. When they advanced down forest tracks, felled trees blocked the way, and as they paused to clear these they came under withering fire from invisible Murids. Vorontsov himself got separated from the main body of his troops, and one of his subordinate Generals was killed. When he reached Dargo, it had been evacuated and put to the torch. Now he had to decide whether to go back or pursue his enemy further into the forests. Vorontsov decided he needed more rations before he could advance further, and despatched the veteran General Kluke von Krugenau to lead what was subsequently to become known in the legends of the Tsarist army as the 'Biscuit Expedition'. It was another desperate struggle through Murid-infested forests. When the remnant of the Biscuit Expedition got back to Dargo, they had lost their second-in-command – General Passek – and most of the provisions they had gone to fetch. They had had to clamber over brush-wood barricades grotesquely decorated with the mutilated bodies of their fallen comrades.

No longer were Count Vorontsov and his staff the well-groomed officers that had set out: they were wounded, unshaven and depressed. His force was reduced to not much more than half its numbers. Survival at all seemed improbable. He had ventured into the enemy's lair and found himself incapable of coping with a terrain and a method of fighting with which he and his troops were quite unfamiliar. The Cossacks and the Caucasian regiments were the most adaptable; but even they, once dismounted, were no longer masters of their environment. Here in the dense and steamy forests there was no place for the Cossack's lightning cavalry charges over rough open country, nor for the parade ground disciples of the line regiments of infantry. In his Order of the Day, Vorontsov told his men, 'Our main care must be to get our sick and wounded through; that is our duty as Christians, and God will help us to fulfil it'.

When eventually Vorontsov's column was rescued by General Freitag, whose headquarters were beyond the forests to the north, the original 10,000-strong task-force had been reduced by the loss of three Generals, 200 officers and 3,533 men. The Kourinsky regiment had set out 600 strong and returned numbering 24. But the Tsar, whose brain-child the expedition had been, did not allow himself to be deterred: he advanced Vorontsov from the title of Count to that of Prince, and wrote on his report 'Read with the greatest interest, and with respect for the courage of my fine troops'.

But still Shamyl was frustrated. He had trounced the mighty Prince Vorontsov. He had widened the sphere of his control. He had shown that the whole weight of Orthodox Christian Russia could not extinguish the flame of Moslem Muridism in the mountains and forests of his native Caucasus. But his eldest son and heir, his beloved Djemmal-Eddin, was still a hostage in the Tsar's capital.

The boy was no ordinary hostage. After his upbringing in a courtier's family, all the expenses of which had been met from the Tsar's own purse, he had been placed in the Cadet Corps school in St Petersburg along with the sons of other noblemen. From there he had graduated with military honours to a commission in the exclusive Vladimirsky Lancers. He had led the life of a young princeling: hunting, gambling, womanizing, speaking French and Russian rather than his native Caucasian tongue. The Tsar had made him his ward and viewed him almost as a son. By 1854, when the Crimean War broke out, Lieutenant Prince Djemmal-Eddin was twenty-three years old and serving with his regiment on garrison duty in Warsaw; he had integrated happily into a more sophisticated world than he could have ever known as Shamyl's son in the Caucasus; he viewed the Tsar as his patron and surrogate father. But Shamyl had not forgotten him; he was looking for some bargaining counter of sufficient value to get his son back.

Georgia had its own aristocracy, and at the pinnacle of this were the two grand-daughters of the last King of Georgia – George XII. They were Her Serene Highness the Princess Anna and her sister the Princess Varvara. Both princesses had acted as ladies-in-waiting to the Tsarina, wife of Nicholas I, and were well known to the Tsar and to St Petersburg society in which they had shone. They had both married eligible Georgian princes who were serving officers in the Russian army; and they had returned to live in Tiflis, the Georgian capital. But Tiflis was very hot and dusty in summer and in June 1854, as in other summers, the princesses

decided to uproot their families and young children and seek the cooler and more agreeable climate of their country estate at Tsinandali, fifty miles to the north-east of Tiflis in a remote valley on a tributary of the Alazani river. It was perhaps uncomfortably close to the Murid-infested mountains of Daghestan, but Princess Anna's husband was nearby commanding the local militia and did not seem unduly perturbed.

A Cossack civilian in the Caucasus at the time of Tsar Nicholas I's expansion into the region.

Life at the spacious Tsinandali estate must have had a certain Chekhovian quality; the ladies sat on the wide wooden verandas with their embroidery; the peasants dutifully went about their rural activities; the French governess – a certain Madame Drancy – gave lessons in French and arithmetic to the older children, and the seven-month-old baby of Princess Anna played with her rattle under the kindly eye of a local nursemaid. It was a reassuringly timeless and tranquil scene.

But there were tensions below the surface. By the beginning of July there were reports of unfamiliar visitors from across the river, rumours of Murids coming down from the mountains, and an unusual nervousness among the local retainers. The mood transmitted itself to Princess Anna, but she was far too well-bred to panic; she decided that the servants should start packing on the night of 3 July and that the whole household should move back to the security of Tiflis in an orderly manner on the following day. She was just too late.

At dawn on 4 July there were suddenly those sounds all too familiar in the Caucasus: the clatter of hooves, the crack of pistol shots and the screams of surprised and frightened women. A detachment of Chechen horsemen clattered into the courtyard of Tsinandali and dismounted Murids surged across the verandas and into the house. The princesses, their children and the French governess were all swept up onto the saddles or tied to the stirrups of the Chechens; in the process Princess Anna had her dress torn off and her diamond ear-rings ripped from her ears, and Madame Drancy was reduced to her stays and 'a pair of kid boots bought in the Rue de Rivoli'. The infant's nursemaid was cut down by a Murid sabre. Children were roughly stuffed into saddle-bags. Within minutes the raiders and their victims were heading at full gallop for the mountains.

Princess Anna was in particular danger and distress. Still clutching her seven-month-old baby Lydia, she had been tied by one arm to the stirrup of a fierce-looking Chechen who then rode off through the river. Only with the greatest struggle did she manage to keep Lydia's head above the water. When eventually she, like the other women, was snatched up onto the saddle, she was still holding the baby, but only by the foot while Lydia's head banged against the stirrup. Half fainting and exhausted, Princess Anna finally lost her hold on her daughter's foot, and saw the child fall to the ground to be trampled underfoot by the hooves of the oncoming horsemen. Lydia was never seen alive again; her body was discovered by her father's troops when they passed that way a few days later.

The whole party of marauders comprised several score of Chechens and Lesghiens (from Daghestan), all of them loosely called Murids (and many of them technically Murids as well since they were Moslem warrior-Mullas). Although violent and vicious in almost every possible way, in one respect only did they show a restraint suggesting they were under orders: none of the young women were raped. The marauders were all well mounted and heavily armed. But there was one brief moment when their brutal mission nearly foundered. As they rode into a particularly steep defile in the mountains, they came under heavy fire from a patrol of Cossacks who were in the region to ambush just such a band of intruders. Had the Chechens stopped and fought, they would have risked losing their captives; so without a moment's hesitation they wheeled their horses around and disappeared up another parallel defile. They clearly knew every turn and twist of the mountain passes; equally clearly they had a specific destination in mind.

It was nearly a month's journey through the snowy peaks and misty ravines of Chechnia before they arrived at that destination.* The journey was not without its horrors. Some of the Princess's retainers had died of exhaustion or been killed by their captors for fear they would hold up the party. At times Princess Anna had become delirious and had asked everyone if they had not seen Lydia. Madame Drancy – who had no head for heights – had fallen from a slippery log bridge into a ravine

*For a recent and vivid description of this wild and precipitous terrain, the reader could not do better than turn to the final pages of John le Carré's novel *Our Game*.

and only been rescued by her Chechen guard catching hold of her feet, still sheathed in those kid leather boots from the Rue de Rivoli.

Their ultimate destination was predictable: the Great Aul, deep in fastnesses of Chechnia, was Shamyl's palace, fortress and hide-away. The captives' hearts must have sunk as they entered through the iron-studded doors in the *aul's* stone walls and looked up at the bleak towers commanding the surrounding country. It was here that they met the dreaded Imam Shamyl for the first time. He was aloof but courteous: they would be exchanged for his son Djemmal-Eddin, and a large monetary ransom would also be expected; meanwhile, provided they did not try to escape or 'deceive him', they would live with his wives in the seraglio of the *aul*; their servants could stay with them; they would not be molested in any way. Having set out the rules, the Imam swept away, accompanied as always by the sinister figure of his Executioner.

So began a gloomy eight-month incarceration. The prisoners all lived in one not-very-large room together: privacy was impossible. Princess Anna incurred the Imam's anger by refusing to write a pleading letter to the Tsar; she maintained their misfortune was her own fault and that the Tsar should not be distracted from the Crimean War by her complaints. There were also special fears for Princess Nina, the sixteen-year-old niece of Princess Anna; it was rumoured that she was not to be ransomed with the others, but kept behind as a bride for Djemmal-Eddin; the very thought of this sent Princess Nina into hysterics, and provoked the Imam's wives to tell her she was an ungrateful hussy.

The great question haunting Princess Anna and her worried husband in Tiflis was whether the Tsar would agree to release Djemmal-Eddin and – even more problematical - whether the young Lancers officer would agree to give up his gilded life as a privileged playboy for the gaunt prospect of life at the Great Aul with his fierce and almost-forgotten father. These fears at least were groundless. Nicholas I for all his austere

Russian troops, including Cossacks, prepare
to assault a Murid aul *in the Caucasus.*

exterior was deeply moved by the plight of the pretty princesses whom he remembered as charming members of his wife's Household. He summoned Djemmal-Eddin back from Warsaw for an audience and explained the predicament. He said the choice of whether to return or not must be Djemmal-Eddin's own, and he urged the young man not to make a hasty decision. He would be giving up much, and he would be missed at Court and in his regiment. He should think it over for two days and come back and tell the Tsar his mind.

Lieutenant Prince Djemmal-Eddin of the Vladimirsky Lancers was not his father's son for nothing. He looked the Tsar squarely in the eyes and said: 'Sire, Shamyl's son and Your Majesty's ward does not need two days to decide where his duty lies: I will go back immediately.' He knelt before the Tsar who embraced him as if he were his own son. When at long last the fateful exchange took place on 11 March 1855 it was a joyful occasion for the Georgian princesses and for Madame Drancy, but a sad one for Djemmal-Eddin. He had heard two days before of the death of his patron Tsar Nicholas I. Now once more at his father's *aul*, he found he had no zest for fighting the Russians, his former comrades in arms, and he pined for the civilized delights of St Petersburg and Warsaw – for the court balls, the opera and ballet, the regimental dinners and tattoos. There was no longer any real common ground between him and his father. He began to feel himself almost as much a prisoner as the princesses had done. He rejected the young women of the harem provided for him and he even lost his enthusiasm for hunting. Finally his health broke down; Russian medicines and doctors were sent for, but all to no avail; he seemed to have lost his will to live, and within a surprisingly short time of his return to his father's *aul* – like his patron Nicholas I – turned his face to the wall and died.

Shamyl too was losing his momentum. After so many triumphs and so many recoveries from disasters, he also was a spent force. The new Tsar – Alexander II – was a more imaginative man than his predecessor, and he realized that the war in the Caucasus, like most guerrilla wars, would finally be resolved by winning the hearts and minds of the people. He set about providing protection for the villagers from the raids and intimidation of the Murids and their hordes of horsemen. He also systematically began cutting down the forests that provided cover for the Murids, or at least cutting great swathes through the forests that meant that never again would a Russian army be sucked into the killing grounds as Vorontsov had been on the trail to Dargo.

But most of all the new Tsar achieved his success by the appointment of a new Commander-in-Chief in the Caucasus. Of all the generals – stubborn, brave, dandified, well-connected – who had held the job over the last decades, Field Marshal Prince Bariatinsky was the most impressive. He had fought in the Caucasus twice before, been wounded and become a legend in his own time. Not only did he inspire the officers and men who served under him, but he impressed Shamyl and his Murids as a worthy opponent, as a soldier whom they could respect, and even as one to whom – if needs be – they could submit without loss of honour.

And that is what eventually happened. In June 1859, Bariatinsky's troops occupied the Great Aul where the Princesses of Georgia had been held captive. Shamyl himself had withdrawn yet further into the mountain fastnesses of Daghestan – to Gounib, a rock plateau a thousand feet above the surrounding hills hemmed in by a natural perimeter wall of stone and with fresh-water wells. Gounib would have been impregnable had it not been for the introduction of Russian long-range artillery. But artillery there was in plenty. And Shamyl was encumbered by his family and other women and children. He was prevailed upon to think it the will of Allah that he should resist no longer. On 25 August 1859 he rode out and surrendered his sabre in person to Prince Bariatinsky saying, 'I could not have allowed my sword to be touched by unworthy hands'.

The following page:
The "Cossack Bay" in the Crimea,
where troops were brought in for
the siege of Sevastopol.

Bariatinsky did not let him down. The Imam's family were respect-fully treated and Shamyl himself dispatched northwards with an escort of two squadrons of Cossacks. At Kharkov his submission was received in person by Tsar Alexander II: 'I am happy to see you here in Russia; I wish it could have happened sooner', was the Tsar's generous welcome to his country's old enemy. He invited Shamyl to join him in reviewing some Russian cavalry units, and later arranged for Shamyl and his family to be settled at the little Russian town of Kaluga a hundred miles south of Moscow. Here Shamyl received visitors, read in his library and remi-nisced about battles fought long ago and far away. When he felt his life ebbing away in 1870, he obtained permission to go on pilgrimage to Mecca and Medina, and there – where the Prophet had died – he too died and was laid to rest. He had successfully resisted the Russian occupation of the Caucasus for some thirty years, and his uneasy spirit was to fuel sentiments and struggles for independence again in the future.

The Caucasian wars had not been an exclusively Cossack campaign. Far from it. By the end most of the fighting units of the Russian army had done stints there: gunners and sappers had been drafted in alongside regular infantry and cavalry regiments. But it was the Cossack line of forts and look-out posts which had been both the launching pad for aggressive raids into Chechnia and Daghestan, and the safe haven to which such raiders returned when repulsed or reduced to disarray. It was the Cossacks, rather than the regular army units, who could match the Murids (whether Chechens or Lesghiens) at their own game. It was the Cossacks who were the eyes and ears of the Tsarist army, who escorted everyone everywhere. When the campaign was finally ended with the surrender of Shamyl, the Tsar and his commanders had come to recognize as never before that they had an asset which could serve them well in other frontier regions of the empire – in Central Asia, for instance, where the recalcitrant Emirs were proving as troublesome as the Imams of the Caucasus.

10: THE COSSACKS AND THE GREAT GAME

PETER THE GREAT was alleged to have said on his deathbed that the aim of his successors should be world domination. From time to time in Russian history this remark has surfaced to inspire or incite tsars and commissars to adopt over-ambitious policies. In particular it encouraged nineteenth-century tsars to turn their acquisitive gaze southwards towards the Indian sub-continent. And what the tsars may have dreamed of, their dashing young cavalry officers talked of wildly and openly: 'the Cossacks would water their horses on the banks of the Indus river'.

The struggle for domination of Central Asia – that buffer region between the tsarist empire of Russia and the British Raj in India – was to be christened by a certain Captain Arthur Conolly of the 6th Bengal Native Light Cavalry (who was in 1842 to become a memorable and fatal casualty of that struggle) as 'The Great Game', and the name was later reincarnated by Rudyard Kipling and has stuck ever since. The most persistent players of the Great Game on the Russian side were to be the

Cossacks. Just as they had formed the spearhead of tsarist penetration of the Caucasus, so they were over many decades to be the storm-troopers of the deserts, mountains and plateaux of Central Asia.

Both the Russian and the British players in the Great Game had considerable provocation. The British were aware of the alarming rate of Russian expansion southwards; as early as 1817 (only two years after the warm welcome extended to Tsar Alexander I and his Hetman of the Cossacks in Hyde Park) a senior British officer who had served extensively with the Russian army – General Sir Robert Wilson – was warning in a widely circulated tract that during the sixteen years that Alexander had spent on the throne he had extended the frontiers of Russia by over 200,000 square miles and had expanded his army to eight times its former size. Moves towards the Ottoman empire and Persia were seen as stepping stones to India.

The Russians for their part saw every reason for what was then called a 'forward' policy. The Turkish Sultan was already showing signs of being 'the sick man of Europe' whose empire was to become a power vacuum; and the emirates and khanates of Central Asia were ruled by corrupt, decadent and vicious despots who made a practice of kidnapping Russian citizens from their estates and settlements on the fringes of the steppe and carrying them off to the slave markets of Khiva, Bokhara and Samarkand. Incursions into Turkey could be presented as moves to protect Christian minorities, and incursions into Central Asia as civilizing missions into a barbarous no-man's-land.

Both sides reconnoitred the region for themselves, using daring military and political officers. Captain Nikolai Muraviev of the Russian army was despatched to Khiva in 1819, ostensibly to establish trade contacts but in reality to spy out the defences of this walled city in the desert. He had to disguise himself as a Turcoman trader and cross 800 miles of bleak steppe, infested by tribesmen intent on capturing travellers for the

By the 19th century the Cossacks had largely been absorbed into the Tsarist army and were decked out in Imperial uniforms that incorporated some of their traditional attire

slave markets of the region. When he reached his destination intact, the Khan of Khiva clearly regretted that he had not been discreetly disposed of earlier and considered – even at this late stage – having him taken out into the desert and buried alive; however, on reflection he granted him an audience and allowed him to depart, but not before Muraviev had seen for himself just how many Russian slaves were being held by the Khan in harsh captivity. Muraviev's report on his return predictably added fuel to the case for sending another military expedition (one had already been sent in 1801 as described in an earlier chapter) to incorporate Khiva into the Tsar's domains.

It was 1839 before the next major Russian expeditionary force set off for Khiva. This time again the army was assembled at Orenburg, the garrison town north of the Caspian and Aral Seas that was a traditional launching pad for thrusts into Central Asia. From here to Khiva was nearly a thousand-mile march, appreciably further than the approach route direct from the eastern side of the Russian-dominated Caspian Sea. The Yaik (or Ural) Cossacks had always had a big presence around Orenburg, but on this occasion the garrison commander – General Perovsky – brought in other Cossacks from the Don and Terek regions to help make up a force of over 5,000 men. The Cossack ponies were supported by a supply echelon of some 10,000 camels. The whole cavalcade moved off for what they thought would be an eight-week march in November, a month that was calculated to enable the Russian army both to avoid the scorching heat of the summer and the worst of the winter cold. It was a serious miscalculation, aggravated by the coming of unseasonably early snows. They should have left in September.

The Cossacks were no strangers to extremes of climate and were better able to cope than the other troops with the rigours of the Kirghiz and Kazakh steppes. They were used to sleeping swathed in their heavy cloaks, while the regular troops wrapped themselves in shaggy sheepskins

Arena of the
Great Game

0 50 100 MILES 250

0 100 250 KMS

Orenburg

RUSSIA

Yaik (Ural)

ARAL
SEA

KAZAKH
STEPPE

KIRGHIZ
STEPPE

CASPIAN

SEA

Khiva

Tashkent

Bokhara

Khokand

Samarkand

Geok Tepe

Ashkhabad

Merv

PAMIRS

Hunza

Gilgit

Teheran

Chitral

Kabul

AFGHANISTAN

Khyber
Pass

PERSIA

Kandahar

BRITISH

INDIA

Indus

jm'99

which froze during the night and adhered to the damp beards and moustaches of the infantrymen. The Cossacks also acted as pathfinders. When the December snows descended, they went ahead of the main column and built pillars of snow along the line of advance to stop their less-well-orientated comrades from wandering off into the featureless white landscape.

But there was nothing the Cossacks could do to prevent the camels collapsing and leaving a trail of dead or dying animals in the wake of the advancing column. Soon there were human corpses too, buried in shallow graves which the wolves opened up. An officer, who went ahead to try to buy replacement camels on the shores of the Aral Sea, himself fell a victim to the very evil which they were trying to remedy: he was captured by Turcoman raiders, trussed up like a chicken, bundled across the pummel of a saddle and carried off to the slave markets of Khiva.

As December turned into January, the Cossack scouts reported ever worse snow drifts ahead. It was not only impossible to find vegetation for the animals to eat, it was also impossible to find wood or any other fuel for the campfires under the all encompassing blanket of snow. The men went to bed hungry and froze as they slept. By now the camels were dying at the rate of a hundred a day, and those that remained were so ravenous that they gnawed their way into the wooden crates containing the remaining rations for the troops. A small band of Cossacks could have pressed on, but an unwieldy army of regular troops could not keep going. Reluctantly General Perovsky gave the order to turn about and retrace their steps towards Orenburg; not a shot had been fired, not an enemy sighted, not even a warning given to the Khan of Khiva – who was blissfully unaware that an expeditionary force had been marching to destroy him.

If the march outwards had been bad, the return was worse. The men were more tired, the rations in shorter supply, the winter further advanced, and the route littered with grisly reminders of their failure. Not only had the wolves desecrated the graves of their fallen comrades,

Wolves attack a Cossack **troika**
on the wintry steppes in the early
20th century.

The following page:
Cossacks in a winter landscape by 19th-century
painter Anton Baumgartner-Stoiloff

but they had gorged on the stricken camels. Wolves had come from far and near and formed menacing packs. On the first days of the outward march, before the last of the wooded country was left behind, the Cossack units had indulged in their favourite sport of wolf-hunting; they had dragged squealing piglets in bags behind their horses and – when the wolves had emerged from the trees to see what the squealing was about – they had shot them from a safe range. Now the roles were reversed and it was the wolves who were hunting down stragglers.

When the remnant of the Russian force got back to Orenburg – over a thousand men and over 8,000 camels had been lost – it was not long before they and their master the Tsar had a further humiliation to face. Spurred on by anxiety to deny the Russians a pretext for assimilating Khiva into their empire, the British had despatched two officers in succession to the Khan to try to persuade him to release his foreign slaves (none of whom were British). The task can scarcely have been easier than that of Moses trying to convince the Pharaoh of Egypt that he should release the Children of Israel. First a Captain Abbott made the journey from the Caspian Sea to Khiva, but failed to persuade the Khan to part with his slaves, and nearly got imprisoned for having the impudence to suggest such a thing. Then a Lieutenant Shakespear made the same perilous desert journey and proved to be more persuasive. His task was all the harder because the Khan had by then heard of the retreat of the Russian expedition a few months before, so Shakespear had to convince him that they would be returning with a larger force if they still had an excuse to do so. Nor was the task simplified by the fact that at least one of the young girl slaves appeared to be destined for the Khan's own harem. However, by dint of courage, persistence and charm, Shakespear eventually managed to leave with a caravan of over 300 released Russians. He had deserved a hero's welcome when he reached the nearest Russian fort on the Caspian, from whence he was sent on first to Orenburg and eventually to St Petersburg, but although he was feted in these places it was an open secret that Tsar Nicholas (him of the 'pewter gaze') was furious that a young English subaltern had achieved single-handed what his own army of Cossacks and others had failed to do.

Although the Cossacks' role in the Khiva expedition had been a substantial one, it had not been sufficient to save that expedition from failure. In many other exploits of the Great Game however their tasks had been both more traditional and more successful. They had operated not as an army, or as part of an army, but as escorts for the prominent Russian 'players' in the Game.

When Lieutenant Henry Rawlinson was travelling through the eastern provinces of Persia in 1837 on a mission to the Shah from the Government of India, he encountered a uniformed Cossack patrol under command of an officer as young as himself. The Cossacks' officer was clearly embarrassed to be discovered on a dubious mission so far from his own frontiers, and told Rawlinson that he was the bearer of gifts to the Shah – a story that turned out (after Rawlinson had checked with the Shah) to be entirely spurious. The real purpose of the Cossack patrol was to cross Persia en route for Afghanistan where they had an altogether more sinister purpose: to persuade the Emir Dost Mohammed to accept a resident Russian mission and to bring his country within the Russian sphere of influence – in fact to pave the way for Afghanistan becoming the route for an eventual Russian invasion of India. Rawlinson lost no time in warning his superiors what was on foot. The sighting of a Cossack patrol had a political as well as a military significance.

The British had already themselves been casting anxious eyes towards Afghanistan, which was undoubtedly the most crucial territory in Central Asia from the point of view of the Great Game because it commanded the passes – both the Khyber and the Bolan Pass – which led through the mountains into the fertile plains of upper India. One of the key British players in the Game – 'Bokhara' Burnes – had been sent to Kabul to win over Dost Mohammed to the friendship and protection of the British Raj.

Now Kabul had two rival emissaries vying for the goodwill of the Emir: Captain Yan Vitkevich and his Cossack escort, and Captain Alexander Burnes with his escort of Indian cavalrymen. Burnes had a chance to undermine his rival's position: the Emir asked his advice about Vitkevich's credentials and it was pointed out to Burnes that the double-headed eagle seal on these documents bore a marked resemblance to the seal on Russian bags of sugar exported to Afghanistan. Could the credentials not therefore be forgeries? But Burnes thought it would be ungentlemanly to exploit this coincidence to cast false doubts on his adversary's *bona fides*. Meanwhile the Cossack escort impressed the Afghans with their displays of horsemanship and generally ingratiated themselves. And in the end, it was the Russian emissary and not the British who persuaded Dost Mohammed to make a defensive alliance.

It was a decision that was to cost both Afghanistan and Britain dear, because it led directly to the First Afghan War. When Burnes withdrew from Kabul and reported to the Governor-General in India that the Russians had stolen a march on us there, the reaction was to back Dost Mohammed's rival for the throne and to send an expeditionary force to seize Kabul and install the new ruler. The British occupation of Kabul in 1841 and the subsequent murder of Burnes and his chief, as well as the massacre of General Elphinstone's expeditionary force on its return march to Kandahar, form no part of the story of the Cossacks. Nor does the punitive expedition that was mounted thereafter which resulted in a further British occupation of Kabul and – despite all that had happened – the reinstallation of Dost Mohammed as Emir. But the conclusion which the Russians were to draw from these unhappy episodes in the history of the Raj was that the Great Game was still one which they could win.

The Bolan Pass which, together with the Khyber, was a route the British feared a Cossack-led Russian invasion of India would take in the 19th century.

A squadron of Don Cossacks makes a disciplined charge during the Crimean War.

Even the Russians' own disasters in the Crimean War in 1855 and 1856 did not do more than check their ambitions in Central Asia, and when – the year after the Crimean War had ended – the Indian Mutiny shook the British army and administration in India to its very foundations, the Russians felt that there was still all to play for. Indeed, had Tsar Nicholas not died in humiliation at the concluding stage of the Crimean War, and had the Russian army (including its Cossack units) not been totally exhausted by that war, the outbreak of the Mutiny might have prompted the thrust towards the Indus for which the more lively and belligerent elements in the Russian High Command had so long yearned. Once his country had recovered from the set-backs of the Crimea, Tsar Alexander II, the successor to Nicholas, was to prove a more ardent player of the Great Game even than his father.

He did not wait long. The year after the Mutiny – 1858 – saw Count Nikolai Ignatiev, a young protégé of the Tsar, setting off with the habitual Cossack escort on a mission to Khiva and Bokhara. Ignatiev was to try to pre-empt British attempts to gain a trading and political foothold in these khanates, and at the same time to gain as much intelligence as he could to facilitate a Russian move into the region. The Cossack escort were somewhat disconcerted to find that they were expected to look after not only Ignatiev but various elaborate presents which he was transporting across the deserts as gifts for the khans – among them a church organ for the Khan of Khiva. The Khan accepted the gifts but gave little away in return. In Bokhara, the Emir Nasrullah was notoriously cruel and unpredictable. It was he who had imprisoned two British envoys – Captain Conolly and Colonel Stoddart – in a vermin-infested pit and had eventually had them beheaded in front of the Ark (the citadel) of Bokhara sixteen years earlier. Now he received Ignatiev and his Cossacks with suspicion tinged with respect for this sample of Russian military might. He also saw in their visit a chance to enlist Russian support in his on-going feud with his neighbour – the Khan of Khokand. The Emir promised to free the Russian slaves he held, but showed no sign of implementing the promise, and Ignatiev and his Cossacks felt that their intelligence-gathering mission had achieved as much as it could and returned to St Petersburg

When Count Ignatiev was received in audience by Tsar Alexander II, he took the opportunity to convince the Tsar that the rulers of these medieval Central Asian states were not to be trusted: their promises were worthless and the prospect of their entering into any durable alliance with Russia was a chimera. The only way of securing these regions – whether as a buffer against the British Raj, as a staging post on an invasion route into India, as markets for Russian goods, or as a source of much-needed raw materials such as cotton – was to take advantage of the military presence of the Cossacks on the southern frontiers of the Empire and seize by force what could not be negotiated by diplomacy. Alexander was to endorse this 'forward' policy.

The first implementation of that policy was an attack in 1865 on the capital of Khokand – the walled city of Tashkent. The attack was the private project of Major-General Cherniaev, the commander of the Russian frontier region facing Khokand, who decided to march on the city on his own initiative, fearing that if he did not do so he would receive contrary orders from the Tsar. It was a risky enterprise because he had less than 2,000 troops under his command and the garrison of Tashkent was nearer to 25,000; failure would not only bring a set-back to the Russian ambitions and reputation in the region, it would also bring down personal retribution on General Cherniaev in the form of a court martial and severe disciplinary action for exceeding his orders.

Undeterred by such considerations, Cherniaev decided to assault the medieval walled city of Tashkent by himself using the techniques of the Middle Ages. There was no massive artillery barrage nor any extensive tunnelling by engineers. Instead, a night attack was made by a scaling party with long ladders who managed to slip over the walls and let others in to support them. While a hand-to-hand fight ensued in the streets of Tashkent on the following day, one of the most remarkable cavalry engagements of modern times was taking place outside the walls. The Khan had launched a formidable cavalry attack on the Russian encampment, to try to turn the tables on the besieging army. But Cherniaev had left a contingent of mounted Cossacks outside the walls to protect his base. These Cossacks, who amounted to no more than some forty men, now rode at full gallop into the massed phalanx of the Khan's 5,000 oncoming cavalrymen. Firing volleys from the saddle as they charged, and then using their sabres at close quarters, they put the Khokand horsemen to rout. Of those who were not cut down in the ini-

Cossacks singing as they ride toward the front in Central Asia.

tial encounter, many were drowned trying to cross the Saidarya river.
The pride of the Khokand army had been decimated by a squadron of
Cossacks.

Cherniaev was forgiven for exceeding his instructions when he
presented the Tsar with a *fait accompli*: Tashkent was a prize worth a
breach of discipline. But although treated as a hero, he was soon
replaced by an even more thrusting officer – General Kaufman. Being
convinced that the Turcoman tribesmen were no match for his Cossacks,
Kaufman resolved to take the first opportunity of bringing the Emir of
Bokhara to heel in the same way as the Khan of Khokand. The opportunity was not long in coming. The Emir imprudently gathered his
forces in Samarkand, apparently for an attempt to move against the
Russians' growing presence in Central Asia. Kaufman decided to pre-
empt him and marched on Samarkand. A series of military engagements
followed, at the conclusion of which Bokhara had joined Khokand as a
Russian protectorate.

Next it was the turn of Khiva. This recalcitrant khanate had
already survived two major Russian military expeditions, those of 1717
and 1839, as well as numerous military reconnaissances, such as those of
Muraviev in 1819 and Ignatiev in 1858. Always these missions had
ended in disaster or humiliation. Kaufman determined that his should
be the decisive stroke. With the Tsar's explicit authority, he set out in
1873 to converge on the oasis city of Khiva with three separate columns
across the desert: his troops marched on their destination from their
traditional forward base of Orenburg in the north, from their recently
acquired base at Tashkent in the east, and from a newly founded
fortress-port on the Caspian Sea in the west. The Khan saw that the writing was on the wall and tried, at the eleventh hour, to buy off the advancing forces with offers to release Russian slaves and other concessions. It
was too late. The Tsar Alexander II and his hyper-active General were

bent on conquest. The Khan fled; Kaufman entered Khiva in triumph; the Tsar declared a 'temporary' extension of his Central Asian empire; and the British – predictably – sent a Note of Protest.

Even louder protests followed the next Russian step forward in 1881. This was an advance from the east coast of the Caspian Sea on the Turcoman oasis of Geok-Tepe, which had for long harboured the desert raiders who looted the caravan routes, and had thus provided a pretext for a Russian attack and occupation. What gave particular offence in Europe – and not only to Britain which was an interested party – was the slaughter that followed the fall of the town. After the walls had been breached by tunnelling and artillery, the inhabitants had swarmed out of their homes and fled across the desert taking their wives and children with them. As they did so, they had been ruthlessly cut down by the pursuing cavalry. It was an atrocity as well as incursion, and the Tsar relieved the commanding General of his command. But he did not give up Geok-Tepe.

In all these campaigns the Cossacks had played a key part, because they alone in the imperial Russian army were able to take on the hardy horsemen of the steppes and deserts on their own terms. They required less back-up than the troops imported from metropolitan Russia, being used to carrying their own provisions as well as their own weaponry. Their horses were as sure-footed and robust as the Turcomans' ponies. Their own horsemanship was more than the equal of the caravan raiders and tribesmen whom they confronted. They were a frontier people, fighting on their own frontier, and had something in common with those US cavalry and cowboys who at the same period (Custer's Last Stand was just three years after Kaufman's Khiva campaign) – were opening up the far west of the North American continent.

But some of the Cossacks made more personal contributions towards the expansion of Russia's southern frontiers. With Tashkent,

Samarkand, Bokhara, Khiva and Geok-Tepe all under Imperial protection or direct rule, there was only one remaining khanate between Russia and Afghanistan – that gateway to India. This was Merv, possibly the most remote and unknown of all the khanates. Before any move could be made against it, it was decided in St Petersburg that more intelligence was needed about the defences of the oasis and the will to resist of the population. A formal envoy would not have been acceptable, and would have been prevented from seeing or hearing anything of value. A clandestine mission was therefore required.

Just as young British subalterns competed to undertake daring missions into the Himalayas and the heart of Central Asia – frequently designated as 'shooting leave' – so it was the ambition of many a young Russian aristocrat or adventurer to make the reconnaissance before another imperial thrust southwards. Those with a flair for languages or disguises were most likely to be selected. In 1882, two such Russian officers were chosen to infiltrate the khanate of Merv. One of them was a figure strangely reminiscent of Lermontov and his exploits in the Caucasus: Lieutenant Alikhanov came from an old Caucasian family and started his career in a smart cavalry regiment, but he had indulged in duelling and had been cashiered, earning his way back into favour by various feats of military prowess. The other was a Cossack Ensign named Sokolev, who shared in all the planning and dangers of the trip but – as he was the junior of the two officers and did not write an official account of the expedition – received far less acclaim than Alikhanov.

The plan was that Alikhanov and Sokolev should join the entourage of a Moscow-based merchant who was taking a caravan of wares to Merv to sell in the local markets. The two officers would be disguised as the merchant's clerks and no one in the entourage would know that they were in fact serving officers. A Russianized Khivan, who had been to the region before, was sent ahead to prepare a friendly recep-

A Cossack trooper as he would have appeared in the confrontation with the British Raj in the 19th century

tion for the caravan at the mid-way oasis of Tejend and at Merv itself. There was also a small escort of native horsemen who were heavily armed in the hope that they would deter casual raiders in the desert, but without any expectation that they could prevent the capture and detention of the party by the Merv authorities if the officers' disguise was penetrated, nor any expectation that they could save them from lynching by a hostile crowd in Merv if things went wrong. It was a high risk adventure which was launched from the Russian port of Askabad on the eastern Caspian coast.

It all nearly went wrong almost before it was started, because the camel drivers refused to go on when they were only two days out of Askabad and had another week's march ahead of them. Threats of arrest eventually persuaded the reluctant drivers to press on, but not before Alikhanov and Sokolev suspected that they had revealed too much of the secret purpose of the mission. When they reached the mid-way oasis of Tejend, with its 3,600 tents, they were received cautiously as the inhabitants had vivid memories of punitive Cossack patrols sent there on previous occasions when they were suspected of molesting Russian traders. When they were still a day's march away from Merv, they were met by guides sent out by the Khivan who had gone ahead to prepare their reception. It was not a reassuring encounter: the guides said it was far too dangerous to pass through the settlements immediately ahead of them in daylight, as the inhabitants were notoriously anti-Russian and would be likely to slit their throats. So a long night march ensued, skirting what Alikhanov described as 'robbers' nests ... where the tents seemed to rise at every step like black mushrooms' and where watchdogs all too often revealed their approach. Even when they arrived on the outskirts of Merv, they thought at first they were walking into a trap and Ensign Sokolev told his companion, 'I shall empty my revolver among the blackguards, and then put an end to myself'. They crossed a river by a narrow rickety bridge, sixty paces long, and were led through the formidable walls into the heart of Merv itself. Only then were they allowed to collapse and sleep off the exertions of a whole day and a night's stressful travel without rest.

In the morning, the word quickly spread throughout Merv that a Russian caravan was in town. The city elders and leading merchants gathered to discuss whether the newcomers should be allowed to trade and move around freely, or whether they were to be apprehended as unwelcome intruders. By dint of liberal gifts and the excellence of their trade goods, the Russians persuaded their hosts that they should be allowed to spend three weeks in Merv.

During the days, the two Russian officers dutifully performed the functions of a merchant's clerk – writing out receipts and arranging delivery of goods. But in the early mornings, at first light and before the populace was stirring, they set out heavily disguised as natives of Merv to survey the defences of the city – measuring the thickness of walls, the height of towers, the width of the river, and so on. Not surprisingly these activities eventually aroused suspicions: local agents tried to trap them into revealing knowledge and characteristics incompatible with being simple clerks – 'If you are mere traders, how does it come to pass that you know all these things?' one interrogator asked them. The answers that Alikhanov and Sokolev gave must have left something to be desired, because soon rumours were circulating in Merv that they were spies and that the right thing to do would be to murder them quietly one night before they could exploit their 'lust of knowing what should not be known'. So persistent were the rumours that the Moscow trader, whose clerks they were supposed to be, decided that discretion was the better part of valour and made a hurried departure from the oasis, leaving his wares behind him 'on credit'. But Alikhanov and Sokolev were not so easily scared off. They carried on until the prearranged date of departure and then insisted on leaving by a different direction from the one they had come – so as to reconnoitre another approach route.

When they finally, after more adventures, got back to Askabad and reported in detail on the defences of Merv, it was decided that a Russian military thrust in that direction would be successful. A force of Cossacks and others set out from Askabad a year later and Alikhanov rode on ahead and persuaded the elders of the city (who were shocked to find the clerk whom they remembered dressed in the uniform of an Imperial Russian officer) that resistance would be futile. Merv surrendered without a shot, and it was Alikhanov, rather then his Cossack companion Sokolev, who was appointed as the first Russian governor of the city. As with the earlier Russian occupations of these desert khanates and emirates, there was a reaction in London. 'England is suffering from Mervousness', punned the Duke of Argyll, a former Secretary of State for India.

These individual exploits found their expression in literature as well as in history. Rudyard Kipling wrote a short story at the end of the nineteenth century entitled *The Man Who Was* about a Cossack officer called Dirkovitch who 'arrived in India from nowhere in particular'. In fact, it is suggested he infiltrated through one of the lesser-known or unknown passes, eventually arriving as a guest in the Mess of the mythical White Hussars at the Khyber Pass. 'He had done rough work in Central Asia, and had seen rather more help-yourself fighting than most men of his years.' Dirkovitch eventually is discredited when a former officer of the White Hussars appears with grievous injuries inflicted by the Cossacks when he was their prisoner. John Buchan also wrote at the turn of the century a full-length – almost forgotten – novel entitled *The Half-Hearted* about players in the Great Game. The villain of his story is a Russian agent 'clad in a Cossack fur-lined military cloak' who travels alone through the Pamirs and stirs up the tribes against the British, while he plans for an invasion force of Cossacks to penetrate the mountains by a formerly undiscovered pass and descend on Hunza and Gilgit. Buchan's hero dies defending this pass single-handed for long enough to allow the alarm to be sounded and the forces of the Raj to rally to the defence of the Indian frontier. It is all the stuff of *Boy's Own Paper* heroics. But the realities were not very different.

One regiment of the Indian Army, raised and employed specifically to counter these missions of intrusion by individual Cossack officers, and later by Cossack units, was the Corps of Guides. Raised by Harry Lumsden in 1847, by the end of the century they provided the eyes and ears of the army, and shared with the Gurkhas the escort duties which the Cossacks performed on their side of the frontier. The Guides had cavalry as well as infantry, and saw their role as being 'to give *accurate* information ... to stop and see whether it is only a few wild horsemen who are kicking up all the dust'. These were the prototypes for the heroes of John Buchan, while Cossacks such as Sokolev – the hero of the Merv adventure – were the prototypes for Kipling's Dirkovitch.

One such real-life prototype was Captain Fred Burnaby of the British Household Cavalry. This adventurous officer, who was reputed to be the strongest as well as one of the tallest men in the army, set off in 1876 to ride to Khiva, which had only three years previously been taken under Russian 'protection'. He somehow contrived to get the necessary documentation in St Petersburg to get as far as Orenburg and he then set off by sleigh, with a native servant as his sole companion, on the 600-mile drive to Kazala on the Aral Sea. The going was as awful as that encountered by the ill-fated expeditions of 1717 and 1839: deep snow, blizzards and arctic temperatures. At one point Burnaby fell asleep on the sleigh under his bear-skin rug, without noticing that his hands were not covered by the rug. The consequent frostbite was so severe that he was in danger of losing not only his hands but possibly his arms as well.

Captain Burnaby of the British Household Cavalry made a memorable ride to Khiva at the height of the Great Game, being saved by his Cossack rivals from losing his hands to frostbite.

He was saved – happily but improbably – by being intercepted by a Cossack patrol who, rather than apprehending him, treated him as a fellow traveller in need of succour; they rubbed spirits into his hands and arms and eventually restored the circulation and sent him on his way. It was a rare but not unique example of Great Game opponents treating each other with some chivalry.

Burnaby was of course, at least technically, a guest of the Russians. When he reached Kazala, the governor insisted that instead of going on to Khiva he should report to the nearby Russian garrison town of Petro-

Alexandrovsk. Burnaby was sure that if he did that he would never be permitted to reach Khiva, so he declined the offered Cossack escort and bribed his guide to turn off the sledge-track and take him to the forbidden city. The Khan, who resented the way that the Russians now treated him alternately as a puppet or a bogey-man (they had told Burnaby that the Khan's executioner might gouge out his eyes), warned him that Russian intentions were directed towards India. When eventually Burnaby retraced his steps to St Petersburg, he was this time given a compulsory Cossack escort; his hosts by now realized they were harbouring a gentle-man-spy in their midst. In fact, Burnaby turned this to his advantage and in his eventual report included a long passage about the operational methods of the Cossacks and the threat they posed to British interests in India. Everyone, including Queen Victoria, listened to his tale of daring and his note of warning. It was to prove timely, even if the precise direction of the threat was to change slightly.

Although Merv was now added to the Russian possessions in Central Asia, the possibility of an advance into India through Afghanistan had receded during the early 1880s, because the British had fought a Second Afghan War and had – under the leadership of Lord Roberts of Kandahar – re-established their influence in Kabul. Russian attentions were therefore focused further east – on the Pamirs, that remote part of the Himalayan range that bordered both the Sinkiang province of China and the petty independent states of Hunza and Chitral which formed the northern extremities of India. It was here that the next clash between players of the Great Game was to occur.

Francis Younghusband, a young British cavalry officer who had been seconded to political work, was sent in 1889 to explore the passes of the Pamirs and report on possible 'back doors' into India which should be blocked, either by defence treaties with the local rulers or by the presence of British garrisons. On his first expedition he was surprised to encounter a Russian explorer on a similar mission to his own: Captain Gromchevsky was also reconnoitring the passes and gauging their efficacy as a line of advance for the Russian army. Gromchevshy was accompanied by an escort of seven Cossacks, whereas Younghusband had an equivalent escort of Gurkhas. While these very different bodies of men eyed each other warily, the two officers sat down to a friendly dinner together, in the course of which Gromchevsky was remarkably frank about Russian invasion intentions. He called his Cossacks over to the tent where he and Younghusband were drinking vodka and asked them what they would think about such a venture; the response was an enthusiastic cheer which left Younghusband in little doubt that it was just what they had been looking forward to for long enough.

One finds oneself wondering exactly what these Cossack contingents, on far-flung service beyond the frontiers of the Russian empire, looked like to a British officer used to the spit and polish of Indian sepoys. Fortunately, a generation later one of the very last players in the Great Game gave a vivid description of a similar Cossack escort. Gerald Uloth was an officer of the 28th Light (Indian) Cavalry on special duties in Central Asia during the First World War and came in frequent contact with opposite numbers from the Imperial Russian Army in the years immediately preceding the Revolution. He recorded that:

> The escort of eight Cossacks from the 1st Caucasian Regiment was a striking body of men, fair, well-built and very theatrical looking in their uniform: a black fur hat, slightly tilted back, long blue *tcherkaska*, open at the front to display a bright red shirt, with pockets on each breast containing silver cartridge cases, pleated and taken in at the waist and falling below the knees. Their full pantaloons were tucked into soft, high, black Russian boots. They possessed no less than five concertinas.

It was just such a band who doubtless confronted Younghusband in the Pamirs.

Two years later, Younghusband was back in the Pamirs and this time he encountered not seven lone Cossacks but a veritable regiment of them under command of a Colonel. They had come not on a reconnaissance but to occupy the strip of no-man's-land which the Russians saw as a vacuum to be filled by them, and which the British saw as part of the buffer zone of Afghanistan. The Cossacks, who far out-numbered Younghusband's party, at first treated him as a guest and fellow explorer: dinners were exchanged and toasts were drunk. But as soon as news of this contact with a British scout reached the Russian Colonel's superiors, he received orders to behave in a very different way. Younghusband was arrested – albeit with expressions of regret – and obliged to withdraw from the Pamirs.

The repercussions in London were more than the Tsar had anticipated; protests were lodged in St Petersburg; belligerent articles were published in *The Times*; Lord Roberts mobilized a division of the Indian army on the frontier. Eventually the Russians backed down: the officer

Cossacks manning machine-guns in the Pamirs, the mountains through which the British feared a Russian invasion of India might take place in the early years of the twentieth century.

who had arrested Younghusband was censured (in public though not in private); the Cossacks were withdrawn; an apology was made. The British were prompted 'to lock the back door to India', by occupying Hunza and Chitral.

By now, at the end of the nineteenth century, at the nearest point only twenty miles separated the empires of Imperial Russia and the British Raj, whereas a century earlier the gap had been more than 2,000 miles. The British had done their share of closing it with the annexation of the Punjab and the acquisition of the smaller Indian states in the extreme north. But the bulk of the gap-closing had been the result of the Imperial Russian drive southwards into the heart of Moslem Central Asia. Peter the Great's dying injunction had not been realized (it was to be left to his Communist successors to come nearest to achieving this) but with the help of the Cossacks – without whose involvement it would never have been possible – a visible stride had been made in that direction. These horsemen from the steppes had shown their worth to the Tsar as frontier troops, now they were to be called upon to act as internal policemen as well.

11:
THE COSSACKS IN THE REVOLUTION: THE SWORD TURNS IN THE HAND

WHEN THE FIRST BLOOD was spilt in the abortive revolution of 1905 (the opening of which was described in the Prologue to this book) the Cossacks were viewed by the Tsar and his Ministers as the natural first line of defence against urban unrest. They had slashed with their whips and sabres into the crowds in St Petersburg and other cities where strikers had taken to the streets. They had no local loyalties to these disaffected communities; their brothers were not factory workers; it was not their sisters and mothers who thronged the pavements and public squares. They came from a martial breed and from distant corners of the Russian empire; if they had an equivalent in the British empire, it was probably the Gurkhas. Besides, their loyalty to the House of Romanov had been assiduously cultivated throughout the previous century; when the Tsar Nicholas II was still Tsarevich, or heir apparent, in the 1880s he had been granted the title of 'August Ataman of All the Cossacks' and encouraged to wear a Cossack uni-

The Tsarevich Nicholas, later to be the last Tsar, presented in the uniform of 'Ataman of All the Cossacks' to strengthen the latter's allegiance to the crown.

form with the famous cartridge bandoliers across his chest; in the eyes of the Tsar, the Cossacks were a Praetorian Guard by 1905.

But like other Praetorian Guards, their loyalties proved undependable. Despite the cosseting by successive tsars, there were grievances: the cost of mounting, arming and equipping a young Cossack trooper had always fallen on the family and not on the state, and in the early years of the twentieth century it had escalated to a point where many Cossack families had had to sell farmlands or livestock so that their son could have the dubious privilege of serving in some far off part of the Tsar's domains. Although they had little in common with the urban populations they were called upon to discipline, they equally had little in common with the state police who were their unnatural and unpopular allies in this task.

Between January and October 1905, the army (which usually meant the Cossacks) were called out no less than 2,700 times 'in aid of civil power', not only against urban strikers but frequently also against rural peasant uprisings. The disquiet in the regular units of the army was spreading to the Cossacks too. They found the work distasteful: guarding the frontiers of empire against Caucasian tribesmen or over-running the emirates of Central Asian tyrants was one thing, but acting as mounted policemen in the metropolis was quite another.

The Tsarist authorities were sensitive to the Cossacks' distaste for some aspects of this work. It was referred to in official documents not as 'counter-revolutionary action' or even 'action in support of civil power', but merely as 'service within the Empire' (as opposed to service on the frontiers or in the Russo-Japanese War). Doubtless this was not entirely due to consideration

Cossacks of the Imperial Bodyguard: splendid uniforms helped to attach them to the Tsar before the Revolution.

for the Cossacks: the authorities wished to minimize all mention of the country-wide disturbances during 1905 so that the threat to the regime should not be seen to be as real as it was. The Cossacks themselves did little to glorify their domestic campaigns; there were no regimental battle honours to compare with those won on the frontiers of the Caucasus or Central Asia.

But this lack of trumpet-blowing should not obscure the effectiveness of the Cossacks' actions in towns and cities throughout the country. Their ferocious reputation and brutal force sent shock-waves before them. The funeral procession of one dissident in Moscow in the autumn of 1905 was broken up merely by a panic cry of 'the Cossacks are coming!' In Odessa that year, thirty mounted Cossacks dispersed 300 armed peasants, and 100 Cossacks broke up a factory-workers' mob of over 1,000 within minutes in Astrakhan. Flying squads were despatched to distant corners of the country. Regiments were fragmented, as it transpired that even the smallest contingent of Cossacks could usually break up an urban demonstration or disturbance.

One such instance at the Gena Factory in Odessa in June 1905 was the subject of a near-contemporary published account (quoted by Robert McNeal in his *Tsar and Cossack*) and gives the flavour of many. The reporter was one of the disaffected workers:

> In the distance a Cossack unit appeared ... the workers threw rocks and the Cossacks retreated ... the Cossacks stopped and regrouped ... a trumpeter sounded his horn ... the Cossacks came forward at a gentle trot ... everyone scattered in flight ... ten paces in front of me a Comrade stumbled ... a bullet had passed through his back ... there were other corpses lying in the gate of the factory.

Often the Cossacks did not even need to fire or use their sabres. Their infamous *nagaika* whips, made of plaited hide, could inflict savage wounds

and when wielded from horseback tended to impact not only on the shoulders and backs but on the heads and necks of the fleeing demonstrators. Boris Pasternak recounts in his autobiographical book *Safe Conduct* how he was struck by such a whip during a street demonstration in 1895, and he describes a Cossack street charge in one of the early chapters of *Dr Zhivago*.

Putting down urban and rural unrest was not only unappealing

Cossack marauders attack a village during the Russo-Japanese War of 1904-05.

The following page:
A postcard from the front during the Russo-Japanese War shows how Cossacks would stand on their horses to observe or shoot.

Казаки.—Les cosaques.· № 41.

Merci — cette échange

M. Denest

*Cossack horsemen attack Kunguz tribesmen who sided
with the enemy during the Russo-Japanese War.*

work, it was also deeply corrupting. Cossack officers got into the practice of whipping dissident suspects until they divulged the names of their leaders, and the rank and file Cossacks expected the peasants to abase themselves like serfs in front of the truculent horsemen from the steppes. Discipline was harder to maintain on these domestic campaigns than when they were patrolling the frontiers of empire; vodka was too readily available; rapes and assaults all too frequently committed. Worse still was the Cossack propensity to string up troublemakers from trees without trial and after only minimal investigation; Orlando Figes, in his recent work on *The People's Revolution*, calculates that the regime – often through its Cossack instruments – executed some 15,000 people between October 1905 and April 1906 alone.

If the role of the Cossacks was equivocal and inglorious in the 1905 troubles, it was to be much more so when the Russian Revolution reached its climax in 1917. Cossack regiments had been mobilized early to fight the Germans from the beginning of the First World War, and the number of units had been augmented by vigorous recruiting which had drafted older men and young boys to the Front. Many of them had borne the brunt of bitter fighting, inadequately equipped and under an ineffectual high-command. These units, like most others in the Tsar's army, had been infiltrated by Communist revolutionaries. Traditional allegiances often succumbed to a combination of old grievances and new ideologies. Nowhere is this process better described than in Mikhail Sholokhov's classic *And Quiet Flows the Don* – the greatest twentieth-century novel about the Cossacks.

When the war had been going for three years and bread riots broke out in Petrograd (as St Petersburg had now become) in February 1917, the bulk of the protesters were women. As usual, the authorities ordered the Cossacks to break up the protest. But the units involved were inexperienced and had no stomach for the job. They rode up to the mass of women, turned their horses and retreated. The word got around that even the Cossacks were really on the side of 'the people'. A few days later, when the bread riots had escalated into a general strike, the Tsar's chief of police – a certain Shalfeev – was dragged off his horse, beaten to the ground and shot dead. None of the nearby Cossacks intervened to save him. Later the same day – 25 February 1917 – a young girl emerged from the crowd of demonstrators and offered a bouquet of red roses to the Cossack officer confronting them; he accepted this apparent symbol of goodwill and of revolution with a good grace; from then on, there were those among the revolutionaries who referred to their 'Cossack comrades'. Later still, in Znamenskaya Square, when the mounted police charged into an unarmed crowd and started laying about them, the Cossacks pursued them into the crowd and instead of joining in the assault on the rioters attacked the brutal police – slashing the police leader to death with their sabres.

But throughout 1917 the role of the Cossacks remained equivocal. They were wheeled out in July to line the streets for Kerensky's triumphal return to Petrograd as Prime Minister of the Provisional Government and treated as a shield against the Bolsheviks. But on other occasions at this period they were deliberately held back by the Provisional Government from acting against its left-wing opponents for fear of contaminating that government with the Tsarist associations which still clung to the Cossacks' bootstraps. There were Cossacks among the motley assembly of troops guarding Kerensky's Provisional Government on the night of the storming of the Winter Palace in Petrograd; but they did not show any more determination or discipline than the other soldiery crowded into the corridors and salons of the Palace. The mere presence of Cossacks on that occasion did, however, instil an extra element of fear into those who stormed the Palace; when the mob finally broke in and, having rushed down a ground-floor pas-

*Cossack cavalry patrols protect the Trans-Siberian
railway and telegraph, vital lines of communication
during the Russo-Japanese War.*

Tsarist might and majesty: a military parade in front of the Winter Palace in St Petersburg.

sage, turned a corner, they fell back in alarm claiming that 'mounted Cossacks were charging down the corridor'; it turned out what they had seen round the corner was not a horseman but an enormous equestrian portrait of a cavalryman with raised sabre.*

During the unhappy periods in 1917 when first the Tsarina and her children and then – after the Tsar's abdication in March – the entire Imperial family were virtually under house-arrest at their palace of Tsarskoe Selo outside Petrograd, the Cossack Guards regiments who were among those guarding the family showed no personal loyalty to their former master and patron. At first their behaviour was distant but correct; later it became stern or insolent, though never as threatening and insulting as the conduct of the non-Cossack guards at Ekaterinburg

*This incident was described in vivid detail to the author by Anastas Mikoyan, Khrushchev's deputy, in 1958 when he conducted me on a tour of the Winter Palace in the course of preparations for Harold Macmillan's visit to the USSR. Mikoyan claimed to have been present, as a very young man, at this momentous event, but a number of his stories did not carry complete conviction.

during the final stages of the Romanovs' incarceration prior to their murder in 1918. So any lingering thoughts the Tsar and his family might have had during their sad final year of life of a 'special relationship' with 'their' Cossacks were to prove without substance.

The civil war, and the intervention of foreign forces in support of the White Russians, which followed the revolution, found the Cossacks as divided and confused as ever. Admiral Kolchak, the improbable leader ('an Admiral without a Fleet') of the White Russian forces in land-locked Siberia in 1919, had a substantial Cossack element in his force; but as the campaign floundered on its disorganised course many of them deserted and went home. There was also a major Cossack element in General Denikin's White army based on Rostov, and – possibly for that reason – instead of linking up with Kolchak, Denikin went to the rescue of the Cossack homelands on the Don which were being invaded by the Reds and made the subject of a campaign of terror; it has been calculated that as many as 12,000 Cossacks were slaughtered by the Reds in early 1919 since the latter feared, not surprisingly, that the former would prove an independent and intractable element in any Communist state.

Admiral Kolchak (left) and General Denikin (right), leaders of the White interventionist forces who had Cossacks under their command between 1918 and 1920.

There was a moment in 1919 when it looked as if the three-pronged White assault on Moscow might succeed; Lenin and the Communist Central Committee were preparing for flight (they had acquired false passports and a stock of Tsarist bank notes); but the White forces were too thinly spread and too far from their supply bases; their attempt to live off the country antagonised the local peasantry on whose support they ultimately depended. Most damaging of all to the White cause was the reluctance of the Kuban Cossacks, on whom they had been relying, to quit their own homelands and join in the march on Moscow. Instead of joining in the attack, they started to lay down unacceptable conditions for the establishment of a separatist Cossack state in the Kuban region. It was the old story of the Cossacks trying to turn a national crisis into a bargaining counter for regional autonomy.

A number of the other less-attractive traits of the Cossacks came to the fore during the civil war. One was their propensity for looting: out of the 8,000 Cossacks in General Mamontov's White army, nearly 7,000 deserted to carry back to their native Don the spoils of their campaigning. Another was their anti-Semitism. This had always been a national failing in Russia, but it was more pronounced in the Cossack homelands of the Don than elsewhere. The White advance into the Ukraine was attended by appalling atrocities committed by Cossacks of Denikin's army against the Jewish communities in Kiev and elsewhere. These acts were frequently encouraged by the Cossacks' officers who accepted the widely held view that the Jews were not only profiting from the Revolution but were among its main instigators. This was an exaggeration: Orlando Figes well summed up the position when he wrote, 'Not many Jews were Bolsheviks, but many of the leading Bolsheviks were Jews.' On the pretext however that the Jews were their enemies, Cossack commanders allowed their men after taking a town or city to indulge in days of extortion and torture of Jews to reveal imagined or real caches of hidden treasure; as the White cause became ever more desperate, and

as the White officers cared less and less for their own reputations, these anti-Semitic crimes extended to murder, gang rape and pillage.

The ambivalence of the Cossacks towards Reds and Whites was never clearer than in 1918 when many of the former Tsarist supporters from Petrograd assembled in or around the Don capital of Novocherkassk. They were a motley assembly of senior officers of the *ancien régime*, intellectuals, civil servants, actors and dancers, prostitutes and professional gamblers. They assumed – wrongly – that the Cossacks would be welcoming hosts. In fact, the Cossacks were split in their sympathies, both geographically and in age groups. In the northern Don region, where most of the settlers were smallholders and life had always been hard, there was

Cossacks fought on both sides in the civil war following the Russian Revolution: this is a typical scene from that period.

Cossacks swimming their horses across a river during the First World War.

And it was not only death that had taken its toll of numbers. As the Cossack strongholds crumbled at the end of the Civil War, tens of thousands fled. The quayside at Novorossisk saw the embarkation of a large number of White Army veterans. Others who could not find a place in the ships marched south into the Caucasus. Many of the emigrants ended up in Turkey where Cossack communities mushroomed. As with the highland clearances in Scotland in the previous century, a strong culture – including song, dance and a warlike tradition – was transplanted to alien shores. The Cossacks were to become an international phenomenon and not purely a Russian one, a wistful and nostalgic phenomenon where previously they had been a boisterous and self-sufficient one.

For the Cossacks who stayed behind in what was now the Soviet Union another grim chapter was just beginning. Although the Soviet

Government tried to lure the emigre Cossacks back with promises of amnesties and free sea-passages home, the land that some of them came back to was not the land they remembered. Their own distinctive structures were systematically destroyed by the Communist authorities who had no room for the old *atamans* with their special responsibilities, nor for the special privileges of Cossack land tenure, nor for the exclusively Cossack regiments. Worse still, the traditional Cossack dress, which had been associated by many of the Red Army with the Intervention forces ranged against them, was prescribed in the same way as Highland dress was prescribed in Scotland following the 1745 rebellion.

Collectivisation was the order of the day. This involved not only merging private land holdings, horses, cattle and farm machinery into communal units, but it also involved classifying the Cossacks – like the rest of the rural population – into farm labourers (who were – in theory – to 'inherit the earth') and *kulaks* (who were to be stripped of their rural properties and treated as a threat to the Revolution). These crude distinctions did not fit the Cossack communities, where every man thought of himself as independent – more like a sturdy English yeoman of the Middle Ages than like either a peasant or a rich landowner. The calls for 'class struggle against the *kulaks*' seemed to the remaining or returning Cossacks to be both irrelevant and offensive.

Sketch of a mounted Cossack by Valentin Serov (1865-1911).

All this confusion led not only to disarray but to a severe fall-off in agricultural production. The regions of the Don, Kuban and Ural Cossacks were already devastated after the twists and turns of the Civil War; now they were left desolate rather than being re-planted and re-stocked. By 1921 there were only half the number of horses there had been in 1917, and other indices of wealth showed an equal reduction. Grain production flagged and when the Communists tried to pay for what little there was with dubious promissory notes the Cossacks refused to part with their meagre stores. This is turn provoked scavenging parties who would raid the barns and store-houses of the Don in search of secret caches of food. Some of the scavengers were officials carrying out government sweeps, but more of them were desperate men who took to combing the countryside in criminal gangs to provide for themselves and their dependants.

There was a brief period in the mid-1920s when it seemed that the Communist regime might be prepared to placate the Cossacks to some extent. Mikoyan, already one of the most prominent of the younger Party *apparatchiks*, when addressing the Regional Committee of the Northern Caucasus in November 1925, spoke of the need to end a vendetta against them and praised some aspects of their life style. Cossack horsemanship – and even Cossack hats – could be harnessed to the cause of the Revolution. At one moment Stalin, who like Mikoyan came from the Caucasus himself, declared himself to be a Cossack at heart. But the rapprochement was not to last.

By the end of the 1920s, when Stalin had already been in full control for over five years following the death of Lenin in 1924, the heat was once more turned on the Cossacks as a more widespread series of purges were beginning. The collectivisation, which had up to then been only half-hearted in the Don and other Cossack homelands, was now intensified; the aim was to abolish once and for all the independent spirit of the Cossacks; the few remaining *kulaks* were driven to give up their lands and labourers, and those who declined to do this even under pressure were dubbed enemies of the Revolution and deported to slave labour camps further east.

Not surprisingly the Cossacks did not go under without a struggle. Many slaughtered their horses rather than see them used as farm animals on Collectives. Others looked out rifles, sabres and other weapons from hay-lofts and barns. Predictably it was in the wild Caucasus that the revolt against authority took its most extreme form. Towns and villages were captured by the rebel Cossacks as in the days of Pugachev. Armoured trains – those dinosaurs of the Civil War – were ambushed. At the small township of Mineralnyye Vody in the northern Caucasus – near the place where Lermontov was killed in a duel in the previous century – the disaffected Cossacks fought a full-blown battle with heavily armoured units of the Red Army. From the Caucasus the troubles spread to those other Cossack redoubts: the Don, the Kuban, the Urals and even Siberia.

It has been estimated that some 20,000 insurgents were killed in the fighting, and many tens of thousands more starved out on their uncollectivised farms. Starvation was not just achieved by neglect, but by deliberately blockading some of the Cossack villages and refusing at rifle point to allow food supplies through. The scale of this atrocity has to be set against the millions who were starved out in other parts of Russia during the worst years of Stalinism. While therefore the Cossacks had no monopoly of repression, it remained the fact that they were more systematically eradicated as a social phenomenon than other less-identifiable racial groupings. A cruel twist of fate added a natural famine in the early 1930s to the unnatural hardships inflicted on the Don Cossacks.

Where deliberate starvation by the authorities was impracticable, and where natural starvation did not occur, whole *stanitsas* from the Kuban and other disaffected regions were uprooted and transported – often in cattle trucks – to quite different parts of the Soviet Union, including the arctic wastes of northern Russia where the warm-blooded Cossack families had to struggle for existence in a totally alien climate. The Soviet scholar V. P. Danilov revealed in the 1960s that Mikhail Sholokhov, the author of *And Quiet Flows the Don* (which was first published in Russia in 1929), had written to Stalin in the early 1930s protesting at violations which included rape and torture. Although he was a friend of Stalin's – to the extent that Stalin had any friends – his protests were ignored and Stalin insisted that the Cossack *kulaks* were among the most intractable enemies of collectivisation. In this view he was probably correct.

To fill the vacuum and work the new Collectives, peasants were brought in from other regions and some of the starving urban overflow from the cities was encouraged to settle in the former Cossack lands. The character of the Don in particular was being deliberately destroyed in favour of non-Cossacks who docilely accepted the Party line. Fifteen years after the Revolution of 1917, Cossacks were still escaping over the frontiers to begin lives in exile – often as taxi drivers in Paris – while others were taking to the mountains of Georgia and Daghestan as the followers of Shamyl had done nearly a hundred years before.

Inevitably there were a few Cossacks who allowed themselves to be used by the Soviet regime. In March 1936 a letter was published in *Pravda* (already the official organ of the Communist Party) by one such group. Having declared that the 'old' Don, Kuban and Terek Cossack communities existed no more, they went on to write about new Cossacks who were 'Soviet, collectivised and happy'. This article was taken by the authorities as evidence of a change of heart in the Cossack homelands; as a reward for their new-found 'loyalty', a number of cavalry units were designated as Cossack and the wearing of Cossack uniform was again permitted in those units. Cossack military bands and choirs were once more allowed to make themselves heard in the Don region and even, on occasion, in Moscow itself.

However, the real reason for this softening of attitude towards them was not gratuitous goodwill: there was a strong element of national and Communist Party self-interest, and this was the possible need once more to think of the defence of Mother Russia in the face of external threat. By 1936 Nazi Germany was already beginning to cast its sinister shadow eastwards.

12:
THE COSSACKS IN THE
SECOND WORLD WAR:
DESERTION AND BETRAYAL

THE COSSACKS HAVE NEVER been strangers to controversy, but few chapters in their history have aroused such sharp emotions as their role in the Second World War.

As has been seen, the Cossacks had suffered appallingly under Stalin's imposition of collective farms. But despite all the ravishing of the Cossack homelands – through resettlement and starvation – which accompanied this process, large communities remained in the Ukraine and the Caucasus. These Don, Kuban and Terek Cossacks were inevitably a disaffected population.

Nevertheless when Hitler invaded the Soviet Union in 1941 most Cossacks, like most of their fellow Russians, rallied to the defence of their homeland. It has been estimated that there were more than 100,000 Cossacks in the Red Army at the moment of the invasion, and volunteers and conscripts swelled these numbers. Under General Dovator, Cossack cavalry units took the field against the invading Panzer armoured divi-

sions; they made forays into the forests picking off tank commanders with rifle fire as the latter emerged from the turrets of their tanks; they lured German tanks onto frozen rivers which would not bear their weight; they penetrated behind the enemy lines and sabotaged supply trains and attacked SS field headquarters.

Several Cossack regiments were designated 'Guards' – as in the old days – for their outstanding bravery, and the Kuban Cavalry Corps won tributes from the Soviet High Command. Although General Dovator himself was killed in action early on, the Soviet government continued to publicize the activities of the Cossacks and to release photographs of them in action, to raise morale at home and among their allies abroad. Legendary stories were propagated – consciously emulating the exploits of Platov's irregular cavalry against Napoleon – telling of

A Soviet Cossack cavalryman passes an abandoned German tank in the Ukraine.

Pro-German Cossacks as depicted in Nazi art during the Second World War.

Two Kuban Cossack veterans who were recalled to colours after Hitler's invasion of Russia in 1941 and were said to have sabred twenty-six Germans during a charge.

raids with muffled hooves across frozen tributaries of the Don. Just as Stalin reactivated the Orthodox Church to swell the chorus of patriotism, and allowed the concept of Holy Russia to be superimposed on the atheism of the Soviet Union, so now he encouraged a revival of the Cossack ethos to inject an element of dash and daring into the cumbersome and battle-weary Red Army.

But even with this evidence of Cossack loyalty, Stalin could not bring himself to rely on all those of Cossack origin. Many were not trusted on front-line operations and were drafted into pioneer units which undertook arduous non-combatant duties maintaining supply lines and mending bridges battered or destroyed by the German blitzkrieg – duties resented by the Cossacks.

And events proved that Stalin was right not to trust them all. The

Above left, General Kirichenko commanding the Soviet 4th Cossack Corps of Guards.

Right, a Soviet Cossack mounted nurse on the Don.

German High Command was well aware of the potentially disaffected nature of many of the Cossack communities which they overran, and much propaganda was directed at them. There were isolated instances of Cossack *stanitsas* mobilizing themselves and going out to greet the invaders as liberators from Communism. More frequently, there were cases of Cossacks in the Ukraine and the Caucasus passively welcoming the Germans when they arrived, and volunteering to join them – or at least not resisting attempts to recruit them into the Wehrmacht. When the Germans overran Novocherkassk, the Cossack 'capital' on the Don, a disaffected Cossack called Sergei Pavlov set himself up as a local *ataman* and actively recruited his fellow Cossacks to form a unit to fight alongside the Germans against the Red Army.

Worse still was the desertion of Colonel Kononov with a whole

curious cavalcade: there were covered carts with whole Cossack families living in them; there were – of course – horses and also mules; there were even one or two camels that had somehow been acquired as pack animals. The moving column was more like a Don *stanitsa* than a battle formation. Having reached Italy with difficulty and tribulation, they were not to stay there long. As the British armies advanced northwards in Italy, and the Cossack settlements there came under bombardment, Domanov had no wish to fight the British and decided it would be prudent to move northwards over the Carnian Alps to Lienz in Austria. Here their long and curious peregrinations were almost over.

Meanwhile von Pannwitz's Cossack Division, which was essentially composed of various cavalry regiments from the Don, Kuban and Terek regions, had also withdrawn from Yugoslavia to the relative security of Austria. When the German surrender was announced in May 1945 both the main Cossack military formations were therefore close together in what was to become the British Zone of Austria. And it was to the British commanders that both Cossack leaders – Domanov and von Pannwitz – surrendered, having tried in vain to secure special terms and guarantees for their future.

Before the surrender of their arms, von Pannwitz's cavalry had held a final parade at Griffen, a village in the British Zone of Austria. This was the last time that Tsarist Cossacks were to form up on a parade ground as a mounted unit with their traditional trappings: well-groomed horses, riders with drawn sabres, white fur hats, ammunition bandoliers, and corps of trumpeters and Orthodox chaplains in attendance. Squadrons of Don, Kuban and Siberian Cossacks rode past their General (Colonel von Pannwitz had been promoted) at full gallop. They were not only a splendid sight, but – unlike the straggling columns under Domanov – they were also a formidable fighting unit, and this was at once their *raison d'être* and their undoing. After the parade, von

*War photographers in 1942 show Soviet Cossacks fulfilling their
traditional role of reconnaissance in the snowbound forests.*

Pannwitz himself, though given the chance to escape and join the Chetnik (royalist) partisans in Yugoslavia, decided to stay with the Cossacks he had led and who had elected him – despite his non-Cossack origins – as their Field Ataman.

There were now probably as many as 30,000 Cossack prisoners of war in British hands in their zone of Austria. Unknown to these Cossacks who had surrendered, a far-reaching decision had already been taken about their fate at the Yalta Conference between Stalin, Roosevelt and Churchill in early 1945. Stalin had insisted that all Russian prisoners in the hands of other Allies should be returned to the Soviet Union promptly at the end of the war. This had not been challenged, largely because it was realized that there were many British prisoners in German POW camps who would be liberated by the Red Army, and it was understandably considered an over-riding priority that nothing should be done which might impede or delay the return of these veterans to the UK. Equivocation with Stalin might have had the effect of tempting him to hold on to the British as bargaining counters.

It was also relevant that many of the Cossacks and others who had fought with the Wehrmacht had either deserted to do so, or – having been captured – had volunteered to do so as an alternative to remaining in – admittedly harsh – German POW camps. Churchill and others were uncomfortable at the prospect of repatriating Russians to the Soviet Union against their will and in the realization that Stalin was likely to be vindictive. He asked explicitly in May 1945, 'Did they fight against us?' and received the reply that they (the Cossacks and other minority groups) had 'fought with ferocity, not to say savagery, for the Germans'. This was certainly true of many of them who had been implacable enemies of the Red Army and the Communist partisans in Yugoslavia. A very few Cossacks had even fought against the Americans and British on the western front at D Day. The term 'savage' probably applied with more accuracy to a Tartar Caucasian Division who boasted of the description than to the purely Cossack units. But the answer was enough for Churchill: there appeared to be no grounds for going back on the assurance given to Stalin at Yalta.

The area of greatest moral concern was regarding those Cossacks and others who had never been Soviet citizens because they had left Russia at the time of the 1917 Revolution or during the immediately following struggle between the Red and White Russian forces. The intention was that these POWs should be distinguished from the others and not handed over. Indeed, Major Ostrovsky and a party of some fifty other White Russian officers (or officers claiming to have left Russia at the time of the Revolution or to have been born abroad thereafter) were reprieved at the very last moment – when they were already in vehicles heading for the Russian Zone – and allowed to return to their camp in the British Zone. But there is no doubt that others in this category were handed back in the confusion and tension of the time.

The fate of the Cossacks who were handed over to the Soviet authorities was grim. They were all treated as being traitors or deserters and no allowance was made for the special circumstances that had led some of them to join cause with the German invaders. The fact that many of them had – ever since 1917 – harboured ambitions to detach their homelands, on the Don and elsewhere, from the Soviet Union was regarded not as an excuse for their disloyalty but as a further indictment against them. The Cossack leaders – including Krasnov, Domanov and von Pannwitz – were tried by court-martial and sent to the gallows. Many of the other more junior officers were shot, often with no trial and within hours of the hand-over. The rank and file and their families (but not *with* their families, as families were usually split up) were despatched to work camps – virtual slave-labour camps – in the rigours of Siberia, from which some emerged many years later to tell horror stories of their treatment.

The Cossacks, and particularly their officers who were more polit-
ically aware, had never doubted that this would be the fate of those who
were handed back to those whom they had fought against. Their leaders
had chosen to surrender to the British thinking that from this quarter
more consideration would be given to their plight; they handed over
their arms without demur, still unaware of the decisions that had already
been made about them at Yalta. When it became clear that they were
indeed to be handed back, many escaped (some probably with the con-
nivance of their captors); some passively resisted and others committed
suicide.

The sequence of events leading to these cruel consequences
deeply distressed many of those concerned in the handover. They had
grown to like and even admire the cheerful, lively Cossacks, with their
fine horses, their Orthodox priests, their hymn-singing and their carousing. Some felt that the deception necessary to separate the Cossacks from
their officers, to avoid a general panic in the camps, and to persuade
them onto the trucks heading for the Soviet Zone, went beyond the legitimate deceptions of war. The sound of rifle fire – assumed to be firing
squads – from the Soviet 'reception' areas sent a shudder through those
who heard it from the safety of the British Zone.

Since then bitter recriminations and extensive litigation have
followed. Individuals have found it necessary to clear their names of
allegations of dishonour. It is no part of this book's purpose to enter that
controversy, but any account of the Cossack peoples and their military
history would be incomplete without recounting the bare outlines of this
divisive and tragic story.

13:
THE POST-COMMUNIST
COSSACK REVIVAL

Afin the Second World War, Stalin and his successors felt no further need to cultivate the Cossacks or the Orthodox Church – those supposed pillars of patriotism – and the harassment and persecution of the
1930s continued through the middle decades of the twentieth century.
Only with the breakdown of the Communist state at the end of the 1980s
did things change. And then they changed rapidly.

In June 1990 the Union of Russian Cossacks was established, representing broadly those Cossacks who had kept the Cossack fire alight
during the long years of Communism; many of these 'Soviet' Cossacks
were descended from fathers and grandfathers who had fought on the
Red side in the Civil War and with the Red Army during the Second
World War. In July 1991 the Union of Cossack Hosts in Russia and
Abroad was established, representing broadly those Cossacks who had
been dispossessed, dispersed and otherwise persecuted during the
Communist era; many of this Union's members were descended from
those who had fought on the White side during the Civil War.

Both groups set about trying to re-establish the Cossack identity and tradition in all its forms. They had one marked distinction from all the other nationalistic groups that were emerging inside the former Soviet Union: they did not want to break away from Russia, indeed they stood strongly for preserving the territorial integrity of their country. This was to lead to problems, to fighting and to mistrust.

But most of the initial objectives were innocent enough. The declared policy of *glasnost* allowed the publication of historical material which had hitherto been suppressed: details of Stalin's purges and other enormities against the Cossacks emerged for the first time inside Russia. Historians took prominent positions in the Cossack organizations. A history professor at Krasnodar – Vladimir Gromov – became *ataman* of the newly-formed Kuban Cossack organization, and in 1991 Krasnodar University set up a special department for the study of Cossack history and customs. A Cossack school was reopened in the town of Novocherkassk where several hundred boys studied Cossack traditions and history alongside their normal curriculum. Outside universities and schools, Cossack historical societies flourished. A handbook of Cossack organizations published in the mid-1990s ran to over 200 pages for the Russian Federation alone, with another twenty pages of Cossack groups in other parts of the former Soviet Union. Usually and significantly, the historical societies tended to be merged with military societies which were to become more activist.

One of the less controversial activities of these military clubs was sponsorship of equestrian training for young Cossacks – or aspiring Cossacks. Summer camps have been established where the traditional skills of horsemanship have been inculcated into a fresh generation. Townsfolk have been struggling to mount frisky Cossack ponies. But observers have noted that nearly always these equestrian activities are closely tied in with military training which is more emotive: time in the saddle is matched with time on the firing range.

The reintroduction of Cossack costume was also a priority. Tailors

set themselves up in most of the southern Russian towns with Cossack populations – notably in Rostov-on-Don – and started manufacturing outfits which were often a blend of the Don, Kuban, Terek and Siberian military uniforms. The professional tailors were supplemented by wives and sisters of Cossacks who sewed together uniforms based on a study of faded sepia photographs of the pre-Revolutionary period. Since no uniform was complete without a *shashka* (sabre) and/or a *nagaika* (whip), these

Horse and rider rear as one: a typical Cossack scene reenacted on the banks of the River Don.

too have been manufactured by local craftsmen and made available. The cost of such an outfit is high, but those attending Cossack Union rallies are expected to turn out in the appropriate gear. Many Russians who have – or claim to have – Cossack origin now wear their Cossack dress in Moscow or St Petersburg, in the same way as Scotsmen sport the kilt south of the Border – or even in Hong Kong. The more rural and genuine Cossacks from the traditional areas view these costumed urban citizens with some mistrust and dub them 'asphalt Cossacks'.

The ceremonial, administrative and religious aspects of Cossack life have also been revived to some extent. New members of Cossack organizations are expected to swear an oath of fealty to Russia and to Cossack values; this is usually administered by an Orthodox priest in church in front of an icon. The traditional *krug* (or circle) is assembled to elect Elders and decide matters of regional policy. Where Cossacks have displayed bravery or been killed in action (in circumstances which are described below) these events have been recognized by the award of Crosses of Honour (similar to the St George's Cross awarded by the Tsars) and by the granting of 'Heroes' Funerals' respectively.

To breathe life into all this new Cossack activity, more than fifty Cossack newspapers were founded in the first few years of the 1990s. These gave prominence to reports of the activities of the new Unions and *krugs* and to contacts between regional organizations and emigre groups. But they also tended to play down various aspects of Cossack life and history: while much was made of the role of the Cossacks in expanding the frontiers of Russia, little or nothing was reported of the unpopular 'policing' activities performed in the Tsarist era; similarly, while much was made of Cossack common ground, little was reported of the differences between the various Hosts and of the bitter disputes that had arisen between Red and White Cossacks.

Probably the most controversial of all the new Cossack activities

Contemporary Cossacks strike a proud pose as they celebrate the founding of the Cossack fortress at Sevastopol.

was the revival of the practice of publicly whipping, with a *nagaika*, offenders against the declared Cossack code of conduct. In Samara and in Krasnodar such public spectacles have taken place in recent years, usually for such offences as molesting young girls. The dubious legality of such punishments, and the fact they have most frequently been inflicted on Armenians or other non-Cossacks, has however given rise to more widespread protests in Russia than has been the case with even more violent public punishments which have been inflicted in Islamic fundamentalist states in recent years.

But the essence of being a Cossack has traditionally been military. Important as these other aspects of a Cossack revival have been – the resurrection of past glories, the reintroduction of Cossack dress, the reinstatement of rituals, even the renewed emphasis on horsemanship – the real *raison d'être* of a Cossack has always been to take up arms for the greater power and glory of the Host or – in recent centuries – of Mother Russia. The last few years have not been without opportunities for military adventures.

The first call for such military intervention was when Kuban Cossack reservists were called up in Krasnodar in January 1990 as a reaction to the threat of a violent overthrow of the authorities in Azerbaijan in the Caucasus. In the event, the feared Armenian massacres did not take place, and the wives and mothers of the conscripted reservists – by no means all of whom were Cossacks – protested at this arbitrary mobilization of their menfolk. But the idea behind the mobilization – that where there was violence and mayhem on the frontiers of Russia it was appropriate to call on Cossacks to put it down – was established and was to recur.

The next rallying cry to appeal to the new-found Cossacks was the fate of the Russian population of Moldova – that relatively small part of the former Soviet Union which nestles between the Ukraine and Romania. Here the Cossacks responded in their thousands to calls to come to the assistance of the ethnic Russians in 1992. Russian nationalists interpreted the efforts of the Moldovan authorities to dominate the self-styled Trans-dniestrian Republic of Moldova as a Romanian attempt to subjugate the resident Slavs. The Republic of Moldova which emerged has much in common with the Bosnian Serb Republic, being a region where Slavs have come to the assistance of fellow Slavs to ensure their predominance.

The following year, in 1993, the Cossacks were again in action in North Ossetia in the Caucasus. Here they were called to the rescue of the Ossetians in their struggle with the Ingush, a fiercely independent people who were trying to stake out their own corner of the Caucasian mountains. The Terek Cossacks had been allied with the Ossetians in the nineteenth-century struggles described in an earlier chapter. The Ingush had no friends, and something of the flavour of their desperate anguish in their inaccessible mountain fastnesses may be gleaned from a reading of John le Carré's novel *Our Game* about a British intelligence officer who defects to join their lost cause. Few non-fictional details of this struggle ever reached the Western press. But one thing was clear: the Cossacks were back in their old stamping grounds fighting with guerrillas as tough as themselves. It was the story of Shamyl over again.

There were other calls to the colours too. In October 1993, Ussuri Cossacks from the Vladivostok region in the furthest eastern corner of the country started to patrol the frontier with China. Unknown numbers of Cossacks flocked to Bosnia to assist their Serbian 'brethren'; some went to Abkhazia and others to the Karabakh in the Caucasus. When the Taliban forces in Afghanistan approached threateningly close to the borders of Tajikistan and the Russians sent 25,000 troops to that independent Central Asian republic in August 1998, a substantial proportion of them were rumoured to be Cossacks – intent on preventing an Islamic fundamentalist incursion into that part of the former Russian empire for which they had campaigned so hard during the nineteenth-century

Great Game. Wherever a scrap appeared to be brewing, there would be a Cossack presence – sometimes requested, sometimes resented.

The real challenge was to be the war in Chechnia. When the Chechens decided they wanted to be separate from the Russian Federation, and to set up their own republic based on Grozny, many Cossacks saw this as an opportunity to fight as they had done in Moldova or Ossetia 'to preserve what our ancestors had achieved by their blood and sweat'. Some of them even claimed Grozny as a Cossack city. There were press reports of some 12,000 Cossacks anxious to join the Russians in fighting the Chechens.

However, in reality the position was not quite so clear cut. To start with, by 1995 Boris Yeltsin was already doubtful about depending on the Cossacks in this theatre of war. There were two main reasons for this. Firstly, he realized that by allowing the Cossacks to enter the arena the chances of a peaceful solution would be diminished. The Cossacks' reputation for heavy-handed, not to say brutal, treatment of opponents and for looting had not evaporated over the years. Secondly, there was some ambivalence about the Cossacks' own commitment to the cause. In 1994 the chief *ataman* of the Don Cossacks had signed an agreement with Dudayev, the Chechen leader, which provided for special treatment of the Cossacks in Chechnia and special trading privileges in return for imposing some restraints on the Russian military machine. There were business aspects of this deal which seemed dubious in the extreme to the Russian authorities. When later, in 1996, the *ataman* made up his differences with Yeltsin about this, some of the suspicions remained. And they were not confined to Yeltsin. Even General Lebed, the Russian defence chief who had a Cossack mother, thought that the Cossack links with Mafia-type business and organized crime were too close to be ignored. To Moscow it seemed the Cossacks wanted to have it both ways: they were spoiling for a fight, but they were also looking to make personal fortunes out of chaos.

Cossacks honour their dead at a reburial service
for those fallen in the Second World War.

Despite or because of this confusion many of the more militant Cossacks were disappointed when in the summer of 1996 General Lebed negotiated a peace which allowed the Chechens to consolidate their position in Grozny. A meeting of Cossack leaders was called in January 1997 at Stavropol at which they demanded that their fighting units should be incorporated into the Russian army and that they should be sent to Chechnia to defend their own traditional lands and peoples from Chechen domination. The fact that some score of Cossack civilians had been murdered in northern Chechnia in the days immediately following the Russian military withdrawal added heat and force to their argument. The Terek Cossacks in particular felt passionately about their right to hold the north bank of the Terek river – that region for which their tussle had been immortalized in Tolstoy's novel *The Cossacks*. Their own Terek *ataman* had been killed in 1996 by a Chechen mine when attempting to visit a Cossack community in northern Chechnia.

In spite of all the rhetoric, there was very little Cossack intervention to assist the occasionally beleaguered Russians inside Chechnia. But there was from time to time a Cossack blockade, or at least a series of road patrols and road blocks, on the routes leading into Grozny. Ostensibly these were trying to prevent the movement of weapons into Grozny, but in fact the road blocks were a means of extorting money and possessions from travellers into Chechnia. Such activities got the Cossacks a bad name in the region. One Chechen trader told Anatol Lieven, a distinguished foreign correspondent there at the time, that 'the conscripts are worse than the police, the regular troops are worse than the conscripts, but worst of all are the Cossacks. They ... threaten to kill you, sometimes they steal everything.' When the Chechens seized a hospital in 1995 and took hostages, the Cossacks threatened to take massive reprisals against the Chechen civilian population. They repeatedly showed an inclination to heighten the tension and the stakes of war. It was little wonder that

Yeltsin and his advisers were wary of involving the Cossacks more deeply.

Whatever Yeltsin's private reservations might have been about using Cossacks in Chechnia, in public he applauded them. In April 1996 he said that the prospect of Cossacks fighting against the Chechens had thrown the latter into a state of panic: 'They know you cannot mess about with the Cossacks!' As early as 1992 Yeltsin had issued a decree classifying the Cossacks as one of the 'oppressed peoples' of the former Soviet Union who qualified for discrimination in their favour and financial subsidies as compensation for past injuries. Presidential decrees offered the return of some traditional Cossack lands to their own administration. Yeltsin had also, both in 1993 and later in 1996, promulgated a number of decrees establish-

Boris Yeltsin, the post-Communist Russian president who did so much to resuscitate the Cossacks, at a ceremony in 1998 to commemorate the anniversary of his country's victory in the Second World War.

ing specifically Cossack units in the army. Two Divisions were renamed to give them a Cossack flavour and it was officially suggested that the Cossacks should resume their traditional role as frontier troops. But Yeltsin's measures did not receive parliamentary confirmation and most of the decrees seem – in the event – to have been still-born. When on electioneering tours in the provinces of Russia, Yeltsin has on more than one occasion employed spectacularly-clad Cossack bodyguards and guards-of-honour; but he has resisted suggestions that he should install them in the Kremlin as an elite Presidential Guard. There are limits to the extent that the ghosts of the tsars can be invoked. However, in April 1996 on a visit to the Kuban Cossacks, Yeltsin accepted with evident pleasure the gift of a Cossack uniform, complete not only with sabre but also with horse. Cynics maintain that Yeltsin seeks Cossack electoral support but is not in reality interested in giving them a more operational role in military affairs. Certainly the experience of Chechnia seems to confirm that.

In many ways the revived Cossacks have been their own worst enemies. They have been too quick to make belligerent remarks: 'We will ram pork down the [Muslim] Chechens' throats with our bayonets, as the Cossacks have always done!' one of them told Anatol Lieven; and they have too readily associated with the rougher end of the Russian Mafia.

In his authoritative book on *Chechnya* published in 1998, Lieven describes in detail one such Cossack political boss and owner of casinos, night-clubs and petrol stations. He stands as an example of many such. Determined, physically brave, tough and cynical, this Cossack 'baron' moved around with a uniformed Cossack bodyguard and a 'small but quite dazzlingly beautiful harem'. Inevitably he had his brushes with the Russian Mafia, but seemed quite able to look after himself and his various enterprises. When threatened with a forced take-over, he managed to mobilize some 300 armed bouncers ('old friends from the Sports Club') who sound about as gentle as Winnie Mandela's infamous 'Football Club' in Johannesburg.

With the reservations about the use of Cossacks in frontier wars, and with the increasing problem of violence, crime and corruption throughout large parts of Russia, two obvious roles began to emerge for the revivified Cossack entities. One was as reservists rather than as part of the standing army. This was in a sense a traditional role, and it also had the advantage that the requirement for expensive and sophisticated weaponry was less than it would have been as all-purpose regulars. Indeed it is hard to see how an irregular cavalry – in First World War uniforms – could easily fit into the nuclear-age regular army of a former super-power. The Cossacks' detractors, of whom there are many, scoff even at the idea of their being reservists and ask who needs weekend soldiers in fancy uniforms in this day and age?

The other role which the Cossacks have been increasingly asked to take on in recent years has been that of uniformed *gendarmes* or policemen. As early as 1990, when the Krasnodar civilian police force found itself unable to cope with the volume of smuggling of subsidised produce out of the region, the first Cossack volunteer patrols were put on the town streets and rural roads. There was definitely an element – as there has been throughout Cossack history – of setting a thief to catch a thief, or of turning a poacher into a gamekeeper. Sometimes it worked well; sometimes – as in the case quoted above of the blockade of Grozny – less well. But always the use of Cossacks in support of law and order has aroused suspicion and protest in certain quarters: liberals tend to see this as a retrograde step, and Jewish organizations fear that the anti-semitism of past times has not been finally laid to rest.

More recently – in 1998 – General Viktor Vlasov, the chief of police in St Petersburg and himself of Cossack origin, has introduced on an experimental basis a plan to deploy mounted Cossack patrols on the streets of this former capital city. The members of the patrols will be paid out of police funds but will be expected to provide their own horses; they will be provided with side-arms – but these are more likely to be pistols and truncheons than the traditional sabres and whips. One of the problems of this plan is that it has echoes of a throw-back to the grim days of 1905 when the Cossack patrols charged the crowds and laid about them. To start with, the patrols will only operate in selected areas of the city; but if they prove effective, and if a public outcry does not develop, then they will be introduced more widely. One thing is certain: the appearance on the streets of St Petersburg of mounted Cossacks in vast sheepskin hats and with cartridge bandoliers across their chests will add substantially to the city's attraction for tourists.

Of course, with the Ukraine now a separate country in practice as well as in name, the Russian Federation cannot claim a monopoly of the Cossacks. Indeed elements of the Kuban Cossacks have recently flirted with the idea of trying to join the Ukraine. But ever since Catherine the Great broke up the enclave of Zaporozhian Cossacks on the lower Dnieper in 1774, and since the unhappy experience of those Ukrainian Cossacks who threw in their lot with the Germans in the Second World War, the Ukrainian claim on Cossack loyalties has had to take very much second place to Russia.

Even with all the Cossack organizations mentioned above, and with all the renewed interest in the Cossack 'nation', it is very difficult to reach any estimate of overall numbers. The most official figure available is 4.5 million, but wilder claims – which include so-called neo-Cossacks (the 'Asphalt Cossacks') – run as high as 20 million. It is not a minority which any nation, even one the size of Russia, can afford to overlook. And because of the intensity with which so many Cossacks feel their identity, it is a powerful network for those seeking jobs, contracts or preferment both in their home country and among the communities of the Cossack diaspora abroad.

As Russia is poised at the threshold of the twenty-first century, most of the old Cossack questions and predicaments remain unanswered, or at least incompletely answered. Is there a case for separate Cossack states on the Don or elsewhere? Probably not. Is there a real role for the Cossack militarists to play on the frontiers of the new Russian Federation? They have tried to find such a role, but it has neither been clear nor popular. Do the Cossacks still hanker after a Tsar with whom they can have the special relationship of old? Probably many do, but few would expect to find their hopes fulfilled. Is there enough real cohesion within the Cossack movement for it to endure as a strand in the Russian national character and ethos, and to be a factor in the military and political equation? Contrary to what most observers and writers about them

where concluding until very recently, the answer would seem to be a resounding 'Yes'.

All sorts of terms have been used to describe the Cossack phenomenon. One of the most popular in recent Western scholarship and serious journalism has been that they provide a 'super-ethos' in the Russians' ribs – an intense nationalism provided by a people who are a

Looking sharp as his sabre, a young soldier of Russia's contemporary army witnesses a ceremony marking his country's recognition of the Don Cossacks.

'nation' but not a nationality. As one Cossack put it: 'We are Russians, only more so!'

But whatever the politicians and administrators, the scholars and historians, the weighty foreign correspondents and the more ephemeral journalists may say, one picture stays in the mind, based on scores of paintings in the Tretyakov and other galleries and on the volume of Russian literature from Lermontov through Tolstoy and Sholokhov to Pasternak. It is a picture of a horseman spurring his pony across the snowbound wastes of Russia, causing a whisper of fear to run ahead of him like a Siberian wind blowing through the tall grasses of the steppes and the clumps of silver birches. His face is hard, etched with lines of courage tinged by cruelty, of mirth tinged with suffering. His destination is unknown. But one thing is sure: he is firmly in the saddle and likely to remain so.

SELECT
BIBLIOGRAPHY

ABBOTT, CAPTAIN JAMES, *Narrative of a Journey from Heraut to Khiva, Moscow and St-Petersburg, during the late Russian invasion of Khiva* (London 1843)

ALEXANDER, JOHN T., *Catherine the Great* (Oxford 1989)

ANON, *A Relation Concerning the Particulars of the Rebellion lately raised in Muscovy by Stenka Razin* (London 1672)

ARMSTRONG, TERENCE, *Russian Settlement in the North* (Cambridge 1965)

ASCHERSON, NEAL, *Black Sea* (London 1995)

AVRICH, PAUL, *Russian Rebels 1600-1800* (London 1973)

BAKHRUSHIN, S.-V., *Nauchnyye Trudy*, Vols 3 & 4 (Moscow 1955-59)

BLANCH, LESLEY, *The Sabres of Paradise* (London 1960)

BUCHAN, JOHN, *The Half-Hearted* (London 1900)

BURNABY, CAPT FREDERICK, *A Ride to Khiva: Travels and Adventures in Central Asia* (London 1876)

CAULAINCOURT, ARMAND DE, *Memoirs of General de Caulaincourt, Duke of Vicenza*, Vol 1 (London 1935)

CLAUSEWITZ, KARL VON, *Campaign of 1812 in Russia* (London 1843)

CRANKSHAW, EDWARD, *The Shadow of the Winter Palace: Russia's Drift to Revolution 1825-1917* (New York 1976)

CURZON, HON GEORGE N., *Russia in Central Asia* (London 1889)

DANILOV, V.-P. (editor), *Ocherki Istorii Kollektivizatsii Selskogo Khozyaistva v Soyuznykh Respublikakh* (Moscow 1963)

DERLUGUIAN, GEORGI M., and CIPKO, SERGE, *The Politics of Identity in a Russian Borderline Province: The Kuban Neo-Cossack Movement, 1989-96*, published in the journal of Europe-Asia Studies, Vol 49, No 8 (Glasgow 1997)

EDWARDS, MICHAEL, *Playing the Great Game: A Victorian Cold War* (London 1975)

FIELD, CECIL, *The Great Cossack* (London 1947)

FIGES, ORLANDO, *A People's Tragedy: The Russian Revolution 1891-1924* (London 1996)

FREDERICKS, P.-G., *The Sepoy and the Cossack* (London 1972)

GOGOL, NIKOLAI, *Taras Bulba* (St-Petersburg 1842)

GOURGAUD, GASPARD, *Napoléon et la Grande Armée en Russie* (Paris 1825)

HARCAVE, SYDNEY, *First Blood: The Russian Revolution of 1905* (London 1965)

HATTON, R.-M., *Charles XII of Sweden* (London 1968)

HOPKIRK, PETER, *The Great Game* (London 1990)

JEFFERYES, JAMES, *Captain James Jefferyes's Letters from the Swedish Army 1707-1709* (Stockholm 1954)

KATAEV, I.-M., *Stenka Razin* (Moscow 1906)

KELLY, LAURENCE, *Lermontov: Tragedy in the Caucasus* (London 1977)

KERNER, ROBERT J., *The Urge to the Sea* (New York 1971)

KIPLING, RUDYARD, *The Man Who Was* (London 1890)

LIEVEN, ANATOL, *Chechnya* (New Haven USA 1998)

LONGWORTH, PHILIP, *The Cossacks* (London 1968)

MACLEAN, FITZROY, *To Caucasus: The End of all the Earth* (London 1976), *Holy Russia* (London 1978)

MCNEAL, R.-H., *Tsar and Cossack 1855-1914* (Oxford 1987)

MARVIN, CHARLES, *Reconnoitring Central Asia* (London 1884)

MASSIE, ROBERT K., *Peter the Great* (London 1981)

MERLIEUX, EDOUARD, *Souvenirs d'une Française captive de Shamyl* (Paris 1857)

PALMER, ALAN, *Napoleon in Russia* (London 1997)

PARES, SIR BERNARD, *A History of Russia* (London 1925)

POPKA, I.-D., *Chernomorskie Kazaki* (St-Petersburg 1858, Krasnodar 1998)

PURCHAS, S., *Purchas His Pilrimes* (London 1625)

PUSHKIN, ALEXANDER, *Kapitanskaya Dotchka* (Moscow 1836)

ST GEORGE, GEORGE, *Siberia* (London 1969)

SCHUYER, EUGENE, *Peter the Great* (New York 1884)

SHOLOKHOV, MIKHAIL, *And Quiet Flows the Don* (London 1934)

SKINNER, BARBARA, *Identity Formation in the Russian Cossack Revival*, published in the journal of Europe-Asia Studies, Vol 46, No 6 (Glasgow 1994)

SOLOVEV, S.-M., *Istoriya Rossii s drevneishikh vremen* (Moscow 1960-66)

TOLSTOY, COUNT LEO, *The Cossacks: A Tale of the Caucasus in the Year 1852* (London 1928)

TOLSTOY, NIKOLAI, *Victims of Yalta* (London 1977)

ULOTH, GERALD, *Riding to War* (London 1993)

VERDEREVSKY, M., *The Captivity of two Russian Princesses*, trans. H.-Sutherland Edwards (London 1857)

WILSON, SIR ROBERT, *Narrative of Events during the Invasion of Russia* (London 1925)

INDEX